The

VILLA

of

DEATH

Also by Joanna Challis

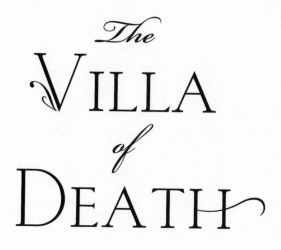

The VILLA of DEATH

A Mystery Featuring Daphne du Maurier

JOANNA CHALLIS

Minotaur Books ✹ New York

This is a work of fiction. All of the characters, organizations, and events portrayed in this novel are either products of the author's imagination or are used fictitiously.

www.minotaurbooks.com

Library of Congress Cataloging-in-Publication Data

Challis, Joanna.
   The villa of death : a mystery featuring Daphne du Maurier / Joanna Challis.—1
      p. cm.—(No. 3 of 3)
   ISBN 978-0-312-36717-6 (hardback)
   1. Du Maurier, Daphne, 1907–1989—Fiction.   2. Women authors, English—
20th century—Fiction.   3. Weddings—Fiction.   4. Murder—Investigation—
Fiction.   5. Aristocracy (Social class)—England—Fiction.   6. Manors—
England.   7. Cornwall (England)—Fiction.   I. Title.
   PR9619.4.C39V55 2011
   823'.92—dc22

                                                                    2011026900

First Edition: December 2011

   10 9 8 7 6 5 4 3 2 1

For my siblings: Tony, Jason, and Amanda

The
VILLA
of
DEATH

CHAPTER ONE

Cannon Hall,
Hampstead, London
Home of the du Mauriers

"Daphne, come away from that window at once. You haven't answered Lady Gersham."

Pulling at the curtain edge, I set my mouth into the acceptable and pleasing afternoon-tea smile: vacant and supercilious. "Dear Lady Gersham, I haven't fully considered the notion. I imagine rolling one's clothes into packed carry cases is the best way to travel."

"Daphne's clothes are always crumpled." Grinning, Jeanne cut Lady Gersham another piece of seed cake. "She packs in a hurry."

"It is ill-advised to pack in haste," observed Lady Gersham. "Perhaps you ought to get her nose out of a book, Muriel."

Lifting a brow, my mother's smile, for once, exuded a little patience for my social shortcomings. "Oh, but crumpled clothes or not she has managed to secure the interest of a certain gentleman."

Lady Gersham sat up. "Oh?"

"A certain gentleman of *impeccable* quality."

"Oh?"

"A man of property and breeding."

"Oh, yes?"

Feeling my face grow hot, I glared at my mother. Surely, she'd not say his name. Surely, she'd not embarrass me in front of one of London's most notorious gossips.

"Sir Marcus Oxley."

"Oooh."

Lady Gersham bestowed her aura of approval on me.

"I thought you were going to say Major Browning," Jeanne blurted out to my mortification.

"Younger sisters never get the current favorite quite right," my mother assured Lady Gersham. "Daphne, take Jeanne to her room and see that she finishes her sums. I have something *particular* to say to Lady Gersham."

Thus dismissed, I did indeed take Jeanne upstairs but with the intention to box her ears. "How dare you? You *promised* you'd not say a word."

Jeanne, bearing the trademark of a younger sister, had developed the unsavory habit of eavesdropping on Angela and me. "You've broken your oath." Halting, I crossed my arms. "And if you can't keep a secret, then you're not coming to Ellen's on Friday. There's no room for silly little girls."

Lowering an instantly glum face, Jeanne sank onto her bed and wept. "Sorry, Daph, I didn't mean to . . . I want to go to Ellen's. I've never been to a bridal shower . . . oh, Daphne, please, *please* let me go."

"No." Slamming the door, I retreated to my room. It was a fortunate thing she hadn't overheard Roderick Trevalyan's name, too. Angela and I alone shared the secrets of Somner House but for one careless mention of Major Frederick Arthur Montague Browning.

"Was he at Somner, too?" Jeanne hunted me out later that day. "Mama doesn't know."

"And nor shall she," I had replied. To guarantee her silence, I relayed a little of my private affairs and agog with the news, Jeanne gave me her solemn promise.

"Daphne!"

I expected my mother's summons the moment Lady Gersham departed.

"Yes, Mother?"

"Why did Jeanne mention the major? Have you received more word from him?"

I turned away. I didn't want my mother to detect the truth in my face. Faces had a way of betraying one and mothers possessed the uncanny knack of unlocking such secrets. "Mother," I sighed, "Sir Marcus is a *friend* of mine, not a beau. I wish you would cease spreading rumors about us. He won't find it amusing." In fact, Sir Marcus *would* find it amusing but my mother needn't know it.

"Well, the way you two whisper in corners would suggest otherwise."

"We're just *friends*."

"I was a friend of your father's before we married."

Oh no. The marriage subject again. "Mama, I told you. I'm not getting married anytime soon and to make it seem as if I were to Lady Gersham of all people!"

"I am merely advertising your marketability," came the swift retort. "Really, Daphne, do you intend to become an old spinster? For you will be one if you continue on this way. Gentlemen need *encouragement* and I despair you've got too sharp a tongue. It didn't help Elizabeth Bennett with Mr. Darcy, did it?"

"I beg to differ. Her sharp tongue secured his interest early on and later he praised her for her mind, more than her 'fine eyes.' "

My mother's eyes rounded. "Oh, then you have an *understanding* with the major as I suspected. When shall he be calling again? Your father was sorry to have missed him last time."

I drew away to the window. The affair she referred to had occurred the Wednesday before. Without any warning, he called upon us. Heart pounding, for I was not properly dressed and my hair looked horrid, I crept down the stairs to see him smilingly entertaining my mother and sisters in the tearoom. Angela caught my gaze. She wondered, as I did, what this call meant since our last meeting at Somner House.

I had to wait. Upon his departure, he raised my hand to his lips and murmured, *"Au revoir.* Until we meet again."

"When should we expect him again?"

I wanted to know the same thing. "I don't know, Mama. I *do* know he is invited to Ellen's wedding."

"Ah, weddings." My mother grinned. "A perfect location for a blossoming romance. Your father has given his full approval. Though," she paused to reflect, "we are not yet fully aware of the major's circumstances. Your father wants the best for his Daphne . . . that is why I think you shouldn't rule out Sir Marcus as a candidate. What a splendid catch!"

Poor Sir Marcus. "Hunted like a fox."

"Well," my mother's lips pursed together, "foxes should expect such and let's hope some of this wedding season will inspire you or your sister, for otherwise I shall feel like Mrs. Bennett and lament I have three daughters, all unwed and what does your father do about it? Nothing! Nothing at all."

The gloomy pathway beckoned. She paid no attention to its dilapidated state, neither seeing nor hearing the windstorm brewing around her. Such was her state of mind as she progressed toward her destination, knowing this was the last time—

"Daphne! The car is waiting."

Sighing, I scribbled down the last sentence. They could wait.

The world could wait.

This sentence could not.

"Oh, dear." Running up the stairs, Jeanne pushed open my door. "You're not even dressed!"

"I am *mostly* dressed," I corrected, sweeping up notebook and pen to put a few final items in my bag. Mentally reviewing my list,

I was satisfied I had everything I needed and followed Jeanne downstairs.

Angela was already in the car, waiting. She, too, had curlers in her hair and we prayed no one saw us on our way to Ellen's house.

"How fun this will be." Clapping her hands, Jeanne exuded the younger-sister excitement of a first grown-up party. "I can't wait to tell Bethany; she's always going on about her rich German cousins yet she's never been invited to a *bride's* party."

"Nobody likes a braggart," Angela warned. "And whatever you do, don't monopolize the ladies with your questions. You're there to sit and learn and if you're good, we'll let you have some champagne, won't we, Daphne?"

Busy staring out the window, I agreed. I didn't know what I'd agreed to for Angela's babble faded against London at night. Still early, dusky embers bathed the streets, catching the lights on the passing motorcars. The city had its glow and its attractions but my heart longed for Cornwall and the wild, open rural country, and the sea, the sea . . .

"Daphne, you didn't forget to bring Ellen's present, did you?"

I gave my sister a woebegone look. "We've been writing to each other for how many years now? I'm not likely to forget, am I?"

"One never knows with you," Angela teased. "Did you finish the chapter?"

"No," I lamented as I'd much prefer to stay at my desk and work on my book. Wrong of me, but apart from Ellen, what business did I have going to a bridal shower? I abhorred these kinds of parties for they invariably attracted giggly females chatting of men and marriage.

Since the war, the men and marriage subject became my mother's favorite as we came of age. Among certain acquaintances, it turned into a competition, mothers airing their daughters' successes a great part of it. I didn't want to disappoint my mother but I wasn't sure whether I wanted to get married. I regarded the idea of enduring love with cynicism, perhaps because I had yet to experience what Elizabeth Bennett felt: "I am convinced only the greatest love would induce me to matrimony."

Such deliberations accompanied me through the gate to Ellen's smart London house. Well, to be accurate, the house belonged to her rich fiancé. Walking up to the door, I admired the crisp hedges and the neat row of flowering pots. Of course, it was nothing compared with Thornleigh.

"What's Ellen's fiancé's name again?" Jeanne whispered.

"Teddy Grimshaw, but don't you call him Teddy. He's *Mr.* Grimshaw to you."

"Oh, that's right. He's old, isn't he?"

"It's a matter of perspective," I murmured back. "Did you think Colonel Brandon too old for Marianne in *Sense and Sensibility*?"

Jeanne reflected. "I suppose not because he was a good man and Willoughby was the devil. A handsome devil, mind."

"Handsome devils do not make good husbands," Angela advised, tearing off her gloves. "And though Mr. Grimshaw is sixteen years Ellen's senior, he's not ancient. Didn't you see the picture of him in the paper? He's very good looking."

"He has gray temples," Jeanne pointed out.

"He's very rich," Angela also pointed out. "And if Ellen minds his gray temples, she can boot-black them out."

We all laughed at this, glancing at each other guiltily when Ellen came down the stairs.

"There you are, darlings! Fashionably late as the term goes."

Sweeping to us in a purple satin peignoir and smelling of expensive perfume, Ellen Hamilton looked every inch the society bride. With her honey-blond hair bouncing on her shoulders and dancing lights in her green eyes, she presented a very different picture since the last time I'd seen her.

Upon seeing me, the sparkle left her eyes for the sincere graveness I knew so well. "Oh, Daphne, I'm so glad you're here. There's so much to do—I never thought a wedding could be so complex."

"It's a society wedding," I reminded. "Were you happy with the name cards?"

"They're perfect! Honestly, I don't know how I'd manage without you and Megan to help me. It's sad my mother never lived to see this day. She would have relished every little detail."

Wistful, her face returned to bridal jubilation as we entered the room full of girls.

At twenty-eight, Ellen Hamilton exuded a confidence none of us possessed. Perhaps her experiences during the war and afterward had taught her self-reliance in the face of poverty, heartache, and oppression. I'd shared so much with her through our letters, yet I still felt gauche and inexperienced in her company.

"No, Daphne," she drew me aside later. "You mustn't envy what I've been through. Yes, I've learned much from it and it is fit for a novel," she smiled faintly, "but don't envy me. You have your whole life ahead of you and innocence is something you don't want to part with too early."

"I am *not* innocent."

She sighed, her perceptive green eyes knowing better.

"Have you any word of your stepdaughter-to-be?"

"Well, Rosalie *is* coming to the wedding. Teddy's gone to meet her at the station. Oh Daphne, I'm dreading it . . . dreading it all."

"The wedding or his daughter's arrival?"

"Both. You know how much she hates me."

"Pressed by her mother," I reminded. "Surely she's excited to have a little sister? I can't imagine growing up without my sisters . . . I suspect only children are very lonely."

"And spoilt," Ellen added. "Unfortunately, Rosalie is more concerned with losing her inheritance than gaining a sister."

"Again spurred on by the mother?"

"Oh, Daphne, you know all of my history but not many others do. If word were to leak out, it would ruin me."

"It *won't* leak out and it won't ruin you," I assured her. "The daughter or her mother would be fools to try something like it."

7

"I think they will try. They can't stand Teddy to be happy again. Oh, I wished they'd just stayed in Boston!"

I pressed her hand. "Now, where's little Charlotte?"

"Not so little now. She turned eight last month."

"Eight! I remember when she was born . . ."

"Yes, so do I." Ellen smiled. "She's with Nanny Brickley at the moment and she loved those books you sent her. We read them every night. *Hansel and Gretel* is her favorite and reminds me of the summers we spent together in the woods at Thornleigh."

I was glad she noted the connection for I had thought the same when I looked at the illustrations.

"And, my darling, have you seen the major since your last letter? You must keep me up to date, you know, for otherwise how can I look out for you? Is he a good man or is he a cad? He seems very popular with women; I don't know whether that's a good thing or a bad thing."

"As is your Teddy."

Ellen reflected before returning with a fond smile. "Yes, I suppose you are right. He is the darling of his family. You should see how his sisters dote on him."

"Have they all arrived for the wedding?"

"Mostly, yet I am anxious to get to Thornleigh first."

"To prepare for the invasion."

"Exactly so." Grinning, Ellen asked what I thought of the new painting of Charlotte on the wall. "Teddy commissioned Rudolf Heinemann to do it. See how she's smiling? That's her smile for Daddy. He so adores her. He always wanted more children but he never thought it would happen."

"Nor did you," I gently reminded with a laugh. "I remember your horrified letter in which you confessed to me your *mortal sin*."

"It was a good thing I kept it hidden from Mama," Ellen reflected. "News of the pregnancy would have killed her. *Scandal of the century.*"

I laughed. "Well, for a time."

"One would have thought after the war people would be more accepting and forgiving. But some things they never forget. They hold onto it and it festers until it becomes poison . . . that's why I dread if . . ."

"Nothing will happen. Years have passed since then."

"Dear, wise Daphne! I am so relieved you are here. Adding the crystals to the dresses was a great idea."

"You'll be a radiant bride, the most radiant of the season."

A sudden pallor crept into her face. "Please don't say such things. You know how I hate being the center of attention. I just want the wedding over and done with so we can begin our lives at Thornleigh."

"But does Teddy agree? He has his business in America."

"Yes, he does," she sighed, "so we've reached a compromise. Half year there and half year here so Charlotte gets the best of both worlds."

"You're brave to take on the 'Boston Brahmins' again." I smiled.

"It will be a challenge, but then my whole life has been a challenge. I suppose, in a way, I am used to it."

"You'll triumph, I am sure," I proclaimed. "And I want to see many pictures of you in the paper defeating the Boston Brahmins. Agreed?"

"I'll do my best." Ellen laughed.

CHAPTER TWO

I did well to hide my disappointment from the wedding party.

On the morning of our departure, my mother telephoned, saying, "Major Browning has not called. Do you wish to leave a message if he does?" I said no, with more vehemence than I intended. Why hadn't he kept his promise? Why hadn't he called?

"Daphne? Are you all right?"

Ellen found me slamming down the telephone.

"What's the matter? It's him, isn't it? The major?"

"Y-yes. He promised he'd call."

"He will," Ellen soothed. "From what you write of him, he sounds like a man of integrity."

Her words failed to placate me. Biting my lower lip, I hunted through the usual excuses. Perhaps he'd been summoned away without any notice? Summoned to a secret assignment where he planned to write at the first opportunity? "He *did* accept your wedding invitation, didn't he?"

"Why, yes." Ellen sounded surprised. "He said he'd be delighted to attend and would come with the Rutland party."

I blinked. "The *earl* of Rutland? He's coming to your wedding?"

"Indeed, he is." Ellen's self-satisfied smile grew wider. "They were great friends of my parents, if you recall. They came to my mother's funeral so I thought why not invite them to my wedding? I daresay the papers will be abuzz with it. I only let them know this morning."

"Dear Ellen." I laughed along with her. "You're a great success."

Her smile vanished. "Don't think too highly of me, Daphne. Sometimes I feel compelled to do these things I don't want to do."

"You mean playing the social game? Returning fire with fire?"

"Yes . . . and more." The shadow left her face and the bright sparkle in her eyes returned. "We're to train it then as Harry has organized cars to take us to Thornleigh."

"Harry. How is he?"

"Oh, well. He's Harry, isn't he? Always looks on the bright side of life. To be sure, I couldn't have managed without him all these years."

"He's been a good friend," I said softly. "What does Teddy think of him?"

"He's happy for Harry to stay as estate manager. Who better than Harry? And we have so much work to do. You'll be amazed when you see Thornleigh."

"Thank you for sending me a copy of the renovation plans. You know how much I adore old houses."

"And your input is crucial." Ellen squeezed my hand. "I want Thornleigh restored to its former glory, like in the painting."

I remembered the sixteenth-century painting gracing the main hall at Ellen's family home.

"It's a huge enterprise," Ellen went on, "but Teddy loves the house too and being a man, likes to 'fix' things. We plan to be abroad for the winter when a lot of the major renovations will take place. Repairing the roof and restoring the west wing, et cetera."

"So you'll travel back to Boston sometime after the wedding?"

"Yes. It's Teddy's mother. She's too ill to travel and she hasn't seen Charlotte."

"But you'd prefer to stay at Thornleigh," I finished for her with a tease. "I'd hate to leave, too, but think of the changes when you return! And winters are miserable here."

"You're right and you cheer me up immensely. Now, I suppose we have dallied long enough. I think that's the last of the packing by the door. Can you be a darling and take down my wedding dress? I don't trust anyone else with it."

I was happy to comply. It kept my mind from thinking about *him,* Major Browning. The missing major who failed to honor his promises.

Arriving at Victoria Station, I did allow myself to search for his face among the crowds. As he hadn't called at the house, surely he could have troubled himself to see me off at the station? Or at least send a note?

I thought my apprehension had gone unnoticed by our party.

"You're in love with him, aren't you?" Ellen pulled my arm.

"I'm not sure I know what love is." I swallowed, watching my step lest I fall over and give in to misery.

"Then there's two of us." Grasping my gloved hand in her own, Ellen propelled us toward Nanny Brickley. "Charlotte has brought Teddy and me back together, I know that for a fact."

I almost tripped in shock. "Don't you love Teddy?"

"Of course I do, but sometimes I wonder if Charlotte hadn't come along, would this wedding be happening? It seems like a dream, after all we've been through, and I suppose I'm afraid to believe it lest it evaporate before my eyes."

"It *is* happening," I assured her as we reached our designated carriage.

"Teddy made all the arrangements," Ellen said, handing our tickets to the attendant. "He wanted us to travel 'in style.'"

Once on the train, Ellen paused, looking the epitome of the elegant sophisticated bride in her dove-gray suit and fine pearls. "I may look the part but I am not one for the center stage. I like dark corners like you and would much prefer to travel second class than first."

She whispered this so the others didn't hear, the others being too overwhelmed by the opulence of our carriage to care. Like a palace on wheels, the beautifully appointed Pullman carriage assigned to us (thanks to Mr. Teddy Grimshaw, millionaire) abounded in unprecedented luxury.

Resisting the urge to jump on the burgundy upholstered couch, I admired the elaborate royal interior. From the brass handles to the drapes on the wide scenic windows, every little detail had been considered and incorporated to ensure a comfortable journey.

Drawing to the window, I scaled the length of the platform, oblivious to my train companions cooing expressions of "oh, this is glorious," "what style," and "this trip must have cost a *fortune*."

Yes, a small fortune, I thought, remembering the face of a beggar I'd seen recently on the streets. My peevishness intensified as hope faded from my eyes. There was no sight of Major Browning, no glimpse of the face I wished to see above all emerging out of the station mist.

"Are you expecting someone?"

The soft American voice caught me off guard. Peeling my gaze away from the window, I watched Nanny Brickley putting away her hand-box. In my experience, Americans were very direct while we English remained inherently coy about our private affairs.

"A gentleman, I gather?"

"A *friend*," I was quick to reply.

Alicia Brickley smiled to herself.

I didn't like the calculation in her doe-brown eyes. As a poor relative of Teddy Grimshaw, he'd seen that she had a place in his household. Formerly a secretary and now a nanny to his newfound child.

"She's Teddy's niece; the poor cousin," Ellen once explained.

"Has she any experience?"

"Four younger sisters and two half-brothers. Who can go against that?"

Nobody, evidently, and Alicia Brickley intended to keep her exalted post. She was treated more like a member of the family, and little Charlotte loved her and that was all that mattered.

I consulted my wristwatch. Five minutes to go. Had he called at the house? Had he received my message?

"All aboard!"

My heart sank as the whistle blew. Frowning at the window, I promised myself to vilify Frederick Arthur Montague Browning in a future novel.

Preferring to read a book or play with little Charlotte over mixing with my lively companions, I buried my disappointment.

I had to do so. I was here as chief bridesmaid and I had a job to do.

"It'll be the most beautiful wedding of the season," declared Megan Kellaway. As number-two bridesmaid, Megan was optimistic, infectious, and engaging, a personality I loved perhaps because it was alien to my own. "Thornleigh at dusk! How unusual . . . I can't wait to read the write-up in the papers."

"As much as meeting all the available men?" Angela teased and Megan grinned.

"Well," said she, "I don't want to be a spinster."

As the daughter of Sir Roger Kellaway, Esquire, Megan had her choice amongst the season's offerings.

"Maybe one of the American relatives?" Eyes dancing, Megan asked Ellen again for the names of those gentlemen attending the wedding.

"I like the sound of the nephew," Megan pronounced afterward. "Jack Grimshaw . . . hmm; can I see myself living in America?"

"Poor man." Jeanne grinned. "Hunted like a fox."

"Are you sure you want all of us sharing part of your honeymoon with you?" The third bridesmaid, Mrs. Clarissa Fenwick, crossed her long legs on the lush upholstery. "After all, darling Ellen, you and Teddy have been too long and too cruelly parted."

With Charlotte on her lap, Ellen's face radiated that of a contented mother. With her bouncing blond curls and mischievous little face, Charlotte had no idea of the scandalous drama her entry into the world had caused. "It doesn't bother us at all, does it, princess?"

"I heard the Spencers turned their nose up at the invitation," Angela commented. "Better for you, I say! I can't stand that pretentious Bertha."

"And Mama says don't be upset about the West-Mortons," Jeanne put in. "They are not at all 'the thing' anymore."

"I don't care a fig about any of them," Ellen retorted, roused to the conversation when Charlotte wriggled off her lap to go to Nanny Brickley. "The past is done with and those who judge me for it I'd rather not know at all."

"Hear, hear." Tapping the sideboard, Megan called for champagne.

I had no complaints about the train. The new S-class sleeping cars painted blue with gold lettering and lining and accompanied by its exquisite wooden marquetry and brass fittings radiated the essence of grandeur and wealth.

Grandeur and comfort didn't always come automatically together but this train outdid itself. From the sleeping quarters to the dining car and lounge, every tiny comfort had been addressed. It made me think whimsically of the *Titanic* and its tragic voyage. I prayed we experienced no such catastrophe again.

"Doom and gloom is Daphne," Jeanne said, her eyes lighting up at the prospect of pink champagne. "Wherever we travel, she regales us with the worst stories. Last year, she frightened Mama out of her wits!"

I smiled.

It was true.

"Oh do humor us with a story, Daphne," Megan insisted.

"But we should wait 'til after dinner," Clarissa advised.

"Yes, after dinner," Angela seconded.

* * *

The elaborate preparations to attire oneself for the dining car amused me. Clarissa curled her hair, Angela absconded with our mother's hand mirror, Megan changed her dress five times, and Jeanne begged me to wear some lipstick.

Since I had the merest pink lipstick in my possession, I obliged her while Angela scowled in the corner. She didn't like to see Jeanne growing up too fast. She liked to think of her as our baby sister.

Tinkling crystal greeted us as we entered the long carriage and the designated dining car.

"Wise of Teddy to prebook a table," Megan whispered in my ear. "Oh, my goodness, is that Lionel Adams over there? I'm going to die!"

"Please don't obstruct the aisleway then." Angela winked her amusement, smiling at the famous actor. "Papa knows him, I think."

"Papa knows *everyone* in the business," Jeanne affirmed, stopping by Lionel's table to ask for his autograph.

"I can't believe she's doing that." Rolling her eyes, Angela shared Clarissa's mortification.

"Oh, let her be." Ellen shepherded us away. "We were all her age once."

Until now I hadn't realized how much one grows up from fifteen to twenty-five. I imagined the jump from thirty to forty would yield further mysteries as to one's true character.

"We are all shaped by circumstance," Clarissa said, reminding all of us we were here for Ellen's wedding and not to gape at the plethora of notables on the train. "When I first met my Charles, I despised him. I thought him a great rogue and very vain."

"And now?" Megan teased.

Clarissa's face softened. "And now I think he's adorable . . . and *so* good to me."

Putting all thoughts of men aside, I tried to drink in the atmosphere from the gleaming silverware on our table to the various faces, voices, and food selections under the lulling hymn of Vivaldi's *Four Seasons*.

For tonight's dinner I'd chosen a dress Lady Kate Trevalyan had so generously bequeathed to me when I was a guest at Somner House. Silver gray, its soft satin folds reminded me of a dove's belly. Drop-waisted, it suited me well and the black lace overlay with its mock sleeves added glamor. To my hair I slipped on the headband bearing one silver star and a black feather. I believed I looked rather fine and much older than my twenty or so years.

"That dress is a bit old for you," Clarissa, the eldest of us all at twenty-nine, observed as we ordered from the menu.

"It belonged to Lady Trevalyan," I replied. "And she is reputed to have the best of taste."

"I hear she is to marry Sir Percival Clements. A *splendid* match."

"You mean he's splendidly rich," Angela snapped. "He's old enough to be her grandfather."

"Father perhaps," Ellen soothed, laughing. "Now ladies, I do believe we're attracting certain attention from that quarter."

Following her sweeping lashes to a table of four gentlemen diagonal to us, I daresay we made a fine impression. Honey-haired Ellen's quiet grace contrasted to Megan's exuberance as much as her raven hair and mischievous dark eyes. On the other hand, we du Maurier girls were often called "attractive" though not endowed with any great beauty. I considered my nose too *retroussé,* Angela's chin too determined, and Jeanne a shadowy version of our mother.

"They look French to me." Megan sighed. "Oh, what I'd give to be romanced by one of them!"

"French men don't make good husbands," Clarissa informed her. "I have it on good authority from my cousin, who is married to one of them."

There was a slight superciliousness to her tone and I braced against it. Clarissa had come from a rich family and had married into an equally rich family. They had money but no title or exalted connections. She appeared the kind of person to make up for this lack by being haughty and using condescension to elevate herself.

As our meals arrived, a couple entered the carriage on the far end. I blanched, my face turning a maggoty white. I could feel the blood draining from it as I looked on, sickened at the sight of yes, *him*—Major Browning accompanying a dark-haired lady and assisting her to her seat, attentively arranging her sparkling shawl and grinning fondly down at her.

"Daphne, what is wrong?"

Squeezing my hand under the table, Ellen's eyes radiated sympathy.

"It's him, isn't it?"

Words stuck in my throat. I could only stare, astonished, hurt, and angry. Who was *she*? She wasn't his sister, I knew that much. And were those her parents seated opposite them?

Angela made a scene by openly glaring at him. She turned back to me, countless questions in her eyes.

"Who is he?" a startled Clarissa and Megan breathed.

"Daphne's boyfriend," Jeanne answered. "Ouch! Don't kick me under the table, Ange; it's true!"

"Jeanne, *shhh.*" I didn't want to believe it, nor did I wish to acknowledge his presence. Searching for an escape, I figured I could leave the table and stealthily make my way back to our carriage. I could do all this without being noticed.

I had to collect my thoughts. My stomach burned. I felt like one disembowelled and weak. Sickening betrayal haunted my steps as I fled, and I paid no attention to the curious whispers.

Once in our quarters, I caught my breath, sagging against the wooden panelled door. I wanted to beat my fists and wail. Curses left my mouth as angry tears spilled down my face.

"It's his fiancée, Lady Lara Fane," Angela brought the devastating news. "They are going to Cornwall for the wedding but they're not staying at Thornleigh. He seemed embarrassed to see me and kept looking behind me to see if you were there."

"*Please* don't say you told him I was on the train."

"Of course he knows you're on the train. He's not an imbecile. He asked after you in a strange way."

I waited for her to enlighten me. I didn't know if I wanted to hear any more.

"He said: 'Are all your family travelling with you?' to which I replied: 'All but my parents who are coming a week later.' Then he introduced his fiancée and her parents. I nodded my head coolly and left."

I was thankful Clarissa hadn't witnessed this interchange firsthand. Angela said nobody else could fit in the aisle and as it was, she barely shared five minutes with them. She added the major looked decidedly ill at ease. "How dare he toy with my sister! I've a mind to box his ears and I will."

"He's not worth it," I whispered. *Now* I understood why he'd not bothered to call at the house or send a note. He was too busy with his fiancée, somebody he should have mentioned. *Was he engaged to her when we shared that kiss at Somner together? Was he?*

I glared out of the window.

Suddenly, the world had turned very bleak. I vowed never to trust another human soul for as long as I lived. I vowed never to surrender my heart again. Never.

Angela sat beside me, a silent companion. Neither of us spoke and she kept the others away from me. I needed to be alone . . . to think.

The wedding and Thornleigh awaited and I prayed the busy frivolities drove all remembrance of the major firmly from my mind.

CHAPTER THREE

"Don't torture yourself," Ellen advised. "Consider it a good thing they are not bound for Thornleigh. Oh, I've got a mind to cancel his invitation. *All* their invitations! I had no idea Lara was engaged. Funny they didn't mention it."

Funny *he* didn't mention it.

"He has ill-used my friend and is no friend of mine. I'll poison his cup if I have the chance!"

I smiled at Ellen's loyalty as we climbed into the waiting motor-cars. Angela stood as sentry to ensure we did not run into *his* party, complete with fiancée. Clutching my handbag, I prayed to be saved that humiliation.

Gulping back painful tears, I fixed my gaze on the passing green countryside. For the first time in my life, Cornwall in the summer-time failed to cheer me. The whole window became a blur of mixed colors, shapeless and moving. A bubbling tightness constricted my throat and I put my hand there to conceal it from the others. Oh why, oh why had I begged Ellen to invite *him* to the wedding? And how dare he accept *knowing* he had a fiancée and *knowing* I was Ellen's maid of honor?

No, I would not cry. Not now.

I am sure I never sat on a longer journey. The minutes seemed like torturous hours and the humming of the sleek Rolls-Royce sounded like swarming bees in my ears. I wanted to block it all out. I wanted to block life out. I wanted to run away.

But I could not.

Duty beckoned and my friendship with Ellen took precedence.

If he had even an inkling of sensibility, he'd have denied the invitation. But no, he didn't. And here was I dreaming of romantic assignations in the gardens of Thornleigh, in the great galley of Thornleigh, in the library at Thornleigh . . . in the woods surrounding Thornleigh. How the very reminder tasted bitter.

How should I conduct myself? Smile at his fiancée and pretend there was nothing between us? Scratch his eyes out in *front* of his fiancée? Scream at him like a fishwife in front of everyone?

My internal guide said to remain silent. To adopt a facade and ignore the situation. Treat him as nothing more than a slight acquaintance.

The great gates of Thornleigh arrested me, as they always did, with their weathered rusty exterior.

"Teddy wants to get new gates," Ellen sighed, "but I can't. The gates may be old but they are part of Thornleigh."

"Yes, I agree. It would be a crime to remove them; they are so full of character."

Entwined on the gates glistened the Hamilton coat of arms, given to Ellen's ancestor five centuries ago. A knight of fortune, Sir Winston saved his king's life and thus won for himself a bride and a castle. Since that day, the Hamiltons had occupied this land. I wished I could boast such a family history. My most infamous connection extended to my great-great-great grandmother Mary Anne who became mistress of Prince Frederick, the duke of York.

Chestnut and lime trees formed a handsome avenue up the house. Sir John Hamilton saw them planted during the Restoration and it was he and his architect friend who designed the Thornleigh standing today.

"Mama, I can't wait to ride my new pony!"

Smiling indulgently, Ellen ruffled her daughter's hair. "Daphne's a great rider. I'm sure she'll take you out this afternoon."

"Yes, I will," I promised Charlotte. Since it had been some time since I'd been on the back of a horse, I looked forward to it, too.

Beyond the trees, Thornleigh stood ancient and proud. Light rain drizzled down the crenulated turrets and the huge Jacobean wing with its endless mullioned windows and pretty gables. Red and green ivy flourished up the three turrets surviving from the original castle and, I was happy to note, had begun creeping across the limestone mansion.

"Think, Daphne, what it will look like in another fifty years." Stepping out of the car, Ellen twirled in the rain. "When we're old ladies, we can sit in that tearoom overlooking the gardens."

I followed her gaze to the far corner of the house.

"Who has need of a drawing room today? We've made it into a tearoom and it's cozy and bright. Our plan is to transform Thornleigh into an English-Italian villa. You'll love it."

I had no doubt I would. I loved all old houses, but Thornleigh remained a particular favorite. Perhaps because I'd come here as a girl, because I'd wandered alone in the woods, because I'd met my pen-friend Ellen here and because I based all my girlhood fantasies around the romantic grounds encompassing the old house.

"Had Xavier lived, you could have been mistress of Thornleigh," Ellen teased as we made our way up to the house and into the delightful tearoom.

I smiled, an image of the handsome Xavier coming to mind in uniform, on leave from the war. Although I was so much younger, scarcely a child, he'd treated me like a lady and I thought of him as a hero. If he had lived, I calculated quickly, he'd be thirty-three now, a perfect age for a man a girl in her twenties like me might marry.

Ellen suggested we take tea before retiring to our rooms. I still could not believe how much had changed. From the new Queen Anne staircase to the fully restored state rooms, Thornleigh was well on its way to returning to its former glory.

"We plan to do one room at a time," Ellen said to me on our way up to the third floor. "Teddy is a great planner. He's pushing the builder all the time."

"I guess money helps." Angela grinned, pausing to admire a painting on the stairway wall. "Is that a Monet?"

"Yes." Ellen seemed embarrassed. "It was an engagement present. I did think of locking it away, but it's insured and Teddy says it should be on display. We put it in the library first but I think it looks better here in the hall."

She moved on, and Angela and I shared a wide-eyed look. This was how millionaires spent their money, obviously.

"It can't have been bestowed on a better person," I said to my sisters later. "And how kind of Ellen to give us the best room over all the American relatives!"

"You *are* her maid of honor," Angela reminded. "And we do have to share this suite with our parents. No late-night sneaking out."

Elated, I skipped about, refamiliarizing myself with the "Queen's Room." Called so for Queen Charlotte herself stayed at Thornleigh while passing through the country, it bore the bed the queen slept in, a massive four-poster carved in oak, a King Louis XVI sitting room, a maid's chamber where we three girls unpacked our luggage, and a separate Regency-style reception room. The old furniture had been tastefully restored and some replaced, and new blue velvet drapes framed the large window. I slipped outside that window onto the private balcony and gazed out at the woods.

I wanted a moment alone. To grieve, to be angry, to dream of what I'd say to Mister Major Browning when he showed up with his fiancée. Lady Lara Fane! The name made my blood boil.

Perhaps I should say nothing at all. Treat him with cool indifference, to pretend he meant nothing to me. Oh, how I wished Sir Marcus was here! I missed his merry humor. Instead, I had to face the vultures—the *haute ton* of English society and their American counterparts, the Bostonians.

I dreaded it. And as maid of honor, I wouldn't exactly be inconspicuous, would I? At the best of times, I had little self-confidence and had no wish to be ogled at by all and sundry. I cheered myself that I only had to walk the aisle, smile, and support Ellen.

If only it were that simple, I thought at the dinner table the next evening surrounded by a host of Bostonians. Two of Teddy's sisters, Mrs. Bertha Pringle and Mrs. May Fairchild, sat there staunch-faced and proud, their children Dean, Amy, and Sophie talking to their cousin Jack and Teddy's daughter, Rosalie. A party of seven, and they did not mix easily with the English, though Megan endeavored to do her vivacious best to fill the void.

Glimpsing Ellen's face across the table, I saw how uneasy she'd become, even shy. Teddy's daughter Rosalie flaunted herself shamelessly while deliberately ignoring her stepmother-to-be. The Americans liked to dance and Angela joined them while I preferred to remain at the table. The men were good looking and loud, the women lively and overdressed. I gathered that the Americans considered us English as staid as old biscuits.

After discussing several neutral subjects with the two aunts, I ran out of things to say. Teddy stepped in then, handsome, boyish, and kind, directing his broad grin to me.

"Daphne here is the daughter of *Sir* Gerald du Maurier. She comes from a long line of English crust as does my Ellen here."

"Oh," they chorused, lifting their brows, and there was a sudden interest in anything I had to say from that moment on. Mrs. May Fairchild eyed me peculiarly as though trying to ascertain whether or not I possessed a sizable dowry. As the mother of Dean and Sophie, I gathered she planned to wed either of them into our English "crust."

The next day hastened my opinion of my fellow guests when upon returning from my ride with Charlotte, Amy asked me outright if my sisters and I had any money to our name.

We were standing in the stable courtyard, and the gentle breeze rustled Amy's corn-colored hair about her face. She was prettier than her cousin Sophie, I decided, and more forward, too.

"Aunt May is determined Dean marries well. She wants a rich English wife for him."

Perhaps too forward.

"So are you . . . ?"

"Rich? No. Well, my father is. As for dowries, I guess you'll have to ask him when he arrives."

Her face fell. "Sir Gerald's coming here?"

"Of course he is. And the earl of Rutland, too, if you are name hunting. In fact, I do have a list of all the attendees if you'd like to peruse it. I can even add a column on the side with their status in life and the amount of their fortune."

She stared at me, her brown eyes thrilled at the prospect before she registered my cynicism.

"You English are far too proud. I meant no insult."

She stormed off, and I let out a little laugh. The confrontation lifted my spirits and I spent the afternoon with Megan making last-minute preparations. The rest of the guests arrived that afternoon, my parents among them, and the hour for the wedding dawned.

"I'm terribly nervous," Ellen confessed as we dressed in her chamber on the far side of the house.

"I'm not nervous, Mummy," Charlotte said, twirling in front of the mirror. "I like my daddy. Why didn't you tell him about me? You said my daddy was dead!"

Half in her dress, Ellen reached out to hold her daughter's hand. "Charlotte, we've been through this before. I told you why."

"I asked Rosalie if she burned the letters and she said she never saw the letters."

"She's lying," Ellen sighed, exasperated. "She was afraid you and I would take her daddy away from her. But hopefully she's grown up enough now and is happy she has a little sister."

Nodding, Charlotte absorbed all this information with unusual solemnity.

"I had thought to make Rosalie a bridesmaid, too," Ellen said, "but I couldn't risk her sabotaging anything. Perhaps it's wrong of me, but *somebody* destroyed all those letters I sent and I know in my heart it was Rosalie."

"Has Teddy confronted her about it?" I asked.

"Yes, but she won't confess. If not her, who else could it be? It was only she and her father living at that address and I can't imagine one of the servants would have tampered with the mail. Although, on further reflection, they could have at Rosalie's mother's bidding. Oh, it's a mess and I'm done with it. It doesn't matter now, does it, darling? We're reunited as a family, even if it is eight years later."

"Don't cry, Mummy." Charlotte threw her arms around Ellen's neck. "We can be happy now."

"Yes, darling," Ellen glanced through her tears at me, "we can be happy now."

Nauseous, I examined the long line before me. The aisle seemed to stretch for miles. Wanting to enjoy the silken tents erected over the prettiest part of the Thornleigh grounds, the candlelight, the shining silver Wedgewood, the chink of crystal glasses, the lulling beauty of the violinists playing Mozart, I took a deep breath and straightened the folds of my dress. Glossy pink satin in a classic cut with touches of white, Ellen insisted we have our hair dressed low under a wreath of flowers.

Standing there in her shining white beaded gown, her curled hair pinned upward using diamond star-clips, Ellen looked like a princess out of a fairy-tale book. I said so and she laughed, scooping my hand as Charlotte, Clarissa, and Megan left us to begin the wedding march.

Swallowing deeply, I prayed my high heels did not give way. My pride demanded I walk with dignity, my head held high and my smile sanguine. I was determined not to feel awkward or humiliated knowing Major Browning was in the audience, Lady Lara poised on his arm. I was a du Maurier, and du Mauriers never succumbed to weakness. Never in the public eye, and I would sooner die than cry.

Blessedly, the wedding ceremony passed sooner than I expected. The romantic atmosphere did nothing for my mood so, at the earliest opportunity, I retreated.

"What excuse do you have for retiring so early?"

The low, amused voice hailed from the shadows near the door to the house.

"Aching feet and a headache," I retorted, "and it's a condition worsened by meeting with a disloyal lecher such as yourself. If you will move out of my way, Major, I have much to do."

His arm waylaid me. "Ah, so you are going to your room because of me."

"Because of *you*?" I scoffed. "Really, Major, you have too-high an opinion of yourself and your charms. When is the wedding, by the way? I suppose you brought your fiancée here to steal tips for your own forthcoming nuptials. I congratulate you both."

"You have the wrong picture, Daphne."

Since he would not let me pass, I stood my ground and crossed my arms. "According to you, I always have the wrong picture. I can't even hope to climb up to whatever exalted limb you imagine yourself perched upon. And that's exactly it. It's *imaginary*. Your overestimation of your intelligence is as misguided as it is laughable. And as for your integrity, well, you have none, sir. Now, please move or I will remove the high heel from my foot and shove it in your face."

He laughed, curse him. And laughed harder when I sought to remove my shoe.

"Daphne, Daphne, it's not what you think . . . let me explain."

"There's nothing to explain," I hissed. "You had better attend to Lady Lara, sir. I am sure she is looking for you."

"Daphne, you don't understand. Yes, she's my fiancée," his savage whisper swept past my face. "But only publicly. I had intended to let you know—"

"That would have been nice."

"—but the details are delicate. I didn't want to speak to you until I was officially at liberty to do so."

"Speak what?" I demanded. "We are only friends, Major. Not even; *acquaintances.*"

"We are more than friends."

"No, we are not. What you have done is unforgivable." I put up my hand. "No, don't speak. Don't breathe another word."

On seeing my father, I rushed to his side. In his concern for me, he did not see the major standing there ashen-faced, but my mother did. She remained silent all the way to our room until I was safely tucked into bed.

"My poor girl, what a shock for you . . ."

She'd known about the major's letters. She had hoped, like I. She had waited for an announcement or omission of some kind and when no omission arrived, naturally commenced her matchmaking venture.

"I don't know what to say."

I drew my knees up to my chin. "There's nothing to say. Yes, he's engaged and she's Lady Lara Fane, daughter of the earl of Rutland. She's beautiful, too; did you see?"

Sighing, my mother sat on the edge of my bed. Her furrowed brow deepened. "He's treated you abominably. I will have your father say a word to him."

"Oh, no, don't! *Promise* me you won't. That would be too humiliating."

"What did he say to you at the door?"

"I don't know. I was too angry to listen and I don't care. The sooner they leave the better. They're not staying here the night, are they?"

"I don't think so. Shall I go and find out?"

"Yes, do," I enthused. "I can't stand it if they are. Ellen would have told me, wouldn't she?"

"Brides have a lot on their minds, my dearest."

She left me and I went to sit on my parents' bed. I had planned to lie there and wait for her return but I couldn't help myself. Turning off the light, I headed out to the balcony. I don't know why. Did I want to torture myself watching the festivities below? Watching the major waltz with his beautiful fiancée in the warm summer evening? See the newspaper man snap their photograph?

Drawn to my senses, I turned to go in when I heard a commotion below. People were running around frantically and shouting.

Jeanne came to tell me the news.

"Quick, come quick! Something *terrible* has happened."

"W-what?"

"You better come down. Quickly!"

I felt suddenly cold and sick. "Something's happened to Ellen?"

"No, to Teddy. He's dead."

CHAPTER FOUR

"Dead?"

Teddy Grimshaw is dead? The infallible businessman on his wedding day? Was it too much for him? Had his heart given way? "Poor Ellen. Where is she?"

"In the sunroom. They were carrying him there to wait for the doctor."

Nodding, I tried to collect my wits. It felt like something out of a nightmare. Teddy Grimshaw, dead? Teddy Grimshaw, Ellen's husband, dead? Pinching myself to make sure I wasn't dreaming, I seized a cardigan and rushed out the door.

Downstairs, chaos reigned. I spied my father looking grim and pacing the corridor. Several other guests followed his lead. What else did one do?

"Let's hope the doctor hastens his heels," my father said to me, searching the inside of his coat for a cigar. "I brought these along hoping to have one with the fellow. Now he's dead. It's devilish unfair."

"Are you sure he's dead?"

"He had a heart attack right before my eyes."

Shaking uncharacteristically, Sir Gerald du Maurier echoed the sentiments of every horrified guest. A man didn't expire on his wedding day.

I found Ellen sobbing on her knees beside the couch where Teddy lay. The still, white face arrested me. Such a vibrant man, reduced to an inertness that did not suit him. I didn't know where to look or what to say so I sank to my knees also. "Charlotte?" I whispered.

"She's abed. She doesn't know. Maybe there's still hope?" She smiled through her tears at the man she loved. "He's such a kind man, oh, I can't bear it! Not now when we've found each other again."

I searched for words but none passed my lips. I wanted to give her hope. I wanted to share her grief.

Others pressed around us. Seeing my father hovering in the doorway, I flung my hands out in exasperation. Ellen didn't need an audience. Roused to action, my father shepherded all the genuinely concerned friends and family farther down the hall.

"This is murder," screamed a voice. "That bitch killed him."

Rosalie Grimshaw pushed past my father into the room. She swayed there a moment, red-faced and bearing the ill-effects of too much champagne. "It's the truth. She only married him to get his money. That's why you had Daddy draft up that new will. Oh, I know all about the will."

Rising to her feet, Ellen faced her stepdaughter. "The new will has not been signed, Rosalie, which still makes you the chief benefactress." Bristling, Ellen squeezed my hand tighter. "Don't you care? You haven't even looked at him!"

Wrath frothing around her mouth, Rosalie glanced at the dead man. "You killed him and I swear you'll pay for it."

Twisting on her heel, she sauntered away.

"Make sure she is all right," Ellen said to me. "It's a big shock."

Following the staggering Rosalie down the hall, I soon left her in the care of her cousins. All their faces resonated their shock and absolute disbelief. The two aunts, Teddy's sisters, had taken the vapors and were sitting in chairs pinched from some room in the house. Leaning over one of the aunts, Major Browning was checking her pulse.

"The doctor's here," my father announced.

The crowd separated to let the doctor and Harry through, and I hastened to meet them. "Harry, it's bad," I warned.

Ellen's long-term estate manager turned very pale. "Ellen. How is she?"

"In shock. I don't think there's anything the doctor can do . . ."

My voice trailed off and it carried no hope. Perhaps if the doctor had been on hand when Teddy had the heart attack? It was difficult to know and I was no medical expert.

There was something very reassuring about my father's presence and I know it comforted Ellen, too. She'd always looked up to my father throughout the years and often said he reminded her of her own father before he became ill.

"I'm sorry," the doctor murmured.

I gathered Ellen into my arms while my father talked to the doctor. I tried to strain my ears over Ellen's sobbing. The doctor said he'd visited Teddy once or twice and that he suffered from angina. He asked if anyone knew where Teddy kept his medication and if he'd taken it today.

"He keeps it in his room by his bed," Ellen wept. "I usually make sure he takes it but we've been sleeping in separate rooms leading up to the wedding."

"It's his heart then?" my father persisted.

"Yes, Sir Gerald, from what I can see. The coroner will make a full report. Shall I do the duties?"

"If you will." Reaching inside his coat, my father slipped out a card. "Here's my details if there's anything I can do. I'll be staying here at the house."

"Very good, sir." Shaking his head, the elderly doctor packed up his little black bag and departed.

Persuading Ellen to sit down, I called for a glass of water. "Do take the sedative the doctor gave you," I said, gently pressing the pill into her hand. "It will help you sleep."

"Sleep," she echoed, her face white. "After today, I don't think I'll ever sleep again."

I met my father's gaze across the room. He'd also taken a seat. "I do advise, Ellen m'dear, you go to your room with Daphne. I'll stand guard, don't you worry."

"No, I can't leave him," Ellen wailed. "I just can't. Please," she begged him, "please keep the others away."

Nodding, my father went to lock the door while unraveling his tie. "Easily done."

The strangest night passed dismally slow. Despite her protestations, the sedative did send Ellen to sleep. My father and I dozed off and on, my father having the good sense to cover the body with a blanket.

I felt ill with a corpse so near. A strong, reasonably healthy man and now he was dead. I had difficulty equating the fact in my mind. True, he was several years older than Ellen, sixteen to be precise, however, he conducted himself like a young man. He had a quick step and he rode well. I'd seen him bound up the stairs and swing Charlotte around a few times. If the man had a bad heart condition, he'd have struggled with such activities, and Teddy Grimshaw seemed a man always in control.

My father had shared none of my qualms that night. Lighting his cigar, he had said to the corpse, "Well, old fellow, I'll still have a cigar with you, though it's not what I had in mind."

I wondered how the other guests fared. I wondered if Major Browning thought the death suspicious. He, like the others, would have heard Rosalie Grimshaw's outburst. *Murder,* she'd cried.

Murder? It looked like a straightforward heart attack to me. Sometimes it happened when one was in high spirits. It wasn't fair, but it happened. I remembered reading in the paper about a young woman coming home to England to be reunited with her family only to perish the night prior. That was also heart failure and the woman only in her thirties.

Ellen still lay sleeping, though fitful and restless and I did not envy her waking up today. Snoring in an armchair by the body, my father remained a neglectful guard. Creeping over to him, I pulled his overcoat.

"W-what . . . ?" he spluttered, his memory sharpened.

"I'm just going to organize some tea. Can you watch Ellen while I'm gone?"

I did not look at the body. I refused to look at the body. Once outside, I was glad to see the house hadn't stirred yet. It was quiet and undisturbed; the only sound the ticking grandfather clock on the hall's mantelpiece.

I entered the kitchen as the cook stoked the fire.

"Ah, hello there, Miss Daphne."

I smiled at the large middle-aged woman. Everything about Nelly Ireson was large—her plump hands, her big smile, her booming voice. "I've missed you, Nelly. You haven't changed at all."

"And ye've grown up so pretty! Very pretty!" Bustling back to the fire, she shook her head. "Sad. It's sad. So nice to see her happy again, after all that. Did she sleep?"

"Yes, a little, with the sedative. I do hope they move the body today."

"Oh, don't ye worry ye little head with it. Dr. Peterson may be old and a little bit deaf but he's not slow about his business. Ye best stay with her every minute, Miss Daphne. She's been through hell and I think this one's near done her in. Good thing that sweet girl is here."

"You mean Charlotte? You believe she'd take her life if Charlotte weren't here?"

Nelly's brown eyes narrowed. "That little girl were the savin' of her, even if she were disowned for it."

"Nelly," I murmured, looking behind me. "You must be careful what you say, for Ellen's sake. Not many know the full story."

"Oh, there'll be knowin' now, if ye know what I mean. Death brings it all out. Ye'll have to help her, Miss Daphne. Don't ye leave

Ellen on her own. I worry about her. I always have, since she were a wee babe."

"Don't worry, I'm not leaving. I have no commitments so I can stay as long as I want . . . or as long as Ellen needs me."

Nelly nodded, pleased. "Ye're a good girl. Not like these other mad young women I see chasin' after every male in a flashy motorcar. Phew! Did ye see the likes of some of them here, thinkin' themselves *all that*."

I smiled, adding that Major Browning could be relegated to this category.

"Don't know him," Nelly reflected, "but I've read about his fiancée, Lady Lara. Beautiful, ain't she? Like a china doll. All that golden hair and a—"

"Yes." I cut her off short. "The *tea,* Nelly?"

"And do try and tempt her to eat." Nelly went on organizing the tray, even pausing to add a fresh flower from the garden. "Strawberry jam on toast. It's her favorite."

"I will try, Nelly."

I couldn't wait to leave. If I heard one more word about Lady Lara Fane, I'd spit in the pond.

"Daphne," whispered a voice as I entered the hallway.

A voice I knew too well. Grinding my teeth, I tensed. "If you say one word to me, Major Browning, I'll throw this tray at you."

"That's not very ladylike."

I ignored his appeasing grin.

"I came as early as I could."

He'd slipped into walking side by side with me down the hall. Looking straight ahead, I seethed beneath my skin. "What are you doing here?"

Whistling, he fell back a step. "Vicious."

Squaring my shoulders, I kept my pace and repeated the question, adding, "You've got no reason to be here, Major Browning. This does not concern you; you yourself said you hardly know the family. You were only invited because Ellen thought—"

"Ah, she did not know I and Lady Lara's fiancée were one and the same, did she? Very economizing for her, I daresay, but I am only a *cover* fiancée"

I paused. "A *cover* fiancée?"

We were nearing the front hall.

"Who let you in, by the way?"

He smiled, producing a knife from his pocket. "A window, in the tearoom. I noticed it had a faulty latch yesterday."

"And you make a business of smuggling yourself into great houses, do you? I should call the police."

"I *am* the police, remember?"

I couldn't win with him and the fact irked me. No, the fact *incensed* me. Yes, that word fit better.

"You won't get rid of me so easily," he called after me. "I've business in the area." He plopped a card on the tea tray. "It's for Ellen. See that she gets it."

He turned and exited through the front door.

Ellen had risen when I appeared with her breakfast. My father had encouraged her to sit by the newly stoked fire. It was a chilly morning and seeing the stiff body under the blanket sent an extra chill up my spine. Could the man really have been murdered? Or had he just died of natural causes?

"I'm living a nightmare," Ellen said to me, struggling to sip a little of her tea. "I don't know how I can go on now. Nothing will seem right. How can I even sit here and eat breakfast? How can I possibly recover? We'd planned our whole lives together. Oh . . . oh . . ."

Choking on her tears, she pulled away to the window. "No, leave me be." She hid her face in her hands and sobbed.

I glanced at my father.

He eyed the toast on the tray but I shook my head. "Ellen," I said softly. "The police will be here soon. Come upstairs with me and change."

"Yes," she cried, tears spilling down her wedding dress. "Cut it off me; I don't want to ever see it again!"

Thankfully, I navigated the way to her bedroom without anybody seeing us. A moment longer and we'd certainly have run into one of the guests leaving their rooms.

Ellen started unbuttoning her gown before I opened the door to the master chamber. In medieval times, this room had been the lord's solar. Stumbling after her, I was amazed at the changes. Shut up for years, I truly felt as if I'd stepped into another time, another era.

"We were to spend our wedding night here," Ellen moaned, sitting on the enormous four-poster in the center of the room.

The room was the epitome of a fifteenth-century wealthy lord's chamber. Medieval weapons stared down at us from the stone walls where four hunting tapestries graced the far wall, each representing a seasoned chase. The tapestries were French, as was the floral and fleur-de-lis design on the bed's coverlet and on the royal blue drapes hanging from the two large windows bearing an easterly view of the gardens down to the river.

Due to the tragedy, nobody had lit the fire so the room had a deathly cold feeling about it. I shivered, assisting Ellen out of her wedding dress and into something plain and comfortable. She couldn't bear to wear anything from her wedding trousseau and I thought it a shame all those fine clothes might end up in the fire. I talked her out of doing so for the moment and considered it a fortunate thing the fire wasn't lit.

"What is the use? What shall I do now?"

I sat down beside her on the bed. I knew I had to get her out of this room, if nothing else. Putting my arms around her, I listened to her heart-wrenching wails.

"I feel like my life is over . . . we had such plans." Smiling through her tears, she recounted the tragedy of the past. "All those years wasted, I thought we had our whole lives together. Do you know Charlotte asked me last night if we were still going on the big ship and if we were, was there a doctor on board who could help her papa? It'll break her heart when she finds out . . . when she finds out . . . oh, Daphne! And to think we could have prevented it."

"Prevented it?"

Blowing her nose, she let me read the card Major Browning had left for her. After his name printed neatly, the messy handwriting said:

> *Mrs. Grimshaw,*
> *I know your husband has many enemies and has suf-*
> *fered a great deal of stress lately. I'd like to talk to you*
> *in private.*
>
> MB.

Of course, I'd already read it. However, I feigned surprise. "Enemies? But he died of a heart attack, didn't he? Do you think stress did it?"

"I don't know." Ellen wept into her hands. "He seemed so happy and relaxed lately, apart from some minor business worries. He never discussed his business with me, you see. He said he wanted to keep our life separate. Who is this Major Browning? I thought you said he was in the army?"

"Yes, but he also works for Scotland Yard."

"Oh . . . perhaps he knows something about Teddy and wants to talk to me. I don't know whether I want to talk to him after what he did to you."

"You don't have to talk to him if you don't want to," I murmured. "Or, if you prefer, I'll find out what he wants to talk to you about."

"Yes, do," Ellen decided. "I have too many concerns on my shoulders at the moment. Oh, my dear Daphne, how am I ever going to be able to face the day?"

CHAPTER FIVE

"I don't envy her," I said to my parents as we stood there watching them take away the body. Ellen stood apart from everyone else, alone, stoic, almost like a dead person herself.

"It's like the Kate Trevalyan affair," Angela whispered to me.

"It's nothing like it," I shot back, my gaze narrowing when I saw Major Browning's face among the crowd of spectators. Was he lurking around in the hope of an audience with Ellen? If so, he must have something important to say.

I burned to know what. He had a knack of knowing things, which irritated me. He took pleasure in proving me wrong. "He should be paying court to his fiancée, not hanging around here," I seethed and Angela too sent him a glare.

He lifted a quizzical brow in response.

"Ha! He even feigns innocence; truly, I cannot abide him."

"Have Ellen whip him off the estate," my father murmured from behind.

I snuck a look at him. Yes, Sir Gerald du Maurier did not approve of Major Browning's treatment of his daughter. He, too, refused to look the man in the eye, preferring to fix his gaze on the black wagon bearing away the remains of Teddy Grimshaw.

"Daphne, Angela, Sir Gerald," Ellen raised her tearstained face to us, "please come to the nursery. Your mother, too. I'm in need of a mother figure today."

Downcast, we followed her back into the house. I deliberately gazed at the ground upon passing the major. Why had I promised Ellen I'd talk to him? No doubt he'd return to wherever he was staying, thereby forcing me to seek him out. Or I could just wait until he returned. My curiosity burned. What did he know? Did he suspect some kind of foul play?

On our way to the nursery, we passed the door adjacent the breakfast room. Voices drifted out: hushed whispers, rapid statements, heated accusations. Ellen's name was mentioned and Ellen paused in her step, holding her stomach.

" . . . and she makes such a pretense! Did you see her just now, dressed in widow's weaves waving off my father's dead body?"

"Don't listen," my father advised Ellen, shepherding her up the stairs.

"My poor darling." My mother took Ellen into her arms.

Nanny Brickley hovered in the background. She had been sitting in the corner with Clarissa and rose to her feet when we entered the room. Megan, who'd been working on a puzzle on the floor with Charlotte also rose and offered her condolences.

"I don't wish any of you to leave," Ellen cried.

"We will stay as long as you need us," Clarissa declared. "Charles has canceled all his engagements and offers his services. His uncle is a vicar in Devon."

Megan frowned.

"What?" Clarissa raised her brows. "It's a necessary business, the funeral."

"The funeral," Ellen echoed, her face turning white.

"What's a funeral?" Charlotte asked, tugging her hand.

"It's a . . . it's a place where people go to say good-bye," Ellen answered through sobs.

My mother reached for her handkerchief and my father put an arm about her. We had had our share of funerals in the family.

"Why is everyone giving me the evil eye?" Persisting in her innocence, Clarissa sailed across the room like a paragon of virtue. "These things simply must be addressed."

"Yes, you are right." Ellen blinked through her tears. "Can you ask Charles to arrange it for me?"

"Certainly." Clarissa bowed her head and I raised my eyes to the ceiling. Of the most inopportune moments, Clarissa Fenwick was a master.

Fortunately, she sailed out of the room in search of her husband.

"You are going to need your strength, my dear," my mother pressed Ellen whilst we kept Charlotte occupied. "It would be best to go down for lunch. Seeing you will halt their tongues."

"Oh, I can't," Ellen started but she soon saw the wisdom of my mother's advice.

"It's staring the enemy in the face," my father added and since he was a man of theater and great intelligence, Ellen acquiesced. "You shall all be with me, I hope. I can't do it on my own. Not with the Fairchilds and Pringles. How they hate me!"

"Two enemy camps," my father observed.

"Gerald." My mother shook her head. "This can't be helpful . . ."

"Nonsense, my dear. You did not see the look in that girl's eye but I did and I can tell you it was positively savage."

"The poor girl has lost her father . . ."

"And her millions," I put in.

"It's true," Megan confirmed. "That's why she hates Ellen. She never wanted her father to marry."

Being the older and wiser one, my mother changed the subject. "The best thing you can do is focus on your little girl."

"That's what I dread the most," Ellen confessed. "He just doted on her. After having no father and then finding him . . . they had a year together at most but in a strange way she became closer to him than to me. Oh, Aunty Muriel, she's in denial. She still thinks he's gone to the hospital. She still thinks we are going to America."

"Let me try with her tomorrow," my mother said softly. "But she will notice everyone's faces and she will have heard things. She's not a little girl anymore."

Ellen cast a look at her daughter. "No," she agreed, somber. "She is not."

"I may have limited experience with children," said the always opinionated Clarissa Fenwick at luncheon, "but isn't it better to tell the truth?"

"We don't know what the truth is yet," I reminded her, keeping watch for Ellen's entrance.

We were all assembled in the great dining room; the silverware laid out and hot and cold aromatic dishes arriving from Nelly's kitchen. For Ellen's sake, I made an effort to speak with the enemy camp. I decided on the less austere of the two sisters first.

"Mrs. Fairchild, I trust all is in order in your room? You must let me know if there is anything you need as I will be staying on to see to everyone's comfort and to help Ellen."

"Oh?" The thin-pencilled brow lifted. "You're the poor cousin, are you?"

My cheeks flamed hot. "Certainly not. I am no relation. I'm Daphne du Maurier."

"Oh, yes, I remember." She smiled anew at me. "Please forgive an old woman's memory, child, for I am quite old, you know. I am the eldest in our family and Teddy ten years younger than I. I had my children late, as you can see." She indicated to where Mr. Dean Fairchild and his sister Miss Sophie Fairchild sat on a Louis XVI couch.

"How is Miss Rosalie coping, Mrs. Fairchild?" I whispered, now that we had established an acquaintance.

She didn't need to answer for the answer stared back at us. Scowling as Ellen came into the room, Rosalie jumped out of her chair.

"Well, if you think I'm going to sit around and eat with her, you're all mistaken. I'm leaving this place."

Pushing past Ellen at the door, she ran off, her cousin Amy Pringle hard on her heels. Miss Sophie Fairchild also made to follow if her mother hadn't indicated she return to her seat.

Lunch commenced then, nobody speaking except out of absolute necessity, like to pass the potatoes and so forth. Occasional remarks were made about the weather between Mr. Dean Fairchild and Charles Fenwick who planned, I suspected, to hunt in the woods this afternoon.

From what I gathered of the American camp, none of them appeared to have had a close relationship with Teddy Grimshaw. His sisters rarely saw him above two times a year; the persons who saw him most proved to be his nephews, Dean and Jack, by way of business. Dean Fairchild managed one of Teddy's companies and Jack was an assistant-manager at another.

I hated to think how their uncle's death affected their livelihoods. Neither seemed concerned. Was their anxiety concealed behind a nonchalant facade? Or, I wondered, were they too good-natured to show it?

Miss Amy Pringle soon returned and resumed her breakfast.

"Isn't she pretty?" Jeanne elbowed me under the table.

Observing the golden locks, pert mouth, short nose, and sky-blue eyes, I did concede a certain prettiness to the debutante. If she hunted for an English husband, I had no doubt she'd find one. And from what issued out of her mother's mouth, I knew the lucky man had to possess a title or he would see the road.

However, Amy Pringle, independent of her mother's designs and wishes, seemed stuck to her cousin Rosalie Grimshaw. Also an only child, Rosalie did exactly what she wanted, no more, no less.

"I cannot understand you English," Sophie Fairchild murmured to me after breakfast. "You never talk in the mornings. Everywhere we go, the breakfast rooms are full of English couples sipping their tea and reading the newspapers. Don't you ever talk?"

I smiled. "Yes. Have you noticed us at parties?"

She considered, tilting her curly brown hair to one side. "I haven't been to many English parties; I only came out this year."

"Ah, then I suggest you befriend Megan. She knows all the best people."

"But Mother says your family is," she blushed, "I mean, oh, you know what I mean."

"Yes, I think I do." I smiled again, beginning to like the girl. She had none of the pretentions of the others and, as we continued talking, it became clear that she adored her brother, Dean. I wished I had a brother. How my father would have delighted to have had a son.

As we turned the corner to go upstairs after breakfast, a commotion occurred in the foyer. Rosalie Grimshaw and her maid ... flinging her luggage out of the door. I thought she'd care more for her fine things, but no, she intended to make a point. She wanted everyone to know she was leaving the house because of Ellen.

A mild frown passed Sophie's face. Was it embarrassment?

"Do stay, Rosalie," she addressed her cousin. "Where are you going to go?"

"Anywhere but here," came the sharp retort, those fierce blue eyes detecting me. "Tell Ellen I'll see her in court after Daddy's will is read."

A car's engine started up outside and I peeked through the window. Cousin Jack sorted out Rosalie's luggage before jumping in the front seat to drive. Rosalie and her maid climbed in, Rosalie tossing her red scarf behind her neck as they hurtled down the drive.

"What a relief." My mother echoed the sentiments of all remaining guests. "Poor Ellen doesn't need trouble like that. It's enough to grieve and look after Charlotte."

"Didn't Rosalie's mother come over from America? Perhaps Rosalie is going to stay with her?"

"Probably," my father snorted. "I don't like to say it, especially not with Ellen around, but she's going to have a fight on her hands."

"You mean about the money?"

"The money. It's always about the money."

"Do you think she caused a scene because she actually truly believes Ellen killed her father? Or because she fears the sudden loss of her inheritance?"

"The suddenness of her father's death has put her in shock," my father said in the privacy of our rooms. "Unfortunately, if her mother has anything to do with it, she'll use the poor girl."

I gaped at him. "It's not an idle threat then? How can she take Ellen to court?"

"Oh, she'll make a noise. An unpleasant noise."

"Poor Ellen," sighed my mother. "But surely, Rosalie's father would have left her something? Someone should tell the poor girl it simply isn't worth making a big fight over."

"When there's millions at stake, yes, there is," Sir Gerald over-ruled. "Yes, there is."

CHAPTER SIX

"So she's left?"

"Yes, she's gone. Jack took her. Where do you think they've gone? Back to the city?"

"Her mother's in London," Ellen replied, pausing to open the old rusty gate at the start of the medieval pleasure garden.

I'd persuaded Ellen to seek some fresh air and the trip did us both good. "My goodness, Ellen, you've been busy!" I gazed around in wonder at the vast changes. Once a labyrinth of overgrown hedges and weeds, it now housed a series of gardens, mostly rectangular with one large oval garden in the center.

"Harry and I worked together on this," Ellen said, guiding me through. "We've incorporated some Renaissance features but I wanted a structured wildness to remain as in the medieval era. That's where I got the idea for the walled garden and gazebo."

I stopped to admire the pond in the oval garden brimming with all kinds of pink and yellow flowers.

"Yellow is happy so I wanted lots of yellow flowers." A sad smile turned up the corners of her lips. "My mother also liked yellow roses. If you remember, she had a rosebush by the stables."

"Yes, I remember. What happened to it?"

"There was a fire. We managed to put it out and repair the

stables, but there was no hope for the garden. And it was in an odd place."

"Very odd," I agreed. "It's nice you have the yellow roses growing here along the wall."

"I knew you'd love the walled garden. There's also a hidden seat in the middle there. It's an ideal place to spend an afternoon reading a book."

"You shouldn't give me ideas," I warned. "You mightn't see me for month."

"Oh, Daphne." Choking back a sob, Ellen crashed into my arms. "My heart feels dead and I feel lifeless. I don't want to go on living. If Charlotte wasn't here, I'd . . ."

"But Charlotte *is* here and even if she wasn't, as hard as it is, we must go on. That's what Teddy would have wanted. Have you heard from Charles for the funeral arrangements?"

"He and Clarissa are organizing it. I couldn't bear to do so. Oh, how I wish we hadn't had separate rooms those last two nights! Then I could have made certain he took his heart medicine. But he was always so diligent, Daphne. Something about it doesn't ring right to me."

I examined her carefully. "Do you think somebody tried to murder him?"

She looked away. "We have been receiving threats. Well, to be more accurate, *Teddy* received the threats. He never wanted me to know about them but one day, about a month ago, the mail came to me first. In it was a note with cut-out letters from the newspaper saying, 'Vengeance is mine, I will repay.'"

I stopped short to blink. "Isn't that from the Bible?"

Ellen shrugged.

"Did you go to the police?"

"No. Teddy didn't want to. He laughed; he wasn't concerned about it at all. He said he'd received many such threats since he became rich. You see, Teddy's investors and his companies are intertwined. While they usually make profits, sometimes they invested poorly."

"And some people lost a great deal of money," I finished for her.

"It doesn't seem fair, but Teddy maintained he conducted all his businesses in an equitable manner and he'd never stoop so low as to cheat to make money. People trusted him, you see, that's why, if anything, he got annoyed when paper threats arrived in the mail. He said it was from people who didn't possess all the facts."

"What did he do with these threats?"

"Toss them in the fire," Ellen answered, gazing down at the ground. "But I did keep one or two of them without his knowledge. I don't know why. Maybe because I thought they might be important one day."

"And you are so right . . ." I began to see Teddy Grimshaw's death differently. I no longer believed he died of natural causes.

Punching her hand through the hedge, Ellen wept. "I believe he may have been murdered. That *somebody* killed him. *Somebody* who was at the wedding . . ."

"At the wedding." My echo faded into the breeze. "But who could want him dead?"

"Those after his money: his family. They all stand to benefit, you know. *All* of them. I know because Teddy had a new will drafted this week. He said he made many changes but his second witness couldn't sign it until next week."

"But surely the new will will take precedence?"

"If the matter is taken to court, I stand to lose everything. Not that I want even a dime of it for myself. If it weren't for Charlotte, I'd wish them all well, greedy vultures."

I was horrified. I knew little of these affairs. The writer in me had always wanted to watch a squabble after a death, greedy vulture-like relatives, as Ellen said, clawing over the money. However, I never expected to land right in the middle of one. "Ellen, don't give up without a fight for Charlotte's sake if naught else."

"Yes, you're right," Ellen muttered under her breath. "But it would give me great satisfaction to spit the money right in their faces."

* * *

I had grave reservations about locating Major Browning on Ellen's behalf.

I didn't want to go, foremost.

What kind of friend was I, though, if I did not?

Swallowing my pride, I asked the remaining guests if they knew of his whereabouts. Apart from the Fenwicks, ourselves, Megan, and the American camp, all had now removed from Thornleigh, shaking their heads sadly as they left.

"I believe Major Browning has rooms at Jamaica Inn," Colonel Ramsay said. "We ourselves are heading in that direction if you'd like a lift?"

I hadn't anticipated such a quick departure from Thornleigh. No time to see to my hair or dress. Not that I *cared* for the major's good opinion but I had intended to go properly dressed. As it stood, I'd simply thrown on a nondescript day gown and my hair lacked luster. It needed a good wash after the wedding-hair arrangement which left it positively coarse and wiry. I'd pulled it back into a severe knot at the nape of my neck and Jeanne said I looked like a governess.

Governess or no, I accepted the colonel's offer. He preferred an open motorcar and to drive himself. I sat in the rear with his wife who frowned at her husband's desire for speed.

"Oh Leopold, you're such a child!"

His grin broadened in the side mirror. "Daphne doesn't mind, does she?"

"No," I shouted back, "but if I had a hat I might."

He laughed at this and I begged him to slow down when we neared the township. There were so many interesting cottages dotted alongside the beautiful countryside. My heart ached to live here, to breathe in the lavender fields each day, to own my own rose garden, to live in a house as grand as Thornleigh. But my heart belonged in Cornwall.

"How will you get home, my dear?" the colonel's wife asked when we motored into the village.

"Oh, don't worry about me. I'll find my way."

I reassured them both, waving them off as my feet landed on the cobbles outside Jamaica Inn. Blushing scarlet as I caught a glimpse of myself, I hurried inside the reflector doors and marched straight up to the lady at the reception desk.

"Hello, would you please tell Major Browning he has a visitor?"

The lady eyed me suspiciously. What did an unaccompanied young lady want with Major Browning, her demeanor insinuated. I refused to give her the satisfaction, drumming my fingers on the desk instead.

"Ye can tell him yeself," she eventually snarled. "Room two, upstairs on the left."

"Thank you." I smiled serenely.

I half expected her to say he was out, dining with his fiancée or touring the countryside. She must have known he had a fiancée and that was why she was curious as to my visit. No doubt she'd ask him upon his return and I wondered what answer he would give. "Oh, she's a friend." "Oh, she's my cousin." "Oh, she's the love of my life I have recently betrayed by my engagement to Lady Lara Fane."

Room two beckoned. Scraping my fist across the wooden door, I glanced around, glad nobody had seen me, though I could hear the maids downstairs whispering.

"One minute," said the voice inside and I cringed.

I almost darted back down the stairs. Coward, coward, I told myself. Remember why you've come. *Remember.*

His face gleamed behind the opening door. Half undressed and halfway through his shaving routine, he invited me inside. If I hadn't blushed because of his deshabille, I might have insisted he see me downstairs.

I tried not to look at him as he floated around the room, happy and relaxed at his leisure. He continued shaving. "I am most privileged to receive you this morning."

"I am here on Ellen's behalf." I got to the point.

"Ah." He scraped a spot on the left side of his face.

"She'll see you."

He paused, glancing at me through the mirror. "That's good."

"Come to the house at three o'clock this afternoon. Good day."

I hastened to the door but he caught my hand.

"Where are you going so early? Won't you at least share my breakfast with me?"

Share his breakfast with him? "Share your breakfast with you," I echoed in utter disbelief. "*Share your breakfast with you?*"

"No need to reiterate the invitation," he joked, toweling dry his face. "Here." He brought the chair from the window to sit opposite his tiny breakfast table. "That's nice and cozy, isn't it? Coffee or tea? No, you take your coffee black and strong in the mornings."

That he'd remembered this minor detail only served to increase my fury. "No, I'll have tea, white and weak. No sugar."

He lifted a devil-may-care eyebrow and I realized the folly of my situation. What was I doing here alone and unaccompanied in the private rooms of a bachelor?

I lingered because I wanted an explanation.

I lingered because I wanted to hurt him as he'd hurt me.

I didn't care a fig for propriety.

Resuming his devil-may-care attitude, he poured his coffee and bit into his buttered toast. "Hmm, a bit cold. I like my toast warm. You?"

Since he wished to play pleasantries, I went along with him. "I prefer a boiled egg."

"Do you?"

I glared at a corner of the tablecloth. He had such a way of showing interest when he didn't mean it.

"Oh, come now. Don't you dream of a nice warm brioche smothered with strawberry jam and whipped cream?"

"No. I'd prefer bacon and mushrooms."

"And spinach? Kippers?"

"No kippers."

"Excellent."

He selected another piece of toast and lathered a good spoonful of plum jam on it. Before biting into it, he offered me half. I declined.

"You don't know what you're missing out on," he murmured, keeping his gaze upon me as he devoured slowly, licking his fingers at the end.

"I suppose you do this routine with your fiancée? Where is she? Hiding behind a curtain?"

The very notion of Lady Lara Fane hiding behind any curtain was ridiculous and we both knew it. He laughed and I managed a miniscule smile.

"Progress," he smiled back. "I'm glad for we are much more than friends, aren't we, Daphne?"

His dark eyes remained intent upon mine, as though endeavoring to lure out secrets. I wished I could hold under such scrutiny, however, I faltered. He was too good looking, too charming, and too practiced, curse him.

"Lady Lara and I are not really engaged. We might have been, if you hadn't come along."

"Oh?" I feigned mild interest though I burned to know everything.

"It was our parents' dearest wish that we one day marry. When Lara's father became sick at the beginning of this year, she asked me to pose as her fiancée publicly. We intend to keep up the pretense until he passes away."

"I see. How generous of you."

"I am not at all generous."

"You could have mentioned something about her to me."

"I could have."

"You deliberately didn't because . . ."

"Because I knew you'd be upset."

He was smiling at me now, warmly. "My dearest girl, how prickly you are! I would have explained at the wedding if you had let me. As it stands, I am despised by your father, and your mother and sisters have daggers in their eyes whenever I encounter them."

A grimace lurked at the corners of my mouth. I liked the notion of *him* being uncomfortable. He was always so polished in society, so liked by everyone. It was good for him to endure a dose of displeasure, I decided. "Why do you want to see Ellen? What do you know about Teddy Grimshaw?"

"Questions, questions. If I'm going to answer any of them, you have to spend a few hours in my company."

I gazed at him askance. My hair was a mess, my dress was atrocious, and I looked and felt ghastly. I had left the house in too much of a hurry to even grab my umbrella. At least, I consoled myself, I had taken Angela's advice last winter and packed my handbag appropriately, now stocked with all kinds of goodies to use for such occasions.

"Unless you have other transport?"

I almost lied and said I had Mr. Dean Fairchild, a handsome and eligible American, waiting for me downstairs.

"Then it's not too bad to endure a little time with the man you love touring the countryside—"

"The man I love? You truly are conceited."

CHAPTER SEVEN

"I know." He grinned. "I cannot help it. Or perhaps it comes out only with you. You have a devil of a way of fanning the fires, so to speak."

"Don't you have an engagement with your fiancée? Luncheon or something?"

"I do," he replied back merrily, "but when a better offer comes up, one must take it."

His gaze lowered as he tilted his head down toward mine almost as though he meant to kiss me. Retreating to the door, I chastised myself for my weakness. I knew this man. His wishing to spend time in my company concealed a motive to find out details. I decided then to see whether he'd try to ask questions on our little outing. Dare I place a bet on it? A thousand pounds he'd try to pry something out of me.

"I don't suppose Lady Lara and her parents are staying in this shabby inn?"

"Snobby." He whistled as we descended the staircase. "It's not at all shabby. It's charming."

He waited for me to prompt him. "Well?" I insisted once on the street. "Where is the earl of Rutland residing?"

"In a house." He grinned, directing me to his motorcar. "In *their* house. They have one here."

"Of course they do. Earls have houses everywhere."

"I wager your Sir Marcus has more houses than the earl."

"He's not *my* Sir Marcus," I began to say then stopped. Why should I? Why not pretend Sir Marcus and I had something between us?

"He measures every woman against you." His dry statement accompanied us across the street.

I paused beside the polished Bentley. "Is this your car?"

"Don't sound so incredulous. Get in."

It wasn't until we were blazing out of the tiny village that he said: "No, you are right. It is on loan from a friend."

"A friend from the Yard?" At his pause, I sighed. "Oh, please. It's just a car; not a state secret."

A secret smile eluded his lips. "One never knows with you. You are entirely too nosy."

"Nosy? I don't like that word. Inquisitive is better."

He changed gears. "By the way, I read your story. It was excellent."

I wasn't expecting the compliment. "Thank you."

A wry grin touched his lips. "I picked all the connections. Your inspiration: Rachael Eastley."

"To begin with, yes, but you will note my widow had her differences. She is more forthright and determined."

"Traits of yours?"

I shrugged. "Where are we going exactly? I do have a life, you know. I am not entirely at your beck and call."

"Oh, but you are." He laughed into the wind. "I have you captive and for a couple of hours or so, you're completely mine."

I refused to allow his charms to win me over. "What is it you wish to discuss with Ellen? I am her ambassador."

"Ambassador! What nonsense. You scarcely know the woman."

"I know her very well," I hissed. "Just because we are pen-friends doesn't mean I don't know her. In fact, I wager I know her a great deal better than my other friends whom I spend time with on a weekly basis."

"Ah," he nodded, "you share secrets."

"To some degree. There's a comfort in being a pen-friend. One can write almost anything about one's life while absorbing another's. It's quite . . ." I stopped. How had he done that? Lured me to talk about Ellen when I'd decided not to?

He realized how annoyed I'd become with the fact and smiled into the breeze.

"I suppose it's pointless to ask what kind of work you're doing at the moment?"

"At the moment," he began, a serious tone to his voice, "at the moment I am working on playing the fiancée."

"Of course you are. I'm surprised the earl of Rutland approves of you. How many houses to your name?"

"Not as many as Sir Marcus." He laughed. "And I have it on good authority I'd make a very bad husband."

"Oh?"

"My godmother says so. I'd like you to meet her one day."

"That's very unlikely."

"Not as unlikely as you think." He consulted his watch. "We should be there in half an hour."

"Half an hour!" He had to be joking.

"She lives in a cottage near Tintagel Castle."

He wasn't joking.

"I promised her I'd take this future famous novelist to come and meet her. She loves books. In fact, I've never seen her without one."

He went on to list the last few books she'd read and the comments she'd made about them. Half-listening, I tensed in my seat. Why did he want me to meet his godmother? Shouldn't he have warned me first?

No. If he'd suggested it, I'd have suggested he take his *fiancée* to meet her. Perhaps he'd already brought Lady Lara here. "What does Lady Lara think of your godmother?"

"She's never met her."

"What was she doing today? An appointment with her dresser? Am I a fill-in?"

Suddenly his foot slammed on the brakes.

I hung onto my seat. He looked angry. I'd never seen him look angry before and the vision startled me.

"What will it take for you to believe me? I don't think you realize what a great risk . . ." His jawline tightened. "No, you don't understand. How could you? You're just a woman."

"I'm just a woman!" I screeched back, ready to jump out of the car and run down the road. I would have done so if he hadn't caught my arm. "Let me go."

"If Lara tells you the truth, will you believe her? What I meant to say was we're asking a great deal of you to conceal the knowledge of our counterfeit engagement."

"When did she ask you?" I needed to know. I needed to know all the details and make the necessary connections.

"Several months ago. Before I saw you on the Isles of Scilly."

I counted in my mind every meeting we'd had together and to my dismay, the cards stacked in his favor. Our relationship bloomed at Somner House and turned into something deeper and intrinsically warmer. Ironic, I thought, that it had done so in the throes of winter.

He started the car again and I remained silent. I didn't want to talk. I wanted to hug the knowledge that he cared for me. More than a friend. More than a passing love interest. He cared for me so much he'd instruct Lara to talk to me. I smiled. I kind of enjoyed that promise . . . the acknowledgement of my place in Major Browning's heart.

Did he have a heart? A heart capable of enduring love?

In any case, I refused to consider it today. I intended to enjoy the day.

As we turned into the tiny seaside village, it started to rain. I'd been watching the clouds form above us, hoping beyond hope that it'd hold. At least until this afternoon when I returned to Thornleigh. It could rain all it liked at Thornleigh but now, no, please not now, I begged the sky.

The sky stared down at me, dark and full. "Oh no," I said, "I've forgotten my umbrella *again*." What had gotten into me lately? I used to be so prepared, always an umbrella within my reach.

"Will this do?"

Reaching over to the backseat, he pulled out a raincoat. "That will keep you dry until we go inside."

I put on the raincoat. The sleeves were far too long but that didn't matter. "What about you?"

He laughed, pulling the hood up over my head. "I'm about to take a morning bath."

And he wasn't far from the truth. What had begun as a medium downfall turned torrential. "Maybe we should wait?"

"No." He encouraged me out of the car. "Head straight for the green door and knock loudly. She's a little deaf."

Tucking my bag under the raincoat, I opened the door and hurried down the path to the green door. Only a few meters from the street, the quaint stone cottage beckoned me. A lone plant swung by the painted green door and in the plant rested a little green frog with big eyes.

"She loves knickknacks," the major murmured, adding one loud thudding knock to my own. "Her house is full of them."

"I hope she answers soon," I said, "or we'll both be drenched."

As I finished saying it, the door rattled and after a succession of turned locks opened to reveal a middle-aged black-haired woman of extraordinary feature. Ushered inside, I had a chance to study her better as she and the major engaged in an excitable witty repartee. Evidently, she hadn't seen him for a long time, her strong brow and square jawline softening as she laughed. I liked the sound of her laugh; it was mischievous and engaging and from her short stub nose and probing blue eyes under a thick wedge of ebony hair, she looked and acted like a European aristocrat. It was a classically handsome face more than beautiful.

She smiled when this observation of her looks tumbled out of my mouth.

"And you must be Daphne." She kissed me on both cheeks. "Welcome, Daphne, to my little house by the sea. You are quite clever. Dare you hazard a guess at which country I come from?"

"Italy?"

"Germany." Her smile faded. "Of course, Germans are not very popular in England and if it weren't for my good husband Wilhelm, we might not have survived the war."

Not caring to elaborate upon this fact, she invited us into her little house by the sea. The darkened corridor lined with a vine wallpaper led us to the heart of the house, a large rectangular room overlooking the ocean. One shuttered window banged open and the sea air drifted up my nose, fresh and exhilarating.

The major went to close the window while I followed his graceful godmother into the tiny kitchen on the right.

"It is small," she said, "but it suits me. Ah, you see I have a passion for copper. Copper everything and books. That is my life. When Wilhelm was alive, we restored books together. He received his first English commission five years before the Great War. We were in London when war broke out and for our safety we came here."

"When did Wilhelm die?" I asked, keeping my voice soft and low. Something about this place inspired quiet and solitude. It was a house of peace and reflection.

"He died in the spring."

Her mouth shut on the subject and I didn't press her. Had he suffered under English oppression, I wondered, recalling how many of my countrymen harbored animosity against anything German.

"Does coffee suit you, Daphne?"

"She likes it strong." The major came into the kitchen, plucking three green clay mugs off copper hooks on the wall. "Susanna makes the best coffee."

"With my tiny little Italian pot." She beamed. "It is good, if I say so myself. And I have meat pasties and almond seed cake for luncheon."

"Susanna *le chef*," joked the major affectionately.

"I bake and cook a little. My neighbor dines with me. He is a widower also."

"Ah, a light o' love?"

Susanna shook her head. "Tommy, you are always thinking along those lines and you have never brought your light o' loves to me before so this girl must be special."

She said it so matter-of-factly it brought fresh color to my face. I busied myself carting out the coffee tray to the main room and offering to pour the coffee. To lessen the secretive smile forming on Susanna's lips, I asked where she kept her books.

"In the reading room," she replied. "I will take you after, but first I want to know all about you and your family, how you met my Tommy, though he has told me some of it."

My face turning red, I concentrated on sipping my coffee. He was right. The coffee was excellent. And I liked his strange worldly wise godmother very much. She didn't miss a thing, taking careful note of all I had to say about myself.

"You have a taste for adventure, no?" she said at the finish. "Ah, you remind me of me when I was young. I used to go riding in the woods for hours and hours. My parents did not approve. But then, they did not approve of much."

"Susanna's family disowned her when she married Wilhelm," the major put in. "She came to England as a bride."

"My family did not want me marrying a book restorer," Susanna explained. "Even though he'd received great commissions from the universities to preserve manuscripts and rare books, he was still poor when I married him."

"Naughty Susanna," the major clicked his tongue, "you ought to have wed the fat count."

"Helmut." Susanna laughed. "How well you remember everything

I tell you. He has a brain for storing knowledge," she said to me, "perhaps you have encountered it?"

"Once or twice." I smiled, gazing out the window. I could just see the jutting point of Tintagel Castle stretching out to sea. The rain obscured part of my vision but I longed to go out there. It didn't look like we'd have time today and for once, I did not care. Susanna interested me far more.

After luncheon, when she took me into her reading room, I thought I'd found a piece of heaven. I'd seen many libraries in grand houses in my time yet none of them matched the simplicity and elegance of Susanna's book room. From floor to ceiling, the room oozed charm, all decorated in warm plum hues. Thick carpet warmed the floorboards and was slightly faded through use, as was the upholstery on the twin set of library armchairs. Solid oak shelves graced two sides of the wall where an antique oval desk with its own embossed green leather writing surface stood empty.

"That is where Wilhelm used to work . . . it is a pity, I have little use for the desk now."

"It's beautiful," I murmured, touching it before turning to run my fingers along the many titles stacked on the shelves. I loved the desk. I wanted to draw out the chair and pen something upon it while looking out the narrow window to the sea.

"Daphne is a writer." The major sashayed around, biting into another piece of Susanna's delicious almond seed cake. "She's published."

"Not novel length," I added, my face burning.

"Is that what you wish? To become a fiction novelist? What do you like to write about? Drama? Intrigue? Romance?"

"Oh." At Susanna's invitation, I tried one of the library chairs. "I don't know exactly. I love history and I love old houses. I also like books with a darker theme, exploring emotions which aren't often recorded in popular fiction."

Lifting a brow, Susanna grinned at the major. "You have chosen well, Tommy. She's smart. I like her. I like her very much and I do hope you will come and visit me again, Daphne?"

"Yes, I will," I promised, not realizing how the time had slipped away.

"You are most welcome to come and stay and write on that desk," Susanna said on parting, the invitation so invitingly warm I thought I just might accept one day.

CHAPTER EIGHT

We arrived back to Thornleigh half an hour late.

"Ellen is very punctual." I sighed, exasperated with him for he refused to share information with me.

"She's in mourning," he murmured, slipping out of the car to open my door. "The world changes when one is in mourning."

It was true. Ellen's words haunted my steps to her room. *How can I go on without him? How can I?* "She loved him and he loved her. The age difference didn't signify at all. It's a cruel twist of fate that his heart should have failed him at this time."

The major said nothing, indicating he knew something. I'd come to know by the slight telltale serration on the left side of his face. It flexed whenever he wished to avoid my inquiries.

Ellen received us in her private study. Thornleigh had two studies, one for the master and one for the mistress. The master's adjoined the library whereas the mistress's overlooked the gardens at the back of the house. It was bright and sunny, like a morning room, and Ellen liked to come here in the mornings because the light warmed the room.

As we entered, I could not help comparing Ellen's study to Susanna's tiny library. Spacious, one large Geroge III desk with floral inlay and complete with numerous drawers stood in the center, with two small plain cushioned chairs before it. Yellow drapes framed the windows, matching the upholstery of Ellen's chair and the sunflower painting on the wall. There was also a smaller Victorian ladies' writing desk in the far corner but it was just for show, not for use.

Ellen rose from her desk. "Do sit down. Do you care for coffee? Tea?"

I saw an empty tea tray on her desk. "No, we're fine and I'm so sorry we're late. It was the—"

"Traffic," the major put in. "Dastardly this time of year."

Ellen looked from him to me. Her face registered mild surprise since last she knew I hated him and refused to spend a minute in his company. I longed to explain matters. I didn't want her to think me a weak-willed woman.

"Well." Ellen resumed her seat wearily.

The question remained in her eyes. I'd gone to invite the major to come at three, not to spend the day with him. But she didn't know why I'd gone with him. I'd gone with him because I suspected he knew something, something he wished to keep private between himself and Ellen.

"The business I have is private," he began, "I think it best if we discuss it alone."

Ellen glanced up from her desk. There were great dark shadows under her eyes. "I couldn't sleep last night. My mind, you know. I was thinking of Teddy's tombstone and what he'd like upon it. Of course, I know he'd prefer to be buried in America but I can't bear the thought of him going home cold on that ship. I've had a terrible row about it with his sisters. They insist he goes back but I can't let him go. Is that wrong of me?"

"Unless there is monetary gain, everybody loses in the business of death," the major murmured, then reiterating the need for privacy.

"No, I want Daphne here," Ellen replied firmly, leaving her desk to walk to the window. She stood there a moment, her slim frame silhouetted by the pale afternoon glow. "I've had two house calls today. Teddy's accountant and solicitor. I knew he was wealthy but I had no idea of how complicated his businesses are. There." She indicated to a box on the floor full of fat blue folders. "It's only a start. Mr. Berting, that's Teddy's accountant, has tried to put things simply but I can't understand it. I wonder if you might help me, Major Browning? If both of you might help me? Apart from my daughter, I have no family and even fewer that I trust. Harry is here, of course, but he manages Thornleigh for me; he has no business head and nor do I."

"Employing a proper business manager might be better," advised the major.

"Teddy loved his businesses. They were like pets to him and as his widow, I feel it my duty to look after these pets, particularly when there are many wolves at large."

Her gaze fell upon a couple walking outside in the garden. I strained my neck so I could see who it was. Dean Fairchild and cousin Jack.

"Your husband," the major began, "was involved in two major deals in the last year. Such business brought him to England."

"Yes. That's true."

"And you contacted him when he arrived?"

"Yes, that's also true. I confronted him with Charlotte. He was astounded by how the child looks like him and offered me money. I refused. He started then to make amends with regular visits and taking us out to dinner."

"During that time, did he ever talk about his work? The two deals?"

Ellen thought back. "A little. I remember the names . . . Salinghurst and Gildersberg. Teddy said he had an interest in those two companies."

"More than an interest. He holds a forty-percent share in Salinghurst and recently acquired one hundred–percent holding in Gildersberg."

"He owns Gildersberg then?" A slight crease showed on Ellen's brow. "What does this have to do with his death?"

"Read the headlines."

Ellen blinked at the newspaper thrust into her hands. *"Gildersberg's share prices collapsed this morning with the news of its director's passing, a Mr. Teddy Grimshaw, of Boston, Massachusetts. It is reported that Mr. Grimshaw had ambitious plans for the German food chain company . . ."*

"Salinghurst and Gildersberg are competitors," the major explained. "I suspect your husband bought Gildersberg and intended to acquire the sinking Salinghurst shares so he would have full control over the market."

"Salinghurst wins?"

"You have a forty-percent share in that company now. It is my belief they will attempt to buy you out."

"So they have full control of the market?" Ellen finished for him.

"I strongly suggest you refuse that offer."

Ellen paused. "Is it your suggestion that I do so, Major Browning, or is it Scotland Yard's? I know you work for them. Daphne told me."

I turned scarlet. I had said so in confidence. To my relief, the major appeared unconcerned.

"We believe some kind of skullduggery is at play between these companies, the central figure being your late husband. If you sell out of Salinghurst, we have no way in to monitor that company."

"Me?" Ellen seemed confused. "But what I can do? I know nothing about running a company."

"The principle shareholders are entitled to attend a company meeting once a month. Scotland Yard wishes you to go to these meetings and report what you see and hear. In simple terms, Mrs. Grimshaw, we wish you to stand in your husband's place."

"Teddy agreed to spy for you?"

There was a pause before the answer came. "He refused; doubtless for reasons of his own."

Ellen sunk into her chair and spun it around. She turned very pale and I knew she was thinking about those threats Teddy had received in the mail.

"I suppose, Major Browning, you can't tell me exactly what all this is about, can you?"

"No."

"Can't you give me some kind of encouragement? Before Teddy died, we were looking at simplifying our lives, not making things more complicated."

I watched the major's face. He didn't want to give out details, any details. Perhaps he thought such details compromised the case. A case of high-class company fraud?

"We believe," the major conceded, casting a surreptitious glance in my direction, "your husband was murdered."

CHAPTER NINE

"Murdered?"

"Of course we have yet to receive the official verdict of death but I'd wager my best fishing set against it."

Turning white, Ellen's shaky hand reached for a glass of water. "I feel ill . . . so Teddy didn't die of a heart attack?"

"So it appears, however, certain poisons are known to produce such a reaction."

"Poisons?" Now Ellen turned completely white. "Who would want to poison Teddy? Would his business competitors stoop so low?"

"That's why we want you to be our eyes and ears at Salinghurst. The first meeting is scheduled on the twenty-eighth. They won't be expecting you—"

"Fine. I will go." Rising to her feet, she rang the bell. "Fetch Harry," she said to the maid, "tell him I will meet him on the green."

After the maid bobbed and left, Ellen picked up her shawl. "They release the body tomorrow. I had thought to have him interred in the parish grounds, but we have an ancient graveyard here, under the yew tree near the woods. Once when we walked by, Teddy joked they ought to put a new 'straight' headstone there to counteract the disorderly ones. Ironic now that they are erecting such a one, isn't it?"

"Oh." She stopped at the door, examining us both. "I am trusting you with Teddy's files and since Scotland Yard is asking me to spy, I think the least they can do is lend me a manager until I can find a replacement. Are you, Major Browning, equipped to handle these matters?"

"I can fill the position for the time being," came the major's smooth reply, a slight smile etching the corners of his mouth, "but I shall need an assistant, a secretary, one equipped with shorthand and dictation."

"Daphne." Ellen touched my shoulder. "Will you help the major? I must go . . . I have things to do."

The door shut, leaving us alone.

"I have a huge desire for a cigar," the major confided, stretching out his long legs.

"Your best fishing set, hmm? Do you really know what you are doing?"

"Not in the slightest. That's why I need a cigar."

This rare display of humility warmed me to him. Normally I'd have a sarcastic reply ready but sensing the inadequacy behind his heavy frown I laid my own hand on his shoulder. "I'll help you."

At my soft murmur, his hand covered mine and drew me to him. The suddenness of the action caught me unawares and before I knew it I was in his arms.

"This working closely appeals to me by the minute." He laughed.

My heart racing, my rebellious mouth sought his. I didn't care if it might be considered forward or even wanton. I wanted him.

"Oh." Nanny Brickley burst into the room. "I was looking for Ellen."

I sprang to my feet, blushing furiously. Had I forgotten that in the world's eyes he belonged to another woman?

"She went outside to meet Harry," the major said, calm, amused, charming as ever. "I daresay it's about the gravesite."

"Yes, of course, yes . . ."

Alicia Brickley could scarcely look at me. And I couldn't look at her, either.

"Oh, the shame of it!" I cursed under my breath when she left.

"Shame?" He chuckled, unaffected. "What shame?"

"You forget you're an engaged man. What if she tattletales?"

"What if she does?"

"Aren't you concerned with the feelings of your fiancée?"

"Not in the slightest. It's a business arrangement."

"Lady Lara might see it differently. She must be on the hunt for a husband, this being her fifth season."

"Oh, she's had plenty of offers," the major replied, taking out the files from the first box.

"Was there none to her father's liking?"

"None to *her* liking is more like it. Lara has . . ." he paused, thinking, "particular tastes."

"And you're to her taste?"

I hadn't meant to sound angry.

He shrugged. "It doesn't signify if I am. You're my girl."

His casual statement caught me off guard. Something sang inside me and I sank to my knees on the floor beside him. Somehow it seemed so natural to do so. "What do you want me to do?"

"Sort those out first," he said, handing me a pile of papers. "In date order." Moving to Ellen's desk, he began reading, his eyes narrowing in the bad light.

"Why don't we use the study?" I suggested. "Or the library? The light is good there."

My suggestion appealed to him and twenty minutes later we were on our way to the library when Angela ran into us. Her hostile stare bespoke her thoughts as she pulled me aside.

"What is going on with you and the major? One minute you hate him, the next Nanny Brickley catches you in his arms. He is *engaged,* you know, and Megan was present when Brickley told me. What if she tells Lady Lara?"

We were standing outside the library and I prayed nobody over-heard Angela's furious whisper. Drawing her away from the closed door (for I imagined the major lingered on the other side, curious as to my sister's "urgent business"), I endeavored to make atonement.

"I can't fully explain but he is . . . I am . . ."

"He is. You are . . . what? Lovers?"

"No!"

"Then why are you creeping around like a pair of schoolchildren? Stealing kisses behind doors?"

Nanny Brickley had wasted no time in spreading gossip. I suppose she, like my sister, scorned my weakness. My friends had supported me against the major, consoled me during dark moments, and now couldn't make sense of my defection.

Nor could I. "He is working on something important and I've been asked to help him. Believe me, if Ellen hadn't asked me per-sonally, I wouldn't do it. I know our being together will generate rumors."

Angela examined me squarely, putting on her older-sister face. "Lady Lara Fane isn't one you want to draw swords with. And you should know the American cousins are dining at Rutland House tonight."

"Then whatever tale they take is their business. As it is, the major and I are working on Ellen's finances. Scotland Yard is involved. I can't say how; I am sworn to secrecy, but don't be surprised if there's a shock in the next day or so."

Angela picked up my insinuation. "It's murder, isn't it?"

I shrugged, slipping back toward where we had left the major. I'd given her enough to keep her occupied and off my back for the pres-ent. I knew she'd not run to our parents. Since Somner House, we shared a special bond of trust.

However, later that evening my father said over his pipe: "Heard Browning came here today."

"Oh?" I feigned mild surprise.

"And he came without his fiancée."

"Ooh." I lowered my gaze so he couldn't read the truth in my eyes.

My father continued smoking. "Thought you'd be interested."

"Why?"

He grimaced. "So as to avoid the man."

"Ah." I pretended to keep reading my book, hoping Angela stayed longer downstairs. If she'd heard our father talking this way, she'd probably say something about it. Glancing across the room to my mother and Jeanne listening to a story on the radio, I breathed an inward sigh of relief. At least, they knew nothing about my sojourn with the major.

He'd decided to take the files back to the inn and asked me to resume our work there the day after the funeral. I had my reservations, working with him unchaperoned.

"Then we can remain in visible view," he said on parting, leaving a light kiss on my cheek. "Good night, sweetheart."

Good night sweetheart. I treasured the memory of those words and the manner in which they'd been delivered. Familiar and fond, a verbal intimacy my father and mother often shared. Dare I hope it led to so much more?

He couldn't be thinking of marriage, could he? I didn't want to trust myself to think upon it, though I lay restless in bed throughout the night. What future did we have? How long did he have to keep his public engagement to Lady Lara? When could we make our romance public?

My father might refuse. I hadn't considered this very real aspect before and now shuddered. Sir Gerald could be a formidable person when he wanted to be. He also exercised great authority and acted the *faire l'important* personage.

And a man like Major Browning had his pride. Assuming he presented himself at my father's door and asked his permission to court me, what outcome dare I expect? I thought of Elizabeth Bennett and her father's grave concerns when Mr. Darcy showed up at his door. She had to defend him. She could do so whereas I could not. I was not privy to certain details and the fact maddened me. I'd sooner prattle out the man's cologne fragrance than where he grew up and in what kind of family environment or how he'd come to work for Scotland Yard or even his current living situation.

"Excuse me," I said to the mirror the next morning. "How much do you earn per year? Do you own a house? Can you expect a legacy from a soon-to-die relative?"

The callousness and yet urgency of such matters plagued me as I dressed for the funeral. Instead of the local church, Ellen had decided to have the service outside by the yew tree.

The day was sunny and chilly. As we made our approach across the green, I picked out black dots arriving from all directions. For a man who didn't belong to this country, the turnout was remarkable.

During the service, I scanned the faces. Relatives, business associates, longtime friends of Ellen's family, neighbors, nosy locals, and an unexpected late arrival: Rosalie and her mother.

I saw Ellen tense as they approached, a large black umbrella shielding their faces from the sun.

"Behold the witch," my father whispered.

Though wrapped in a lush ermine coat, it didn't hide the plumpness of Cynthia Grimshaw's belly or her short stature. Beneath frizzy blond hair, the woman's face, much older than Ellen's, remained fixed and hard. Holding her daughter's hand tightly, they moved to and stopped by the Fairchild family.

". . . we hereby commit thy body to the ground from whence we came. Ashes to ashes, dust to dust."

Silence accompanied the shining coffin to its final resting place. Glimmers of sunlight danced on the bronze handles as they lowered it, down and down into the cool ground. Ellen and Charlotte stepped forward to place their wreath on the coffin; however, Rosalie broke free from the crowd and hurled hers down first.

Astonished whispers echoed all around. Even the priest looked offended and frowned. He quoted some further bible verse to dissolve the incident while Rosalie returned to her mother, triumphant.

I glanced at Ellen. Shaking with grief and anger, she seized Charlotte's hand and turned from the gravesite, my mother steering her away.

"Yes, go," Rosalie urged, completely unabashed. "We don't want you here, do we, Daddy?"

The upper *croûte* of English society frowned. She'd committed a great faux pas without any remorse whatsoever. Slightly embarrassed by her outburst, her American cousins had the sense to take her from the scene. The other attendees soon followed suit, each leaving their token flowers.

Having walked a few yards from the site, I returned to fetch my mother's shawl. She often left it lying around here and there and in her haste to support Ellen, it had slipped to the ground. And, at any rate, I'd seen Cynthia Grimshaw linger and wanted to catch her expression.

The expression had hardened, noticed upon arrival. And then, in the crevice of her mouth the tiniest smile emerged as she stared down at the filling grave.

Shocked, I stepped back onto a dried leaf. Cringing at the loud crackle, I met Cynthia Grimshaw's icy stare.

"Ellen's little friend, aren't you?"

"Yes," I said, holding my head high.

She looked down at the grave, almost smiling. "He thought he was invincible . . ."

"I'm sorry for your loss," I said, lifting a caustic brow.

Throwing back her head, she laughed. "The English; they always have a way with words . . . the right response for each occasion. Well, let me tell you something, I'll see justice done. Let that bitch know we'll see her in court. She won't get a penny of my husband's money."

"He's not your husband anymore," I replied, but she'd swept out of earshot.

Relieved, for I was in no mood to go to war against a woman whom I knew only by reputation, I picked up my mother's shawl.

The moist ground left it damp and I stood awhile watching the grave diggers complete their job.

"Sad business, this is," the older gray-haired one said to me. "I dug her parents' graves, y'know. Poor Miss Ellen. So much tragedy for one so young."

"Do you know the family well, Mr. . . . ?"

"Haines, it is. Me and mine been here abouts me whole life."

"Then perhaps you remember me? As a young girl, Ellen and I used to ride through the woods."

Leaning on his shovel, the man rubbed his chin thoughtfully.

"My hair was cropped short like a boy," I added.

"Ay." Haines grinned wide. "I think I might do. Used to lend a hand up at the manor in those days. So did the Missus." He shook his head. "My Mary's softhearted. She didn't like it when Sir Richard and Lady Gertrude turned out Miss Ellen durin' the war with the lad dyin' and all."

I gazed down at the grave and shivered. "It shouldn't have ended this way. They should have lived happily ever after."

"Oh, that's a fairy tale, miss!" Haines sniffed the air. "Bad bones lie about this place. Ever since Mr. Xavier died."

"He was the darling of the family," I murmured.

"He were that," Haines confirmed. "Handsome lad. He'd not have turned out his sister, either, if he were alive when she got herself into trouble."

"If only." I smiled. "But the 'if onlys' are always ineffectual. The time has long since passed." However, I couldn't help wondering how things might have turned out, as Haines said, if Xavier hadn't died. I could imagine him ensuring the wedding went through between his sister and Teddy Grimshaw. Then Charlotte wouldn't have missed knowing her father for eight years and Ellen wouldn't have suffered alone all those years.

Oh, it was too cruel.

I left the gravesite promising Haines I'd visit his home sometime.

He said it would make Mary's day to have such a grand lady visit, one she might remember as a child.

Grand lady! I didn't think myself one; in fact, the term caused me profound amusement.

I returned to the house through the servants' entrance. I wanted to see Nelly in the kitchen but I only found her helper Annie stirring a stew there.

"Oh, miss, I'll be glad when they all leave. We're overrun here and that Lady Pringle, I can't get a thing right! 'The tea's too cold,' 'the eggs are overdone!' "

"Never mind, Annie. Now the funeral is over, they will pack up and go, one by one."

"Aye, and the sooner the better."

My mother was of the same opinion. Stirring sugar into my father's cup of tea, she expressed their desire to leave the next day.

"We have no wish to burden poor Ellen . . ."

"But she looks upon you as a mother," I protested.

"No, she is old enough and a mother herself," my mother over-ruled. "We do feel it's best, don't we, Gerald darling?"

My father looked up from his newspaper. "Yes, dear."

"And Jeanne and Angela? Are they going, too?"

Noting the forlorn note in my voice, my mother poured me a cup of tea. "Sit down, dear. As Ellen's particular friend, you are the only one who should stay and help her through this difficult time."

I was beginning to feel deserted.

"The Fenwicks are leaving tomorrow, and I believe the Americans will shortly follow suit."

"Megan?" I began, hopeful.

"Megan may stay a little while—"

"No she won't." Angela marched into the room, ablaze in a stage of flurried packing. "There's the Lavingsham soiree next weekend. She'll want to get back to London."

"And what about you?"

"I'm off to Scotland," Angela announced.

"Jeanne?" I appealed to my younger sister.

"I'll stay awhile." She peered up from her book. "Can I, Papa?"

"If you keep up with your studies," my father agreed. "And as long as Daphne promises to look after you."

"Oh, I will, Papa," I vowed, overjoyed to have at least one member of my family stay with me. It was not that I feared being alone; however, since Ellen had Charlotte to care for and I had Major Browning to contend with, I felt I needed a little family support.

Perhaps I did fear being alone.

Death had come to Thornleigh and it frightened me.

CHAPTER TEN

After the funeral, silence reigned in the house.

I spotted Nelly and her helpers putting the final touches to the afternoon tea. It was the strangest wake I'd ever been to; nobody knew what to say so limited themselves to the essential subjects of the news and the weather.

"I can't believe he's gone," Mr. Dean Fairchild said to me, filling his plate with a selection of Nelly's tasty little Cornish pasties. "By oath, I'll miss these when I go home."

"When will you go home, Mr. Fairchild?"

"Not for some time yet. Uncle Ted brought me over here to start up a new branch for our tobacco company."

"What will happen now, with all the businesses?"

"I've no idea. I assume Uncle Ted left instructions in his will."

I nodded, driving my fork into a sweet orange tart. "It's no surprise your cousin and her mother aren't here . . . I had words with Cynthia Grimshaw at the gravesite."

"Ah." He leaned over, interested. "What did she say?"

"She's talking of going to court. For the money."

"She's a greedy termagant. The word is she's low on funds; bad investments and costly living. She'll use Rosalie but she'll want the money for herself."

"Are you close to your cousin?" I asked, guiding him away from the eagle eye of his mother and aunt.

"Relatively so," he assuaged. "Rosalie and I have never seen eye to eye. She gets on better with cousin Jack."

My gaze drifted to where cousin Jack sat sipping tea with Sophie and Amy. The definitive ladies' man, he liked his clothes, combed his fair hair to one side, and wore the thinnest moustache. His demeanor was always suggestive and charming without being too scandalous. "Do you work with Jack?"

"No!" the answer fired quickly. "We do all right in social circles but that's it. Jack's a—how should I say?—man of the moment. He can't stay put anywhere so Uncle Ted uses him to represent us, stir up new business contracts, and that kind of thing."

"Now, Daphne," Megan Kellaway wandered to us, "you mustn't monopolize our American friends. Mr. Fairchild," she extended an arm, "I'd love to hear more about your home, and have you ever been to New York?"

Letting them slip by me to walk in the gardens, I found myself a quiet corner from which to study the other funeral attendees. There were faces I didn't know and I wondered if they belonged to the business world. Quite possibly, as I spied Major Browning speaking with one of them, their voices low and grim.

Across the room, Ellen sat with my mother, her face drawn and vacant. She scarcely blinked when Charlotte sang "Yankee Doodle" under the direction of her doting American aunts. The two ladies remarked how much the child looked like her father.

"Hello there," murmured a smug Jack Grimshaw in my ear.

"Hello," I said, still watching Charlotte.

"I've just been speaking with your father. He's a fascinating man."

"Yes, he is."

"He suggests I should visit the theater while I'm here."

"You should."

"And he says you're the best person to accompany me."

I looked up, horrified. I didn't believe him. He teased with a sincerity I found disturbing.

"Let's make a date, shall we?" Flicking out his little flip-pad, he poised his pencil. "How about next month or the month after? You'll be in town then."

"I'm not sure if I will be." I bristled against his brazen attitude. What did he think? I had nothing better to do than to entertain him?

"Then we will surely meet up at the premiere of your father's new play." He smiled, leaving me to pursue Megan Kellaway.

Angela whispered to me from behind. "What do you think of him? He'd make somebody a great lover."

"Ange! If Mother heard you speak that way—"

"Mother's quite safely out of earshot. Jack Grimshaw's after money. He's heard of Megan's dowry, no doubt."

"Megan's not stupid," I put in, observing the upset look on Dean Fairchild's face. "He may have some competition."

"Oh, the other one. He has more to his name. Do you know Papa has invited them both to our house in London?"

I pursed my lips. "I hope he's not trying to match us to one of them."

"Our parents think our settling down will absolve them of future responsibility. Marriage is the only solution in their book."

"And in our book?" A tight smile crossed my lips upon seeing Major Browning carting a cup of tea to Lady Lara. I had endured his assiduous ministrations to her and her parents during the funeral and found the whole facade sickening.

"Two-timing is he?"

Angela missed nothing.

"What story did he tell you? Something about her father being sick and it was the parents' dearest wish that they marry?"

I stared at her, aghast.

"If it's a pretense," she went on, "why has her mother reserved the Savoy for a wedding reception?"

Holding my breath, I felt the blood drain from my face. "How do you know this?"

"I overheard the countess say so just now."

I looked over her shoulder to see the earl and the countess seated beside their daughter and Major Browning. "Was he there when you heard?"

"Yes," Angela replied.

"And he said nothing?"

"No, he said nothing."

"Did he smile? Was there any expression whatsoever?"

"He did smile once," Angela recalled, "and patted Lara's hand."

Green fury consumed me. Jealousy. I didn't like the emotion; it pained my heart and robbed me of peace. But I refused to believe it true.

"People are staring at us," Angela whispered. "Best turn around and have another cup of tea."

Have a cup of tea. I didn't want a cup of tea. Why did everyone always assume a cup of tea would fix everything?

Not I. I needed to go for a walk and stormed off to the woods without a by-your-leave. I hoped, upon my return, to find Thornleigh rid of the Rutland party.

The chill air arrested me. I shivered. Something about funerals left me empty and cold. And the death of a millionaire on the eve of his wedding was going to attract attention. I wondered what the newspapers would make of it.

Walking farther into the woods, I fancied I heard a faint moan. Pausing, I began to turn back. Then I heard it again.

Ensuring not to tread on any crunchy leaves, I tiptoed toward the noise. Catching a glimpse of clothing and naked arms through the trees, I questioned the wisdom of my curiosity. Lovers in the woods. I almost envied them.

Until I saw who they were . . .

Rosalie and Jack Grimshaw.

Drawing away, my face hot, I hurried from the site. Cousins . . .

and lovers. On the day of her father's funeral? Shocked, I considered all the possibilities such a relationship suggested. Cousins and allies.

Allies in the death of Rosalie's father?

"Daphne," said my father in his most austere tone. "Ellen has asked if you may stay on and who are we to begrudge her tho' your mother and I don't like you so near Ellen at this time."

"Oh?" Leaving the bathroom, I paused. Had Ellen confessed to my parents about the death threats? Had she, as Teddy's widow, received more?

"The policeman came while you were out," my mother informed. "Ellen had retired so your father received him."

Drying my hair with a towel, I thought I'd better sit down.

"Teddy Grimshaw died of cardiac failure due to hemlock poisoning," my father proclaimed as though he were acting in a play.

"The hemlock caused the heart attack," my mother explained. "The policeman said it was a rare form, water hemlock. He'll be back tomorrow to ask Ellen more questions."

"Are they saying it's murder?" I asked.

"Not yet," my father answered. "But whatever it is it's highly suspicious. They might be after Ellen next. Money breeds desperate people."

I stopped, thinking of the entwined lovers in the woods. "You don't think one of the family poisoned him?"

My father shrugged. "Why not? They all stand to benefit from his death."

"The policeman said there will be an investigation. Your father has relayed all this to Ellen and we've asked her to come home with us, but she is adamant she wants to stay near Teddy. So you'll stay with her and try to convince her to come with you when you come home. She'll need people around her at this time, especially if a murderer is out there."

Glancing up at my father, my mother frowned.

My father seemed to read her thoughts. "I don't like it any more than you do, Muriel, but Daphne's Ellen's friend."

"But she is unchaperoned."

Upon hearing this, I searched the room for Angela. She, conveniently, had disappeared. "And what need have I for a chaperone?" I presented innocently.

"Major Browning and you," my father said. "Ellen mentioned he'll be about the place. As an engaged man, I don't want you alone with him, out of respect for you and for his fiancée."

"As it happens," my mother put in, "the countess has raised similar concerns when she heard you are assisting the major with Ellen's papers. She asked quite pointedly if there'd ever been anything between you."

I blushed. I couldn't help thinking of that stolen kiss in Ellen's study. Oh dear! I should have a deeper care for my reputation. "And what did you reply, Mama?"

"I know my daughter. You still are bemused by the man."

"Bemused!" I half choked. "I most certainly am not—"

"A heated reply often betrays a burning heart." My father grinned. "Ah, girl, he's a handsome man. But I thought you were stronger. He hurt you with his engagement and from what I understand from Rutland, it's serious."

I studied both of them. "You think he won't break it off?"

There was a long pause before my father slowly shook his head. "Lady Lara stands to inherit the bulk of Rutland's fortune. I, on the other hand, am not so well oiled. I can't match him."

"Not all men, Father, are after money."

"Don't use a hostile tone with me, young lady. I'm only watching out for you. I don't want my little girl hurt."

"Nor do I," my mother murmured, eagerly scanning my face. "That's why Jeanne will stay." She waved a hand. "Ellen's quite aware of it. When you and the major are working, Jeanne will be there, reading a book or working on her school assignments. She has been instructed that you are not to be alone with the major. I don't want my daughter ruined."

I don't want my daughter ruined. Warming, wasn't it, my parents' faith in me? But they were not privy to the real reason behind the major's public engagement to Lady Lara and I wished I could blurt out the truth. *He's not really engaged at all. It's all a farce!*

However, a niggling doubt had taken root with my father's words, and Angela's comments the day before. The earl of Rutland had only one daughter. He was a very rich man. My heart sank at the hard fact. Why shouldn't a man like Major Browning take up the earl's and no doubt Lady Lara's offer?

I returned to my room in a sombre mood. Rather than wallowing in self-despair, I took out my notepad and began to write. Since my modest success with the *Widow* story, I yearned to complete a novel.

Tapping my pencil against my chin, I decided on the setting: Cornwall. Cornwall and I belonged together, so must my book. And while I was here, I needed something else to focus on than Ellen's grief, her financial affairs, and Major Browning.

What should I start with, character or plot? Character. A character, like myself, in love with Cornwall. Putting pencil to pad, I began to sketch the essence of a woman. *Here was the freedom I desired, long sought for, not yet known. Freedom to write, to walk, to wander. Freedom to climb hill, to pull a boat, to be alone . . .*

Freedom to act as I pleased, a free and loving spirit.

I decided to call her Janet.

CHAPTER ELEVEN

"Is Janet rich or poor?"

Staring at Jeanne over the breakfast table, I nibbled on a piece of toast. "Middle class."

"And where are you setting it?"

"In a Cornish village. I don't know which one yet. I'll have to do some exploring. I want something close to the sea."

"Ah, boats." Ellen smiled faintly, helping Charlotte to crack her egg. "You love boats, Daphne, but you haven't had a chance at sailing much, have you?" A wistful look came into her face. "Teddy loved to sail. We did hope you'd come to Italy with us on the yacht."

"I would have loved to," I replied, keen to change the subject. "I'm really determined this year to write a full novel. It's like a feverish madness burning within me."

"Then by all means work on it," Ellen advised. "It's quiet here, now everyone has gone. I hope you don't mind staying on?"

"Not at all," Jeanne and I answered in unison.

Ellen nodded. "I couldn't bear to be all alone. Please make Thornleigh your home. Do whatever you wish. Horses, cars, day trips . . . Charlotte and I might come with you on one of those day trips. Harry will drive you around. I wouldn't know what to do without Harry."

I had seen Harry earlier that morning working in the garden. "He does everything, doesn't he?"

"He's not the type to sit back and give orders. He's teaching young Samuel how to prune hedges."

" 'Prune hedges,' " I echoed. "I've never tried that. Sounds like fun. Why don't we work in the garden today, Charlotte?"

"Oh, yes! Can we?"

Charlotte was all enthused. She ran off to inform Nanny Brickley of our plan.

Seeing that it was good for her daughter to have her attention diverted from the death of her father, Ellen agreed and so after breakfast, we set out with aprons and gloves.

Not expecting all these female helpers, Harry quickly found something easy for us to work on, sending us in different directions.

"It's a full-time job caring for such gardens," he said to me, directing me to a garden by the wall to weed. "Here's your shears. Start here."

Watching him snip away, I thought he was quite handsome with his light brown hair, crisp overalls, and clean-shaven face. Not a servant and not exactly one of us, he lived in his own world.

"Oh, Harry." Ellen later brushed the dirt off her gloves as I asked her about the groundskeeper. "No, he's never married. I hear he's a heartthrob to the ladies in town. They're all competing to trap him."

"I remember he was the same in London. You wrote me once saying how he made you laugh when he and his girlfriend serenaded you into the night when you were feeling down."

"Oh, yes." Ellen smiled. "I'd forgotten that. Harry has always been there."

"Faithful and loyal like a puppy dog. And Charlotte likes him, too."

Sitting on the bench by the garden, Ellen drew off her gloves. "I need to rest for a while. Sometimes, when I look at Harry and Charlotte together, it breaks my heart. She never got to know her father in those early years. We've been cheated." She began to sob.

"Those letters." I put my arm around her. "How could they all go missing? You'd think *one* would have reached him."

"Not when there's a female in the house receiving the mail," Ellen said bitterly. "I'd like to box Rosalie's ears for it. She succeeded in breaking us up then," she choked, "and now, Charlotte won't know her father. He entered her life—larger and bigger than life—how will she recover?"

"She's young," I observed. "I think sometimes they recover better than we do. You must keep your spirits up for Charlotte's sake."

"I know." Ellen sighed. "But it's so hard. I don't know what the future holds anymore. I can't make plans. I can't think straight. I can't sleep, either. I lie awake all night, thinking, thinking. Is there any way out?"

"Any way out?" I suddenly observed her face. "No, Ellen, you mustn't think along those lines. You have a daughter and a house to care for. Both need attention."

Glum, she looked at me. "You're right. But the future is so uncertain . . . I don't know whether I'll be able to keep Thornleigh."

"Because of the costs?"

She nodded. "I've always just scraped by to keep it. Teddy's money was going to see it restored to perfection. But I can't continue what we set out to do now . . ."

"Why not? Wouldn't Teddy, if he was here, say the same to you? You can't stop halfway through a project."

"But the money . . ."

"The money is *yours,* Ellen. They can't take it from you."

"I wish I didn't have to worry about it. Teddy's affairs are so complex. What does the major think? He's coming here this afternoon, isn't he?"

"Yes," I murmured. "I'm going to tell him about the death threats, Ellen. I think it's important."

Frowning, she searched her memory. "Teddy burned most of them. But there might be one upstairs somewhere. I'll have a look."

"Yes, do," I urged, "and you should have given them to the police."

"Teddy said it was a waste of time. There's little the police can do."

"Maybe then, but now I think you ought to tell them."

She nodded.

"I shall ask Major Browning to have the inspector call upon us. He was going to come back anyway, wasn't he?"

"Y-yes. I think so. After the will is read tomorrow in London."

She shivered. The warmth had left the day. Putting on a false smile as Charlotte, Nanny Brickley, and Jeanne approached, I wondered if Ellen's shiver had to do with the journey tomorrow. The journey she should have been on was a cruise in the warm Mediterranean and later, America, instead of a chilly train ride to London.

I wasn't surprised, then, when she burst into tears and fled the gardens.

"Poor Mummy." Charlotte began to cry too. "I still think we should go to America and meet Grandmama, but Mummy won't go."

"Mummy has a lot on her mind, dearest," Nanny Brickley reminded with her drawling accent.

Charlotte blinked at me. "It's got to do with Daddy, doesn't it? Daddy died and left Mummy all confused. That's why she's sad."

"Yes," I soothed, appreciating the child's remarkable grasp of affairs. "Don't worry. In time you'll make new plans and I'm certain you'll get to meet your grandmama."

"She's very old," Charlotte wrinkled her nose, "and lives in a wheelchair in a great big house. Daddy said she wheels around with her cane and hits the servants."

"I'm sure she doesn't *hit* the servants." I smiled, conjuring up the vision of such a tyrannical matriarch. "Isn't that so, Nanny?"

Ellen addressed Alicia Brickley as "Nanny" so I had followed suit. Behind the coolly aloof face a spark of anger glittered. She was the poor cousin of the family, chosen by Teddy Grimshaw to care for his newly found daughter. I wondered if she expected an inheritance from him? It was highly possible, I thought. "Dear Nanny, do sit down. You've been running after Charlotte all morning. I'm sure your feet ache."

"Well, actually, they do." She smiled back, accepting a seat beside me.

"I can't imagine how different it must be in America," I began. "I suppose we seem so odd in comparison."

"Different," she agreed.

"Forgive me if I seem rude but you aren't close to your cousins, are you?"

"Ha!" She spat. "My mother was a Grimshaw but she married beneath her. The family didn't accept us until my father begged them to do so on his deathbed. He'd run out of money, you see."

"So they took you up under compulsion?"

"Something like that. We survived. We offer the others our services."

"Your mother didn't come across for the wedding?"

"No. She serves Grandmama now."

Studying her face in the pale light, I pitied her plight. "Have you ever thought of marriage?"

"Me? I'd need a dowry for that, wouldn't I? Uncle Teddy always joked he'd give me one if a worthy young man came along."

I was surprised she'd confided as much in me. Death brought out all secrets, I thought. There was no need to hide under petty propriety.

"Do you really think," she said under her lashes, "Uncle Teddy was murdered?"

"Yes, I do."

"But who'd do such a thing!?"

"I don't know . . . perhaps one of your cousins had a motive?"

She paused then, thinking hard. "You mean Rosalie. Or Jack? Both are high spenders. Both want the money."

"And they are lovers, too."

Now she stared at me, amazed.

"I saw them in the woods," I went on, returning her confidence with one of my own. "Do you think they'll marry?"

"They are first cousins," she returned, noncommittal. "And they are both unpredictable. I don't know what they'll do."

"I like your cousin Dean," I said, and when she softened at his name I added: "He says he may stay in England."

"Yes," she replied.

"He seems like a nice person."

"He is."

"Will he marry money like the others, do you think?"

Her frosty expression returned. She shrugged and I knew I'd hit upon a sore point. The money mattered to her. She didn't want to stay a nanny forever. She wanted her independence and her freedom to marry whom she wished.

Unlike Rosalie and Jack, I believed Alicia had genuine fondness for her cousin Dean without any romantic aspirations.

Unfortunately, Jeanne and Charlotte came back from their walk so I could not press her further. I had made my mind up not to like her, but after today I understood her better. All of our lives shaped who we were as people and I felt sorry for her being the poor cousin to a family like the Grimshaws. She desired escape, and money meant escape for her and her mother. They could only hope to access such money through death: the death of Teddy Grimshaw. Was it reason enough for murder?

CHAPTER TWELVE

"That's a preposterous idea."

"It's been done before, Major."

"For a certainty it has. But not by the Nanny Brickleys of this world. Entirely too dependent."

"Dependency can breed desperation," I reminded him. "She intimated she'd receive some kind of inheritance from her uncle."

"They all will," he replied under his breath.

"And they all have a motive." Sitting down in the swivel chair, I tucked my legs up under me. I thought back to just prior to the wedding. Everyone was busy, running from here to there. Anyone could have slipped the poison to Teddy Grimshaw. "The timing depends on a person's cunning, isn't that what Dr. Peterson said?"

Major Browning looked up from the desk where he was working and raised a caustic brow.

"She's talking about the poison." Jeanne tried to help him out.

Clearly frustrated by our endless deliberations, the major rustled several papers and continued scratching down his notes. Since I had been given the meager job of sorting papers in date form, I had no inclination as to his report. The complexity of Teddy Grimshaw's business operations was evident in the buildup of paperwork.

When he found something important, his jawline flickered and I, pausing in my job, made a study of his face. It was a strong and lean face with good bone structure, a heavy brow, inquisitive eyes, and a straight nose. His well-shaped mouth, now holding the nib of his pen, tended to purse on the odd occasion.

"What are you smiling at?" The acerbic brow shot up again as he glanced my way.

"You," I shot back, "and your idiosyncrasies."

"My idiosyncrasies?" Putting down his pen, he entwined his hands together while waiting for an explanation.

I decided to give none. Diverting his attention, I asked if Ellen had shown him the death-threat letters.

"She kept two," he answered, indicating a file, and I immediately deserted my comfortable chair to have a look at them.

"It's the sort of thing one reads about in the newspaper," I murmured, touching the black ink cutout letters, both placed in this form:

Pay £10,000 or you, your woman, and child die.

At the bottom of each letter was a typed strip of paper detailing where and when to pay the money. " 'To be dropped by the grave of Ernest Gildersberg' . . . Gildersberg . . . the name of the company competing with Salinghurst? How did this Ernest Gildersberg die?"

"Of a heart attack," the major replied. "Significant, isn't it? Both great men die of a heart attack within a few months of each other. Ernest Gildersberg, they say, died after selling his flagging company to Teddy Grimshaw. Grimshaw paid a pittance for the company, planning to overhaul it. With his death, the company is worth nothing."

"Unless the plans to resurrect it go ahead?" I frowned. "Surely the share prices would go up then and Salinghurst would have its old competitor."

"Exactly." The major beamed. "You have a fine grasp of it, Daphne."

I blushed. "I didn't just play with dolls as a child, you know.

I paid attention to my father and his interests. He's always willing to explain things to us girls, isn't he, Jeanne?"

"Huh?" Glancing up from her book, Jeanne yawned. "I'm starving! Can we order tea now? I'll go and see Nelly."

She slipped out of the room before either of us could answer.

"The erstwhile chaperone," joked the major.

His jovial mood did nothing to appease mine. "How is Lady Lara? When will you see her next?"

"Tonight." He grinned.

"For dinner?"

"Yes, for dinner."

My heart sank. I had hoped he'd stay here for dinner. Facing another night alone with Ellen and Jeanne seemed depressing.

"But I shall travel with you to London tomorrow."

I was immediately suspicious. "You want to be there for the will reading, don't you? You just have to be first to know everything."

Instead of answering me, he pushed back his chair and examined me as if I were a naughty schoolgirl.

"Well?' I prompted.

"You are not in possession of the full facts."

"I am in possession of certain facts," I retorted, crossing my arms. "Are you aware that Jack and Rosalie are lovers? I saw them in the woods on the day of her father's funeral."

This caught the major's attention. His jaw dropped open. "What?"

"Yes, so you see, I have my uses. *I* am willing to share information, but you are not. And please don't say it's your job."

"It *is* my job. But because you have proven trustworthy and because you are close to Ellen, I will say this: *never leave her alone.* I do not offer my escort tomorrow out of idle curiosity."

"No? Then why?"

"Because she is in danger."

" 'Danger,' " I echoed, sitting down again as Jeanne entered the room bearing a huge smile and a tea tray. "Is Harry still driving us?"

"No. I am. We'll leave at seven sharp to make the train."

I rose early and went up to Ellen's room. Meeting her maid on the landing, she confirmed the mistress was "up and gettin' ready."

Still dark and dreary outside, I shivered in my woollen coat. Choosing comfort over fashion, I had put on a plain dress, stockings, and sensible shoes. The only concession I made was over my hair, having set it in curlers the night before. Fixing the curls around my face, I added a small turquoise-studded comb and a little rouge to my cheeks. My face had the horrendous habit of appearing white and drawn on occasion, especially in the morning.

Ellen had also decided to dress sensibly, though her clothes were infinitely finer than mine. A black dress and a black fur coat completed her ensemble. With her hair, she'd simply dressed it in a French bun at the nape of her neck. She wore no jewelery, except her gold wedding band and diamond engagement ring.

"I am terribly nervous," she confessed to me as we climbed into the major's motorcar. "I shall feel so much better when we are able to return to Thornleigh."

The major loaded our bags into the car. I didn't know how long we'd be staying in town, possibly a night or two. Alicia promised to take care of Charlotte and Jeanne in our absence.

A mist drifted over the grounds of Thornleigh and the neighboring countryside. Beautiful and silent, it curled at the base of the trees, at the mouth of the river, and around the stout village houses alongside the road.

Tightening my scarf, I let the cool air assail my cheeks. The train station resembled a graveyard. Spotting one or two lonely travelers, I patted my dripping nose with a handkerchief. It seemed a crime to travel so early and I thought longingly of my warm bed.

Silence reigned throughout the journey. Ellen continued to stare out the window, her trembling fingers clutching her handbag.

Major Browning read the paper. I read a book.

On reaching London, we took a taxi to Hanover Square.

A line of newspapermen and photographers awaited us. Grasping my hand, Ellen took a deep breath and exited the car.

Following close behind, the major helped us through the onslaught. "Say nothing."

"It's difficult," Ellen breathed to me when a reporter lashed out at her with: "Mrs. Grimshaw! Mrs. Grimshaw! Did you poison your husband?"

"I can't bear it," Ellen whispered once safely inside the building. "All these allegations and presumptions. They are wrong . . . totally wrong."

After locating a chair, Major Browning insisted she rest for a moment. "You stay with her," he said to me, charging off to find what level of the building we were to go.

Standing beside Ellen I had the best vantage point so I saw her first. Rosalie burst through the door, her mother directly behind her, and a moustached man I didn't recognize.

Sallying past Ellen, the ex-Mrs. Grimshaw hissed some vulgar term.

Ellen's face turned white. She was going to let it pass but I didn't. "You pathetic, ill-bred, pernicious woman," I retorted, standing as tall as I could muster. It helped my cause that at that moment Major Browning returned to our side of the wall. His sardonic face questioned the ex-Mrs. Grimshaw, poised for battle.

"Come on, Mother." Rosalie tugged her mother's sleeve.

Reluctantly, the older woman withdrew.

"What a snake," I hissed at her ensuing spluttered curse.

"Daphne, Daphne, don't defend me," Ellen pleaded. "It's my fight, not yours."

"But I'm your friend. What are friends for if not to defend one another?"

She smiled. "It's sweet of you to say so. Isn't it, Major?"

The major gave me a stern frown. From it, I knew he didn't approve of my waging war against my friend's enemies. Did he expect me to remain neutral then?

I seized the first opportunity to find out and asked him forth right as we moved along.

"It's not that I don't approve . . . however, fights between women rarely accomplish any good."

"You speak from your extensive experience, no doubt."

He shrugged. "Well, yes. Yes, I do."

My gaze narrowed. "Do you mean sisters or mistresses? Or women in general?"

"Women in general," he replied, nonplussed. "Ah, here we are. Level four. And the Henderson room is down that corridor."

Leaning against the corridor wall and smoking, Jack Grimshaw saluted us. I shuddered. The vision of him and Rosalie in the woods was too fresh in my memory.

"I'll wait outside," the major offered, but Ellen, fortified by his presence, asked him to accompany her.

The three of us entered the Henderson room, Ellen and I on either side of the major's arms. Eyes scathed every part of us, as the major was quick to find a seat for Ellen.

Most of the family were seated. Standing near the door, Jack Grimshaw adjusted his jacket and spoke in low tones to Dean Fairchild. The tension in the room increased with every passing second. How long must we wait? I prayed not any longer for I foresaw daggers drawn. I purposely avoided the eye of Cynthia Grimshaw and Rosalie.

"Good morning, ladies and gentlemen." The younger of the two solicitors commenced the meeting. "If you are not already seated, please sit down. Mr. Morton will read out the last will and testament of Terrence Bradley Grimshaw—"

"Excuse me," Cynthia Grimshaw interrupted. "Is this the new will or the will he made a few years ago?"

Mr. Morton, seated at the desk behind his young associate, looked at her through his spectacles. "These are Mr. Grimshaw's last instructions."

"But I don't think it was witnessed properly, was it?"

"It was witnessed," Mr. Morton said, grave and despotic. "If you wish to contest the will, Mrs. Grimshaw, you will have to take it to the courts. Now, Frankton, proceed."

Clearing his voice, Frankton appealed to all in the room. "Mr. Morton and I will endeavor to answer your questions at the end of this reading. If you could please hold your questions until then, I would appreciate it.

" 'Last Will and Testament of the deceased: Terrence Bradley Grimshaw, dated this day of May the twenty-seventh, 1927. I do hereby leave the bulk of my estate, my worldly goods, cash, and possessions to my fiancée, Ellen Mary Hamilton. I stipulate that after we are wed, Ellen continues the renovations to Thornleigh. I also wish for my daughter, Charlotte, to grow up on that estate, though, if I die, I would like my daughter to make the journey to America once every two years to visit her grandmother (my mother, Phyllis Enid Grimshaw, of Sevenoaks, Boston).

" 'As for my other daughter, Rosalie Lilybette Grimshaw, I do leave an inheritance sum of twenty thousand pounds, and the—' "

"It has to be the house." Cynthia Grimshaw nudged her daughter. "It has to be the house."

" '—allotted sum of shares (forty percent) for the Gildersberg business.' "

"That's outrageous!" Cynthia hissed. "What about the house in Boston? That's ours! It *has* to be ours!"

"Please be quiet!" Tapping his desk, Mr. Morton gave her a severe frown.

"You may ask any sort of question at the end," Frankton soothed, finding his place to resume the reading. " 'As regards Gildersberg, I do hereby leave a further share of (thirty percent) to my nephew, Mr. Dean Fairchild, and I also leave the final share of (thirty percent) to my nephew, Mr. Jack Grimshaw. The fate of Gildersberg I leave in your hands to do with what you will. Mr Dean Fairchild is aware of my plans for the company and I wish those plans to proceed. I am therefore allocating a trust fund of thirty-five thousand pounds in the hands of these solicitors, Morton and Frankton. The amount is to be used solely on the business and any withdrawal out of this investment by the directors of the company is disallowed.'"

Frankton paused, making sure that if he was to be interrupted it was now and not midsentence.

Cynthia Grimshaw openly seethed across the room. Equally incensed, Rosalie glared at Frankton, waiting to hear the rest.

"'The house in Boston shall be sold.'"

"It's yours." Cynthia Grimshaw put her arm around her daughter.

"'The house in Boston shall be sold,'" Frankton repeated, "'and the proceeds, less the sum of fifteen thousand pounds, are to go in a trust fund I have set up for the restoration of Thornleigh. Five thousand pounds I bequeath to my niece, Miss Alicia Brickley and a further five thousand pounds I do hereby bequeath to my daughter, Rosalie Lilybette Grimshaw, upon her marriage.'"

"The bastard!" Cynthia Grimshaw roared. "He's done it to cut me out."

Her face turning pink at her mother's outburst, Rosalie blinked in pure disbelief. It was obvious to all she expected to receive a great deal more than her father left her.

"Don't worry, honey." Springing out of her chair, Cynthia Grimshaw seized her daughter's hand. "We'll fight this in the courts. You'll get your money."

They flounced to the door where Jack Grimshaw stood. Opening the door, he murmured, "Rosie, looks like you're practically disinherited."

Rosalie flung her hair over her shoulder. "The rest of the money is *mine*. I'll get it back one way or another."

Closing the door behind them, Jack Grimshaw crossed his arms. "Anything for me in there, old boy? Or are we boys cut out of the will?"

Mr. Morton frowned at him. "Mr. Grimshaw, you were never in the will to be cut out of it. Your inheritance, along with your cousin

Mr. Fairchild, is the shares in the company. It was Mr. Grimshaw's plan that you work for a living."

"Oh, that's rich," he snorted, displeased. "Rosie's out to pasture, too, I see. Ha. Smart old man. Never liked us loitering about, did he, Ellen?"

Ellen tensed. His calling her Ellen instead of "Mrs. Grimshaw" was an evident slight.

"No offense intended," he added, quick to heal the breach. "I suppose I have to ask you for a loan now, don't I, Aunty Ellen?"

"Now's not the time, Jack." Dean Fairchild pulled him away.

"No, it's not," Dean's mother backed her son. "Your father, rest his soul, would be ashamed of you."

"Well, I damn well expected *something*. Even a share in the house in Boston. Uncle Ted knew out of all of us I spend more time there than anyone else."

"I agree with Jack," Amy Pringle spoke up. "Rosalie should have got the house."

"It was Uncle Teddy's decision to make," her cousin Sophie reminded her.

"Well how come he gave five thousand pounds to Alicia and not to us?"

"Because we have our own dowries, Amy. Poor Alicia has nothing."

"It's not our problem her father left her nothing. I can see what this is. We should have danced more on attendance with Uncle Ted. Now we're all disinherited. It's not fair."

"It's been a tiresome morning," Dean Fairchild said, taking on the male responsibility for the family. "I think we ought to retire. No doubt Mrs. Grimshaw will wish to talk to the solicitors in private."

"Thank you," Ellen whispered to him as he passed her. "For all your kindness."

He smiled. "Let me apologize for them."

"Don't bother. I can understand their . . . objection. As for the threats, I hope they won't come to pass."

"I shall do my best to persuade Rosalie and her mother to accept things as they are," he promised. "No harm can actually befall you."

"I wish I had your confidence," Ellen whispered. "There was murder in their eyes, didn't you see?"

CHAPTER THIRTEEN

Hanover Square loomed before us like a minefield.

"Follow me."

Tagging behind the major's curt order, we weaved through the desperate reporters and photographers.

"Say nothing."

I admired Ellen's tenacity. Though she gripped my hand tighter, she refused to let them lure her into answering such taunts as "husband-killer," "married him for his money, did you?" and, the worst: "whore."

Once inside the taxi, she burst into tears.

"Ignore it and don't take it as a personal offense," was the major's advice. "They have a living to make. It's called sensationalism."

"I know, I know," she breathed. "But it's difficult. They label me as a murderess and it's not true. I can't even grieve for Teddy because—because—"

Sliding my arm around her, I appealed to the major. I wasn't sure what I had in mind but he seemed to understand.

"The hotel won't be a good place to go now. Driver, take us to the . . . Tower."

My brows rose.

"Well, there we should be unremarkable among the tourists."

He was right, of course.

He was right about most things.

Ellen didn't care where we went. She said that she wanted to brood alone.

"Forgive me, Mrs. Grimshaw, but it isn't safe."

Her eyes filled with tears. "When will it ever be safe? I feel like a hunted rabbit."

"Don't worry." He smiled. "We have a plan to lure out the fox and trap him."

"Him, sir?"

"I would say 'her,'" I put in. "How does one trap a female fox?"

"Why don't we discuss it over tea?" the major suggested and I warmed to him, to his strength, to his reassuring presence. Oh, how I wished he was mine.

"I really don't feel equipped to do what you want me to do," Ellen whispered over a fresh cup of hot tea.

"The monthly meetings aren't formidable," he promised. "And we don't expect you to understand what is discussed there, only that you take notes and report to us."

"All of this means something, doesn't it, Major? But you won't say what it is."

"I can't say because we don't actually know at the moment. Foxes have a way of going underground when they are pursued. Give it time, Mrs. Grimshaw. Give it time."

"Thank you for your support today, both of you."

She gazed from him to me. I registered the query behind her eyes and blushed. The major intensified my blush by smiling at me. It was the kind of smile one gave when holding one's hand.

"I suppose we ought to be getting back now." Ellen broke the awkwardness. "I promised Charlotte I'd buy her a new dress and thought I'd go shopping this afternoon."

"With all due respect, Mrs. Grimshaw, I don't think that is a wise idea."

"Why ever not? You think I'm in danger, too, don't you?"

"Let's get moving, ladies," the major said, firm and serious. "And I think it's in your best interests, Mrs. G., to have a man about caring for your safety. I have already taken the liberty of hiring one for today. He's a trustworthy man and has no current engagements."

"Oh."

The news came as a shock to Ellen.

"How long will I have to have this person?"

"It's hard to say, but you have to realize you are a very rich lady."

Once we were inside the car, Ellen implored the major for his particular advice.

"I would keep a man about for the remainder of the year."

Ellen turned white. "What about Charlotte? They wouldn't seek to harm her, would they?"

"Children are sometimes prey in wealthy families. Once this business is concluded, I recommend going home to Thornleigh and staying there but for the—"

"Monthly business meetings?"

"Yes."

"You suggest leaving my child, Major? When she could be in danger?"

The major looked at me. "It's always advisable to surround yourself with people you can trust. For the time being, you have Daphne. Do you trust her?"

"Of course I do! I'd trust her with my life!"

A whisper of a smile teased the major's lips. "Good. Then you have your answer." Turning to me, his eyes deepened with a new meaning. "And I'm sure Daphne will stay with you as long as you need her. She loves frolicking about in grand old houses."

"I can stay the whole year if you need me," I said to Ellen, open to the arrangement. "You know I love Thornleigh and there's my book to write."

"But your parents . . ."

"They won't mind at all. In fact, they'd be relieved to have me so occupied. Papa's busy with his new play and as you both know, London and I are not the best of friends."

"Then it's settled," the major said, and I thought, pleased with himself.

Back at the hotel, I ran Ellen a hot bath and went downstairs to collect her messages. The elderly concierge shook his head.

"I am sorry, madam, but we sent Mrs. Grimshaw's messages to her room."

I asked whether this was the usual practice.

"Not normally, but Mrs. Grimshaw telephoned this morning. She wished for any messages to be sent directly to her room."

"Oh. I see. Thank you."

Frowning, the concierge began to look at me suspiciously. "And you are?"

"Miss du Maurier."

"Mrs. Grimshaw's companion?"

I paused. To some in my circle being called a companion might be regarded as an insult. I never thought of myself as a companion before and an intriguing possibility entered my mind. What was the life of a companion like? Perhaps I ought to make my character a companion at the start of the book?

Janet, a free and loving spirit finds herself hopelessly at the mercy of her rich relatives . . .

"Did you see them today?" Ellen said from her bath. "Vultures, all of them. The look on her face was priceless. She thought they were getting the Boston house."

Rosalie and her mother.

"And no doubt much more. She's furious with him for leaving her those company shares. It means she'll have to work or at least have an interest in the company to reap its profits instead of being handed them on a silver platter. She'll contest the will, of course."

I said I had little doubt they would try.

"Jack is livid. He thought he had it easy; fetching and carrying for the heiress."

Sitting down in the chair beside the bathtub, I told Ellen what I'd seen.

"Yes, I know. Jack and Rosalie. Teddy found out before he died. He had a man following them."

She paused.

"And now that I think of it, Teddy's been quite clever in leaving that company to the three of them: Rosalie, Jack, and Dean. Dean is the worker. But he won't brook any tardiness, particularly when his future is at risk. He'll make it work. They either have to make it work or risk losing the benefits."

I couldn't imagine Rosalie working at all and said as much.

"No," Ellen agreed. "She'll send Jack to look out for their interests. Remember, she still has the twenty thousand pounds."

"Which will go quickly if her mother gets her hands on it."

"Exactly. But it's not my problem, is it? Once, a long time ago, before I learned Rosalie destroyed those letters, I thought we may have a chance to be a happy little family. Teddy, me, Charlotte, and Rosalie."

"Things could change," I replied, endeavoring to engender hope into this conversation.

"If she becomes her own person, yes . . . but can you see her free of her mother? Or even wanting to be? Her mother has controlled her whole life."

I thought hard. An only child, raised by a domineering mother. But there comes a time when one leaves the nest to find their own home, their own place in the world.

"Jack will press Rosalie to marry him," Ellen predicted. "But Rosalie knows which side of her bread is buttered. She'll marry elsewhere."

I nodded and fetched her a towel. "Oh, by the way, did your messages arrive?"

"Yes," Ellen called out from the bathroom. "They're on the table."

On the table I found a small basket with a bottle of champagne, a box of chocolates, and scented flowers.

"Who are they from?" Ellen asked, drying her hair.

"Frankton and Morton." I read the card.

Ellen paused to admire the flowers. "Nice, but a little bit inappropriate?"

I shrugged. "As your husband's solicitors, they were obviously aware of the likely family squabbles."

"Still . . . it's odd. Care for a glass? After today, I certainly need a drink."

So we sat down in the little reception parlor in our room. Upon our second glass, Ellen reached for the box of chocolates.

"How did they know I like chocolate?" Ripping open the box, Ellen offered the tray to me first.

I always took time in choosing. We loved chocolate in our house. As soon as I saw the box, from the Swiss chocolate company, I knew which one I wanted. While searching for it, the tray flipped from my hands and crashed to the floor.

"Oh, sorry," I cried, leaping down to pick the chocolates off the floor. Turning over the empty tray, I started to stack them but Ellen grabbed my hand.

"Daphne, stand away!"

I did so, startled by her outburst and the intensity of her expression.

"Look at the box!"

Black words obscured my vision.

DIE.

Written across the back of the box.

Shaking, Ellen lifted the telephone. "Help. Help . . . quickly."

Placing down the receiver, she inched her way toward me. "I knew I was right. I knew they'd try *something*."

"Shall I call for the major? He'll know what to do."

"Yes, yes," Ellen murmured. "I should have known the moment the basket arrived. Morton and Frankton wouldn't think of sending such a thing to me; they're men. No, this is the hand of a woman. And the poison is meant for me."

"If they are poisoned," I pointed out.

"They must have planned it . . . they'll be expecting to hear of my death . . ."

I stood with her while we waited. "What about the other death threats you received? Do you think they are from Rosalie and her mother, too?"

She began shaking again. "I don't know. I expect so. And Teddy," she wiped away a tear, "was the first victim. I am clearly the second." Her gaze darted to the door. "Charlotte. I have to get home to Charlotte."

Neither of us felt safe staying on in London. When the hotel manager arrived, he exclaimed at the mess on the floor.

"I'm certain it's poison." Ellen shivered. "And I can't stay here another night. I just cannot."

After a curt knock at the door, a maid appeared. "Excuse me, madam. A Major Browning telephoned to say he is on his way."

"Thank you," I said. "I shall begin packing at once."

"We can move madam to another room?" the hotel manager suggested.

"No." Ellen was firm. "But you can book the first train out of here."

"There is not a train 'til the morning, madam. May I suggest you stay in our luxury suite? There is one on the ground floor next to my wife and myself. I assure you it is safe."

He bent down to inspect the chocolates. "Poison, you say?"

"Don't touch them," Ellen advised.

"My wife loves these chocolates," he went on, tempted.

"I wouldn't do that if I were you." Major Browning entered the room, an anxious maid hard on his heels. "Not until they are tested."

Before the hotel manager could touch them, the major slipped on gloves and put the items into a brown paper bag. At my ashen face, he gestured to the flowers and collected them also.

"The flowers," Ellen whispered, putting a hand to her head. "I sniffed those earlier . . . oh dear, I'm feeling very faint."

"Fear will make you feel faint," the major assured her.

"She's determined not to stay another night in the city," I said to him, and repeated the manager's suggestion.

The major consulted his watch. "It isn't the hour to move hotels. Move rooms, yes. If it makes you feel better, Mrs. Grimshaw, I will put a man outside your door."

"Yes, do," Ellen insisted, "but I should feel safer if you are here as well. I'll pay for your room. Is there one next to us, Mr. Smythe?"

Mr. Smythe was quick to comply. "Why, yes. We have one available down the hall. And may I be so bold as to reserve you a table this eve, Mrs. Grimshaw?"

"A table for three, please, Mr. Symthe. A table for three."

CHAPTER FOURTEEN

Ellen left the table early.

"No, Daphne, you stay. No harm can come to me. I have the major's man outside my door, remember. I thought I'd take him this." She opened her handkerchief to where she'd placed the remains of her dinner. "I know what it is like to go hungry."

"That was thoughtful of her," the major remarked after she'd gone. "What happened to her?"

"It's a long story." I smiled when he had my glass of wine refilled.

"We have *all* night." He grinned back, and ordered another bottle of wine. "Dessert too. Plum pudding I think should be in order."

"Good choice," I said with a shiver. "How long will it take to find out about the flowers and chocolates?"

"A day or two."

"Do you think they are poisoned?"

"Yes, I do. There is someone out there who wants Ellen dead."

"The same person who killed her husband?"

"Possibly."

"I can't believe some think she killed him."

"What do you believe?"

"Of course I believe my friend," I retorted. "Wouldn't you?"

"Touché. Of course you would. You are a loyal person."

"Are you implying you are not?"

He shrugged. "That question you would have to pose to my dog."

I laughed. I liked his sense of humor. And it was nice to have him all to myself for a change. "Missing your fiancée?"

"Not in the slightest."

"She's very beautiful."

"Yes, she is."

"What kind of wedding are you planning?"

He gave me a wearied look.

"Well, for the sake of her parents, I'm sure you often discuss the topic. I am just curious, that is all. What type of wedding would you like?"

"A small one. With only a few select friends and family."

"Exactly my idea. After participating in Ellen's wedding, I don't think I could do it any other way. But then, I am not Lady Lara Fane, am I?"

"No," he replied under his breath. "You are infinitely much more."

"You are a practiced charmer."

He smiled.

"A good one," I conceded. "What do your parents think of Lady Lara?"

"They like her."

"I suppose they've known her for some time."

"Yes. I am something of a family friend, as the term goes."

"You use the term very liberally."

"Perhaps."

"Have you ever indulged your friendly liberties with a woman?" The moment I said it, I wished I hadn't. But it was too late now, and I blamed the wine.

His hand covered mine. "With you, I should always tell the truth. I have known many women."

I felt my face turn redder. "Have you loved any of them?"

He paused to reflect. His tender gaze sought mine over the table. "What I have experienced mostly is lust. You ask of love . . ."

His voice trailed off and I suddenly felt self-conscious. His presence alone evoked within me something akin to love. I wasn't sure if I loved him, but I knew I was *in* love with him. I could no longer ignore the fact.

The waiter soon returned to clear our table. It was getting late and we were the last in the restaurant. I sensed the waiter and the manager wanted to close for the night and said I thought it best that return to our rooms.

"A pity," the major said, leaning over my hand. "It feels early to me."

"Me, too," I replied in a small voice. "If I had a choice . . ."

He lifted a brow. "If you had a choice?"

"I'd like to stay all night. Or, at least, until I felt tired."

"What shall you do? If I were a great rogue, I should ask you to my room."

I smiled. "But you are a great rogue, are you not?"

"Maybe. And you are at my mercy. Are you not afraid?"

"Touché."

"The offer is there . . ."

"And you think I would accept?"

He raised my hand to his lips and lingered over it. "Please, you are welcome."

I had never received such a scandalous invitation. And from a man whose very proximity sent me mindless. I wanted to say yes, how much I wanted to do so, but some moral fiber in me said no. "I'm sorry. I cannot. I wish I could but if I did, I think I'd be . . ."

"Spoiling a good thing?"

"Yes," I answered, at long last. "It's peculiar. Can you read my mind?"

In answer, he rose to his feet and assisted me out of my chair. "Sadly, it is time for us to leave. However much I'd like this party to continue, it is over."

"That was gentlemanly of you," I whispered as we left the restaurant, me clutching his arm.

"Did you not consider me a gentleman before?"

My response was quick, perhaps aided by the wine. "You are the epitome of a gentleman." I paused. "But you also a man of mysteries. Your work with Scotland Yard. You won't tell me anything about it. May I ask you a question?"

"I'm not stopping you, am I?" He smiled.

We were almost at the door to my room. "If I were your wife, would you tell me about your work?"

Stopping at the door, he heaved a sigh. "It's difficult to say. I've always been alone; worked alone. If I had someone in my life, very close, a wife, like you say, I really don't know. I'd like to maintain steadfast in my job and I hope my wife would respect that."

My gaze narrowed. "Then how would a socialite darling like Lady Lara fare? A poor choice in wife, I would think."

"Extremely poor. Which is why I will not marry her. I don't know why you don't believe me."

"Because," the words ran out of my mouth, "I've known and observed women like her before. They are what you call 'femme fatales.'"

"Have you written about them?"

"I hope to," I said. "I will create one the world will never forget, mark my words."

"I believe you," he said in a whisper and I felt my guard begin to melt. It was so difficult to resist this man, this man I loved. However, I knew that if I strayed across the boundaries of moral decorum I would jeopardize our future.

"The future is such an uncertain thing." I laughed to myself. "What future can *we* possibly have? You are not publicly *free* at the moment and I am not sure you would make a faithful husband. But for now, shall we call it a night?"

"Yes." He raised my hand to his lips once more. "Although you know how much I want to hold you in my arms and kiss you wildly, I will refrain. On the grounds of moral decorum."

"Thank you," I said, and rushed inside the door.

Once there, I leaned against it, almost feeling the heat of him and our encounter through the timber.

"Are you all right?"

Ellen, in her nightgown.

"I think so. Oh dear . . ." I put a hand to my head.

"Have you drunk too much? Were you with the major?"

"Yes . . . and I suppose, yes."

She giggled. "But you came back here?"

"I almost wish I hadn't," I confided, collapsing on my bed.

"You would have regretted it in the morning," Ellen said sensibly. And I believed she was right.

The train ride home to Thornleigh proved uneventful.

After seeing us safely home, Major Browning returned to London to await the results of the flowers and chocolates. He also promised to speak with the solicitors and further question the hotel staff as to who delivered the basket and when.

"They won't find anything." Ellen sighed.

Nanny Brickley was shocked. "Who could do such a thing? The same person who killed Uncle Teddy?"

"Ellen was clearly targeted," I replied. "And she's been targeted before."

Ellen sent me a woebegone look. I understood she didn't want Alicia knowing too much. Perhaps she thought she might be afraid to continue her duties if she knew the danger to Charlotte. And Charlotte loved her nanny.

"Is Charlotte in danger?" Alicia's gaze rested on the child.

Charlotte went on playing with her puzzle, unaware of this conversation.

"And who is that man hanging about the place?"

"He's a . . . kind of protector," Ellen answered. "Major Browning thought it a good idea."

Nanny agreed.

"But who would harm a child? Have you received notes before?"

This time, Ellen did not hold back. She relayed all the death threats she'd received. "The police know, of course. There is little they can do."

"Uncle Teddy should have told them earlier." Alicia turned pale. "If he had, maybe . . . maybe he'd still be alive today."

"The doctor says his heart was weak and he was therefore susceptible to the poison. Whoever put the poison in his cup knew of his condition. The only clear answer in my mind is his business associates. Someone wanted him dead for an intelligent reason I cannot fathom."

"Dean thinks the same," Alicia whispered. "He came to visit while you were gone."

"He came to Thornleigh?" Ellen shot out of her chair. "Did anyone else come?"

If Alicia was surprised by the outburst, she didn't show it. "No. He came on his own, expressly to see me." Lowering her gaze, she blushed. "He came to tell me about my inheritance. It was . . . unexpected."

"His promises weren't in vain," Ellen assured her. "He always said he would leave you something."

"But I don't, I mean I shouldn't—"

"Don't feel guilty."

"But the others—"

"You mean Rosalie, of course. Yes, I suppose it came as a shock. But Teddy had his reasons for leaving her what he did."

"She must be angry . . ."

"Very," I said. "It was the most uncomfortable meeting I've ever been to. Daggers drawn everywhere."

"It must have been a comfort to have Daphne." Alicia sympathized with Ellen.

Ellen allowed a little smile to appear on her lips. "And it was a *great* comfort to have Major Browning, too. He's always there watching over us, isn't he, Daphne?"

It was my turn to blush.

Though Alicia knew of the major's engagement, she said nothing. However, I sensed her wondering about me and the fact made me feel decidedly uncomfortable.

Whatever perception I had about my own character, being a femme fatale wasn't one of them. Nor a wanton woman, tempting a man away from his lady.

Lady Lara Fane is not his lady, I told myself.

But if she was not, then why did I see her arriving from the hall window?

Heart beating wildly, I froze. Why had she come? To visit Ellen? To offer her condolences? If so, why didn't her parents or her mother accompany her? Why come alone?

"Excuse me, miss." A maid bobbed before me. "A lady's come to see ye. I put her in the tearoom."

"Thank you, Olivia."

I didn't even have a moment to compose myself. Sweeping out of her motorcar, Lady Lara had appeared dressed for a soiree and here I was barely out of my morning robe.

"Oh, forgive me." Her painted red lips smiled when I entered the tearoom. "I see you are unprepared for visitors."

Ignoring her, I glanced at Olivia. "Tea, please, Olivia."

Looking from Lady Lara to me, Olivia nodded and curtsied and I only imagined what tale she'd carry back to Nelly in the kitchen.

"I will come straight to the point." Poised to her full height, Lady Lara observed me through critical eyes. She was exceptionally beautiful, and she knew it. Tall, slim, not a hair out of place, or a blemish on her face and I felt immeasurably dowdy in comparison.

"What is between you and Tommy?"

I cringed at her use of his nickname.

"There is no use pretending. I have seen you two together."

I stared at her. Was she baiting me to betray something he'd told me in confidence? Did she suspect that I knew her engagement to him was a sham?

I pretended to go along with her game as I took a seat. "I'm sure I don't know what you mean . . . the major and I are friends."

" 'Friends,' " she echoed, sitting down. "There are many different types of friendships, wouldn't you agree?"

I shrugged.

"Varying degrees of attachments, some wholesome, some not so wholesome."

This time she had gone too far. I shot to my feet. "Whatever you are insinuating, Lady Lara . . ."

She stood up. "Yes?"

"I am not—"

"Yes?"

I wanted to say "wanton." Or one who breaks up engagements and marriages. "The major and I have a *wholesome* friendship," I said instead. "You have no reason to be jealous."

"But there are rumors," she insisted as Olivia brought in the tea.

She waited until Olivia departed.

"Shall I pour?" I poured. "Milk? Sugar? Lemon?"

"No milk and lemon."

I put in two sugar cubes and milk and handed it to her.

Stiffening, she set the teacup down. "Tommy is right. You do have a fiery temperament. He told me about your involvement in the Padthaway case and your lucky escape last winter. Does drama find you or do you find it?"

I expected some kind of insult after the one I'd given her. "I don't actually know."

She turned to find fault with the room's decor. "Tommy and I are planning a spring wedding. He has put your name on the invitation list. Will you come, I wonder?"

This news stabbed me like a knife. Invitations. Invitations? If they were sending out invitations, the engagement couldn't be a farce.

"No need to answer yet." Lady Lara smiled. "I really must be going. I just wanted to have a little chat with you. Now we know where each of us stand?"

Without waiting, she collected her umbrella and preened out of the door.

I remained staring after her, a formidable enemy, a woman scorned.

CHAPTER FIFTEEN

"It's poison hemlock . . . a rare kind. Identical traces of the poison were found in your husband."

Ellen turned around from the window in the breakfast parlor. While the inspector and his sergeant delivered their findings, she stood perfectly still. When they finished, her eyes lowered and she wiped away a tear.

I handed her a handkerchief and she blew her nose. "So we're dealing with the same murderer, Inspector James?"

The little middle-aged man nodded. Since the findings, he'd come down from the north country to handle the case. I wondered if he knew Major Browning. In the silence, I asked the question but Inspector James shook his head.

"I have heard of the major certainly, Miss du Maurier. If I may say so, you are both very lucky ladies. If you'd consumed the chocolates, even a small dose, you'd find yourself in the hospital or worse."

Lifting a weary hand to her forehead, Ellen summoned tea for our visitors. "They killed my husband and now they wish me dead." She shivered. "I have a terrible feeling this has to do with more than money."

"Revenge?" I posed to the inspector.

He rolled his shoulders. "Who can ever tell what motive there is for wanting to kill? It could be as simple or as complex as we can imagine."

"What is your plan now, Inspector?"

"To keep close, Mrs. Grimshaw. To interview each member of the family and certain business associates of your late husband."

"Are you taking the files?" I asked.

"Not yet." Inspector James opted for coffee instead of tea. "Scotland Yard has an interest in those files. When the major completes his report, then the files will become police property until the case is closed."

"What if the case doesn't close?" Ellen shrieked. "What about my daughter? Our safety?"

"Rest assured, Mrs. Grimshaw, you have taken the necessary precautions and you are surrounded by friends here. I would advise, however, you keep your daughter close to you, even when you travel to these monthly meetings."

Ellen sat up. "Why do you say so? Do you think they'll strike her next?"

"We cannot predict the mind of a madman, madam."

"Or a mad*woman*," I put in.

"So." The inspector flipped out his notepad. "According to my initial questions, you attest that on the day of your husband's death you never saw him until at the wedding ceremony?"

"Yes, that's true," Ellen whispered. "I wish I had . . . but it's tradition not to see the bride until the ceremony."

"What about you, Miss Daphne? Did you see Mr. Grimshaw on the day of the wedding?"

I stretched my mind back, running past each event of the day. Most of it seemed a blur because of the tragedy. "I believe I saw him in the morning . . . going into the library."

"What time was this?"

"Just before lunch."

"Was he alone?"

"As far as I could see, but as you know, Thornleigh was crowded with visitors."

The inspector nodded. "Did you at any time see Mr. Grimshaw speak to Miss Rosalie on the day?"

"No . . . I was mostly in the bride's room, preparing as brides-maids do."

"Thank you, Mrs. Grimshaw, Miss du Maurier. And now, if you don't mind, I'd like to question the household staff once more . . . I'll start with Nelly, the cook."

I led the inspector and his sergeant down to the kitchen.

"Nelly," I said, "the police are here. They want to talk to you."

Her face turned bright red. "What do they want to talk to me for? There's no poison in my food, I'll have ye know—oh, Inspector," she greeted, "what'll it be? Tea? Custard tart?"

"Nothing, thanks, Nelly—"

"Oh, sir," his sergeant spoke up, "I'll have a custard tart." He grinned. "Thank you, Mrs. Nelly."

"Oh, just call me Nelly, lad. Or Nell. That's what the old master used to call me. And there was never once any trouble with my food, not since I began in service. Ye ask anyone. Isn't that right, Miss Daphne?"

"Very true," I asserted.

"From the postmortem, the poison alone didn't kill Mr. Grim-shaw. He had a heart condition. A healthy heart may have withstood the poison."

Nelly bristled at the word "poison" again. "It's not my cookin', I'll tell ye. Mr. Grimshaw didn't even eat much that day. He said he had no stomach for it. Nerves, and all that."

"When was the last time he ate, according to your knowledge?" the sergeant asked.

Nelly thought hard. "He had the usual for breakfast, eggs and a muffin. He skipped lunch and asked only for coffee. I sent up coffee and biscuits in the afternoon to his room."

"What time was this?"

"About two o'clock, if I remember. Yes, for that's when those Americans complained about the cold tea. They serve it hot in America, I'm told."

"I'm sure it was no slight on you, Nelly," the sergeant soothed her.

"Well," Nelly rolled her eyes, "I've never heard so many complaints in all my life . . . I'm glad they're gone."

"Do you believe any of them had a reason to murder Mr. Grimshaw?"

"They all did. They all wanted his money. That's easy enough to see."

I thought about Nelly's protestation that afternoon. *They all wanted his money.* I hadn't realized until then how they must hate Ellen. His relatives.

Escaping to my room, Ellen safely with Alicia and Charlotte, I scribbled down the names in the back of my notebook. Teddy's sisters had come to the wedding to show their support but I wondered if they really supported it. In any case, they were unlikely to murder their own brother. I ruled them out.

As for the cousins, Jack Grimshaw leapt first on my page. His association with Rosalie put him at the top of the list.

Jack and Rosalie. I shuddered when I thought of them together in the woods. Had they planned the murder? Had they also planned on Rosalie receiving a fair amount of her father's fortune?

Ellen and Charlotte. Though I believed infallibly in my friend's innocence, it still had to be considered. I was certain Inspector James included her in his list of suspects.

Alicia Brickley. Was something sinister hiding behind her calm repose and her seeming devotion to Charlotte?

And lastly, the unknown author of those letters. Someone Teddy Grimshaw bankrupted through his business dealings?

Cynthia Grimshaw. Would she go to any lengths—even murder—to ensure her daughter's inheritance? I recalled her face at the will reading. Shock. Shock upon hearing the news that her murderous attempt bore little fruit?

Now I had my main suspects, I drew a big question mark on the opposite page. A dollar sign took the shape below it.

"Daphne?"

My heart beating, I shut my book and hid it under another.

"I'm glad I didn't wake you." Ellen came into my room. "Am I disturbing you? Are you writing letters?"

"No, working on my book," I lied, scraping my chair along to further conceal the contents of my desk. "But I'm not really in the mood."

"Excellent. Then why don't you join me in the violet room? I can't sit around idly and cry all day so I thought I'd better continue the renovations. You can help me paint."

Feeling guilty for putting her name down in my book, I was eager to comply.

"You'll need an old smock or something. Do you have one? No matter; I have plenty. A souvenir from my poor years."

Her joke carried a bitter tone to it.

"Oh, I don't mind hard work," she said on our way to the violet room. "My brother and I always liked to work in the garden and in the kitchen. Nelly had to chase us out! Mother, of course, disapproved. She disapproved of everything I did."

"You committed the mortal sin," I reminded her. "Fell in love with an American and not Lord Penthrow."

"Yes," she sighed, "and then having a child out of wedlock. I caused a great scandal and my own father disowned me. He refused to meet Charlotte."

"Those were awful years for you . . ."

She wrinkled her nose. "Yes and no. Charlotte and I had each other. And there was Harry. Faithful Harry."

Faithful Harry. I hadn't thought of him as a suspect, had I? But he had more reason than any if he fancied Ellen. "Did Harry ever ask to court you?"

She laughed. "Harry's just a friend. He's always known that."

"But did he?" I persisted.

She frowned. "Where is this questioning leading? You mustn't think any ill of Harry. He'd not harm a garden worm. He's the most gentle man I know."

"And he did look after you during the poverty . . . when your parents . . ." I glanced at the floor. I couldn't even begin to comprehend her feelings when my parents had always supported me. Would they have supported me, I wondered, if I'd had an affair with an American and bore a child out of wedlock?

"Let us not speak ill of the dead. Those years are gone and my parents are gone with them. Sometimes I do think they wanted to make amends . . . but it was too late. Timing has never favored me."

Nodding, I changed the subject by noting that I loved the violet room.

"I plan to make this guest bedroom the best." Ellen led me through the maze of sheets, tools, and utensils. "For the beds and nightstand I've chosen erstwhile lavender—it's lovely against the pink-and-white stippled wall and perfect for the deep violet carpet and the chintz of the upholstery. The dressing table, you can see, is white, and I purchased antique gold for the mirrors. The bedspreads, wrapped over there for when we're done, are crimson and violet with a softer mauve weaved through. And the lampshades, Daphne, you are going to design with me. It'll be our little project."

I said I'd never done lampshades.

"Oh, haven't you? It's great fun. Like making one's own hat for the races."

I said I'd never worn a hat to the races, either.

"Perhaps the major will take you one day?"

Her eyes twinkled. "What did Lady Lara want with you?"

Avoiding her candid stare, I picked up one of the velvet cushions. "To warn me off her man."

"But he's not really hers, is he?"

I fought with myself then. Do I confide in Ellen or do I not?

"The major will make up his mind and if he's any taste at all, he'll choose you."

"But why should he choose me over a rich and beautiful heiress?"

"Because, well, you're different."

I was curious. "How do you mean, different?"

"You're a published writer, for one."

"Only in story form. It's novels which matter."

"Not in everyone's eyes. You're intelligent *and* attractive. It's a lethal combination. Lady Lara, behind her cool veneer, is not so smart."

Helping her apply paint to the wall around the fireplace, I smiled. "You're a loyal friend. I'm not sure his family would consider me a better choice over Lady Lara . . ."

She paused. "Has he asked you to meet his family?"

"No." My heart sunk. "He took me to meet his godmother, though. She said he'd never taken any other girls there."

"That's something. What does your family think of him?"

"After Somner House they knew we had an *understanding*. Angela blurted it out one night so when we came to your wedding it was a shock to see him with Lady Lara."

"He never mentioned her?"

"Not once." I lowered my eyes. I *had* to tell her. "He says the engagement is a sham and he entered into it for the sake of her sick father."

Ellen put aside her paintbrush. *"What?"*

"Yes, that's what he told me. She begged him, and he conceded. It's been an arrangement for some while."

"How *long* is it meant to last? Until the earl is dead?"

"I suspect so." I shrugged. "It doesn't signify. I'm not ready for marriage yet and we've never discussed anything remotely related to the subject."

"But anyone can see you're meant to be together," Ellen insisted. "Wherever you go, he shows up. That's got to be a sign."

I wanted to believe her. Part of me did, but in the game of love, one should heed caution. I'd seen too many broken hearts amongst my peers to suffer alongside them. I didn't mind writing about love, but to *agonize* like my heroines, no, not me. I'd rather die alone like the Brontë sisters.

CHAPTER SIXTEEN

I next saw the major a week later.

In his usual style, he sent no word to warn of his arrival.

Ellen and I received him in the tearoom.

"Forgive my absence," he said, raising first my hand to his lips and then Ellen's. "I was unavoidably delayed. I trust you kept the files safe under lock and key while I was away?"

"Yes." Ellen nodded. "Daphne and Jeanne did a good job of guarding them. There's no one to fear here, in any case. I trust everyone and all the servants."

Something flickered in the major's eyes at this statement.

"Inspector James paid us a visit. He has a very pleasant sergeant. He won over Nelly in a heartbeat."

"I've heard he's a good man, James. Very thorough. Exactly what you need for this case."

"'Case,'" Ellen echoed, turning pale. "If my husband died of foul play, I can't see how anyone can catch the culprit."

"No murder is perfect, Mrs. Grimshaw."

"Murder." She lowered her head and served the tea, her smile sad and reflective. "Teddy was such a vibrant, robust man. Clever and affectionate. I just can't accept that someone would deliberately kill him in cold blood."

"If he had been an ordinary man, there wouldn't be much of a case," the major replied, accepting the fresh cup of tea from her hand. "However," he added milk and one teaspoon of sugar and stirred it thoughtfully, "his will and his affairs are complex. Hence the investigation."

"What of those threatening notes and chocolate?" I brought up. "Whoever perpetrated the crime is not keen to stop. Ellen and I could have died."

"Poisoned chocolates." Resting back on one of the sofas, the major studied me. "I thought you prefer savory to sweets."

"Then you don't know women," Ellen answered. "All women love chocolate."

"And flowers," added the major.

"I'd prefer a book or an antique necklace, actually," I said, feeling the need to defend my sex. "You sound like my father, Major Browning. Encapsulating all women in one sarcophagus. Sometimes the mummy breaks forth, you know."

Ellen and the major laughed.

"See," Ellen beamed, "isn't she a gem? So, so different from most girls, wouldn't you agree, Major? Oh. Is that the time? I promised Charlotte I'd help with her English assignment. Can I leave you in Daphne's hands?"

After she left, he discarded his tea. "My work here is done. I came back to see you."

I swallowed my disappointment to think he'd go away again so soon. I hadn't expected this. "I thought we'd only just begun . . ."

"I came here to investigate a company and its transactions."

"Gildersberg?"

"Yes. The Yard is sending me to Germany. I leave tomorrow."

I swallowed again. *He was leaving. Leaving the country.* "When will you be back?"

"I don't know . . . Dean Fairchild and Jack Grimshaw are already on their way there."

I sat down. "I see. What about Ellen? She feels safer when you are around."

"Inspector James is close by . . . he's working another case in the area."

"But," my mind raced ahead, "what if something happens? How can we reach you?"

"I'm staying at the *Shoenshreider* in West Berlin."

"Berlin!" I cried. "Isn't it dangerous? My father says the Germans will never give up until they win a war. They are warmongers."

"It takes two sides to create a war, my girl."

"And power and greed," I added, my heart pounding inside my chest. I didn't want him to go. It was *I* who felt safer knowing he was there. It was *I* who worried over him leaving the country. And it was *I* who despaired at the thought of never seeing him again. "I suppose your fiancée is seeing you off? She paid me a visit a few days ago."

"Ah."

I could see this was news to him.

"And what was the nature and purpose of her visit?"

"A clawing claim," I replied. "On you."

Tilting back his head, he laughed.

"You might find it funny but I certainly do not."

"My dearest girl." He moved toward me and swept me in his arms. "*My* dearest girl. When are you going to believe those words?"

I lost all my resolve. A buzzing warmth consumed me, and as I slowly rose my eyes to his I saw the truth in his words. He *does* love me. He does. He does.

I'd never felt so happy in all my life as he kissed me again and again.

"Daphne?" Without waiting, Jeanne had burst into the room. At the sight of the two of us embracing, she recoiled and frowned at me. Why was it always my fault? I thought and rephrased, why was it always the woman's fault?

Clearly, she did not approve.

It was time to let a little of the truth out.

"Jeanne," I began, imploring the major for his consent. "I know Mother and Father asked you to chaperone us for our reputations' sake but what they don't know and what the world doesn't know is that the major is not truly engaged to Lady Lara. Isn't that so, darling?"

At the endearment "darling," he grinned, allowing the silence to further Jeanne's suspicions. When I scowled at him, however, he quickly squeezed my hand and bowed.

"Yes, it's true. I can't say why yet but our engagement will shortly end. Daphne and I are much better suited, don't you agree?"

She still stared at the two of us as though we'd committed a great sin.

"Lara Fane is a friend of mine," he explained. "Her father is ill and it is his dearest wish that she and I marry."

"I see," Jeanne finally replied. "Is it fair to subject my sister to ridicule, though?"

"No. It's not fair. Or equitable. That's why we are keeping our attachment a secret. I will no longer be subjecting you to the burden of chaperone as I am leaving the country. I came back to say goodbye."

His confession melted her resistance. He had a winsome way with words, delivered with the charm of his character. I almost envied him for it. I had no such charm.

"What do you say, Jeanne? Do you fancy me as a brother-in-law?"

"I'm not sure," she answered and we both laughed.

"She's brutally honest," I warned him. "Angela will be thrilled, but of course we can't tell her yet."

"We must ask you to keep our secret, Jeanne. Can we trust you?"

She couldn't say no to him. He could have asked her to take away his dirty laundry and she would have done it. Holding his hand, I felt myself glowing. This was love. The romantic love I'd often written about but never experienced.

"This calls for a celebration!"

Ellen appeared at the door with a bottle of champagne and glasses.

"Please, no, humor me. It's a special occasion and you mustn't blame Daphne, Major. She never breathed a word, I promise."

At her smile, he agreed to stay the hour. "But only the hour," he whispered to me, his tone firm, yet gentle.

Half an hour must have passed before Alicia discovered us.

Drawing my hand away from the major's, I heard her excuse for the interruption, something to do with Charlotte who was having a nap. Her doe-brown eyes missed nothing, and continued to survey us with quiet, unobtrusive contemplation.

"You must join us, dear." Ellen extended the invitation to her.

"She's a perfect replacement." The major, to my dismay, prepared to leave. "Duty beckons, alas. I hope you don't mind Daphne escorting me to the door?"

I blushed when Ellen winked at his smile. I was certain Alicia hadn't missed that, either.

I was right.

Upon my return, still warm and flushed from our lingering farewell kiss, she mentioned it was a great pity the major had concluded his business at Thornleigh.

"Oh, he'll be back," Ellen said.

Alicia's thin eyebrows rose.

"His fiancée resides in the area," Ellen added, and I thought how clever of her.

CHAPTER SEVENTEEN

"It's monstrous."

Flinging the newspaper across the room, Ellen marched to her bedroom window and heaved a long sigh.

"Why do they have to bring that up, now? Have they no sense of decency?"

Shepherded to her room at such an early hour, I'd forgotten to put on my slippers and so shuffled closer to the fire, picking up the discarded paper on my way. "What am I looking for?"

"Oh, you'll see. The torn page."

"Oh . . . *Oh.*"

Now I understood. Under the bold headline MURDER FOR MONEY the article read:

After the shocking recent news of millionaire Mr. Teddy Grimshaw's death, new allegations made by Mrs. Cynthia Grimshaw have led to an ongoing investigation.

"What man dies on his wedding day? He was murdered," Cynthia says. "He was murdered by his bride for his money." It is public knowledge now that Mr. Grimshaw died of heart failure and also that traces of poison hemlock were found on his person. Inspector James has no comment at this time except to say, "They

are investigating all aspects of the death." When pressed for a list of suspects, the inspector referred to his sergeant, who says, "We are still working on it."

Mr. Grimshaw was an extremely wealthy man. It is possible foul play is at play here since the surprising details of Mr. Grimshaw's will became public.

"The will's a forgery," Cynthia Grimshaw maintains, and says she has hired a lawyer to ensure her daughter's succession.

It is still not known what Miss Rosalie Grimshaw was left of her father's estate. The bulk of it, attests Cynthia, has gone to the "murderess," Mrs. Ellen Grimshaw (formerly Hamilton of Thornleigh). "My husband left me for her. They had an affair during the war. She (Ellen) broke up our marriage and disinherited our daughter. I will remain in London until everything is restored to how it should be in his real will.

Miss Rosalie Grimshaw has no comment.

One can only wonder what is next in this Thorny affair . . ."

"It's not true." Tearing around the room, Ellen's breath shortened. "It was *she* who had the affair that destroyed their marriage. When I met Teddy, he was *divorced.* Or just about to be. How can she lie without a backward blink?"

"Because she has no morality," I answered, putting down the newspaper.

"What am I to do? Call her out? Will she ever stop?"

I had little advice. I suggested she talk to my father about organizing a counterattack. "He's knows a few newspapermen. Perhaps one of them can interview you over the telephone."

"That's a good idea." Ellen joined me by the fire. "Oh, I'm a horrid friend! You don't even have slippers on. Your feet must be freezing."

"They are. But the drama was worth it. Promise me you'll put this aside until we speak to my father?"

"You're right." She smiled. "And you must keep me in check. I don't want Charlotte mixed up in all of this. Already she has questioned me about the will."

I paused. "Charlotte? Have you told her anything?"

"Only a little. That her father left her money and houses."

"What did she question you about?"

"She asked whether Rosalie got money and houses, too. I said she got money but not a house. She asked why. I said I wasn't sure but that most likely their father felt that if the house had been left to Rosalie, she would have sold it and not preserved the family tradition."

"That must have been awkward. Did she understand?"

"I think so. That conversation was her first real acceptance that her daddy's dead and he won't be coming back."

I did not envy her and tried to picture myself in her shoes. A rich widow. Hunted and targeted by all. Her very reputation in question because of circumstance and money. It didn't matter whether she was innocent in the reporter's eyes; what mattered was that the case attracted great interest and sold newspapers so poor Ellen was destined for discriminatory criticism.

My father confirmed this when we telephoned him after breakfast.

"Ellen, m'dear, you're best to keep your head out of this. They'll be chasing you for a statement after her claims but don't give in to them. You're best to talk to this fellow I know and let him write a report about you. When are you next in town?"

Ellen mentioned the shareholders' meeting.

"End of the month. Good. We'll talk then."

Ellen put down the receiver. "He wants to talk to you, Daphne."

I picked up the receiver.

"How's my little authoress? Written much of the book?"

"A little." I smiled, heartened by his faith in my ability. "I want to research some shipping towns, though. Middle-class families are my focus."

"Have you wheels down there? Is MB still around?"

"No." My heart sunk thinking of the major and I ached to confide in my father. "He's left for Germany."

"Germany!"

"It's to do with the case."

"Well, I'm glad he's gone. I won't have him upsetting my little girl. And besides, you've got a book to write."

"Yes, I do," I echoed, "but it's difficult . . . you understand . . ."

"And Jeanne? Is she behaving herself?"

"Yes," I was quick to confirm. "We're off exploring tomorrow. I was thinking of taking Jeanne with me. Is she allowed?"

"Wait. I'll ask your mother."

I heard my parents discussing it in the background.

"The verdict is yes," my father relayed. "As long as you keep a firm hand on her and don't go wandering off into fairyland."

"I promise I'll take care of her."

"What's that? Wait a minute, Daphne . . . your mother invites Ellen to stay when she's next in town. She's planning a special dinner party."

That sounded interesting. I said I'd pass on the invitation. "Goodbye, Papa. I love you."

"Love you, too, darling."

After getting off the telephone, homesickness overcame me. I missed my parents. I missed my bedroom, and above all, I missed my typewriter.

Handwriting proved slow and I had little patience. I devoted the morning to my story idea, researching in Ellen's vast library. Upon finding a few books on local towns, I spread them out on the floor, flicking to various pages. In one of the books entitled *Country Estates* there was a section dedicated to Thornleigh and the Hamilton family. There was a photograph of Xavier before he left for the war, and a snapshot of Ellen outside a London club. The caption halted me:

Ellen Hamilton and friend.

Behind Ellen stood faithful Harry in much smarter dress than I'd seen him in around here. A handkerchief folded in his dark striped suit and on the date of the photograph he wore a moustache and dressed his hair short and to the side. In such attire, he scarcely resembled the estate manager and gardener of Thornleigh today.

I asked Ellen about the photograph.

"Oh, you found that! How funny . . . that's years ago."

"When you came back from France?"

She nodded, a fondness creeping into her face. "Dear Harry. He's changed a lot, hasn't he?"

"What did you say he did then? Worked at the club?"

"Yes . . . he made introductions; connected people."

"He looks comfortable in the smart clothes," I remarked.

"Harry's just as comfortable in garden gloves and overalls. He loves great houses. He always wanted to work on one . . . so he came to Thornleigh with me."

"After your parents died?"

Her lips tightened. "Let's not speak of the past. It upsets me."

I left my questions there. She didn't want to talk about the past or Harry and I wondered why.

What did she—or Harry—have to hide?

I went to see Harry about the car.

"He has an office down the hall," Olivia said, pausing with her duster as I ventured into that part of the house.

"Near the morning room."

Near the morning room. Well, I knew where *that* room was; how could I forget? The room where the major first kissed me in this house. I blushed when thinking of it. I blushed when thinking of him.

Fortunately, I spied Harry working at his desk.

"Hello," I greeted, inviting myself in and sitting opposite him. "We haven't really met properly but I feel I know you."

"Oh?"

He seemed suddenly on guard.

"Ellen and I have been pen-friends for years." I hoped my blithe explanation put him at ease.

His hazel eyes flickered, calculating, I thought, what might have been said over the years. "It's nice to have a supportive male friend. Last winter I made such a friend and I'm determined to keep him."

Crossing my fingers under the table, I guessed sharing a little may encourage him to talk.

"Do you write to this friend?"

"No!" I laughed. "Sir Marcus despises that sort of thing. He'd rather we meet at house parties. He believes in living life as if it's a party, it being so short and all. Were you in the war?" I lowered my eyelashes at this blunt question. "I don't remember Ellen saying so."

"I served two years as a bombardier," he replied. "When my plane went down, I was the only survivor." He indicated the scar near his hairline on the left side of his head. "The recovery was slow."

"You met Ellen at the hospital, didn't you?"

At my relaxed poise, he continued to chat to me.

"Yes . . . she came back to work there awaiting the birth."

"Were you shocked she was pregnant and so young?"

"Not in the least. This was war. Many crazy things happened."

"And you became friends. You were there for her during the birth."

"Yes." He chuckled faintly. "The raids were going all night. We couldn't get her to the hospital so she gave birth to Charlotte in a barbershop."

"Amazing." I shook my head. "She has amazing fortitude. I couldn't have done it."

"Yes, you could have. When there isn't an option, you have no choice."

I agreed, and decided to leave our little tête-à-tête there. I had no wish to sound like an interrogator. He may become suspicious of me then and I wanted to keep him communicative.

After mentioning in passing a town I wanted to visit, he said he'd drive.

"I'm happy to. I love this country and motorcars are like horses, they need exercise. When do you want to leave?"

We settled on an early start to make the most of the next day.

I showed him the map I'd drawn.

"There's also an old church along this road . . . and a seventeenth-century pub. Shall we have lunch there?"

Our plans concluded, Jeanne and I spent a quiet evening with Ellen, Charlotte, and Alicia. Since her father's death, Charlotte no longer wanted to take meals in her room. She wanted her mother, so Ellen obliged and Charlotte sat with us. By nine o'clock she tired, though, and we all soon sought out our beds.

"I'm getting bored," Jeanne announced when we retired.

"Tomorrow will be fun," I promised. Jeanne was not one to entertain herself. She relied on friends to do that and she had no friends in the area. "You could make new friends," I added. "We'll go to church on Sunday. You might find someone there your own age."

She seemed appeased with that idea and put on a smile for Harry the next morning.

"I don't want to be stuck at ruins all day," she had advised me while we dressed.

"There are shops in the town; and we'll have ice cream at the quay."

Out of the three of us, Jeanne loved to do feminine activities like shopping and making calls. Always surrounded by people at Cannon Hall, she was unused to the quiet.

She chatted most of the way, asking Harry all kinds of innocent questions like, "Why aren't you married?" "Were you ever married?" "Never found a girl you liked?" "Would you like to get married?"

Good-natured Harry laughed off her attempts. He was an attractive man in his forties. He replied he'd had a few relationships but none that eventuated into marriage.

"Ah," Jeanne teased, "there's a local girl. There must be."

Shrugging, Harry turned into the street of our first stop. "Yes, there is someone. Thornleigh. She's my mistress."

Thornleigh's my mistress.

I thought it a curious expression. Ellen referred to Harry as a friend. But had Harry ever entertained ideas of becoming her husband and thus master of Thornleigh? In turn, could Harry have murdered Teddy Grimshaw?

CHAPTER EIGHTEEN

The possibility of Jeanne and me being driven around by a murderer was discomforting, to say the least.

Charming and talkative, Harry behaved like an impeccable gentleman. He proved himself informative and educated and over a quiet seaside lunch, I inquired as to his family.

"Oh, there's no one really left but me. It was Mum and I for a long time. We lived in a small Dorset village. Ma was a schoolteacher. We used to travel down to Cornwall for the holidays."

"That explains your passion for the land." I smiled, sipping my glass of cider.

"Where did you go for your holidays?" Jeanne asked.

"Not any grand house, Miss Jeanne. We'd go to Penzance. Ma had a friend there who ran an inn. Years later I discovered Ma was his mistress. He had a wife and four daughters."

"Oh." Jeanne and I looked at each other in shock. "Is he your father?"

"I suspect so, since he left me a few bob in his will. I was never fully acknowledged, you must understand, so there wasn't any home for me in Penzance after Ma lost her mind. She lives in a home now. She doesn't recognize me when I visit."

"That's sad. What of your half-sisters?"

"They weren't interested in a young half-brother, probably because their mother poisoned them against me."

"That's sad."

He shrugged. "That's life. Life is what you make of it."

"Daphne." Jeanne tugged my sleeve. "Do you mind if I walk down that jetty? I won't go far."

Squinting, I inspected the ground. It seemed safe enough so I said yes and turned back to Harry. "So you went to London to seek your own fortune as the term goes?"

"Yes. I became a jack-of-all-trades. I had a knack for people, though, and through the clubs became an introducer. It paid well."

"Did you see Ellen as a potential client when you met her?"

He paused then, his eyes softening at the memory. "Not at first. I didn't even know who she was. It soon became evident, though. People talk. And she talked. Her family had cut her off. It was my job to structure a reconciliation."

"And you posed as her husband?"

"At first. Her father was dying and her mother was very ill. He wanted to see her settled one last time. I went down to Cornwall with her and the baby. It was a happy family reunion. The father died and her mother asked us to stay on."

"That must have made you happy. You've been a father to Charlotte."

"She calls me Uncle Harry. Ellen never wanted me confused with her real father."

"It must have been a relief when the pretense ended. Ellen's mother never suspected?"

"No. She lingered on a few months and then died. We lived quietly at the house so very few knew about the pretend marriage. After her mother's death, we put it about that I was a distant relation. Nobody questioned it to this day."

I swallowed. No wonder poor Ellen feared what the newspaper people might find out about her. What if they got to Harry? "You'd never do anything to betray Ellen, would you?"

He gave me a woebegone look. "She's like a sister to me. A sister that I never had."

"And she thinks of you affectionately."

"We bonded through circumstance. The war, and the birth. The saving of Thornleigh."

"She owes you a lot," I replied, recalling the letters. "She called you her 'savior' and if you weren't there, she may have been disinherited."

"Despite her father's threats, that wouldn't have happened. Thornleigh is entailed. She's the next Hamilton in line. And after her, it will go to Charlotte."

"Charlotte's a very rich little girl at the moment. I worry for her . . ."

"She's got protectors." Harry's reply was fierce. "If anybody were to harm her . . ."

His tone became murderous.

"What did you think of Mr. Grimshaw," I whispered. "What did you *really* think of him?"

"A swine." He laughed. "At first. How could he have deserted poor Ellen? Then I came to understand the reasons. The missing letters. The miscommunication."

"You must have resented his coming back on the scene?"

"Yes and no. In some ways it settled Ellen and Charlotte. He needed them and they needed him."

"And he brought money to Thornleigh," I pointed out. "A very good virtue."

Gazing at me, he laughed again. I thought he didn't mind me; he respected that I'd taken the time to talk to him and not consign him to his position. In truth, he was much more than Ellen's estate manager. "You'd do anything for Ellen, wouldn't you?" I asked as a final question to our little conversation.

"Anything," he confirmed. "Anything."

* * *

Mevagissey, on the east coast, was a delightful little town. Upon reaching it, I made good my promise to Jeanne and spent an hour or so browsing the gift shops and art galleries. Jeanne found a painting she liked but my haggling failed to bring results and we left the shop downhearted.

Like Fowey, where we had a home, Mevagissey attracted many tourists. Small and unspoilt, the traditional fishing village was an ideal place to begin my research. With Harry's help, I found the shipbuilding company I wanted to talk to on the west quay.

"We are a family business." The owner's wife agreed to speak to me. "Prichards has been in our family for five generations."

After taking me on a tour of the warehouse, she invited Jeanne and me for tea at her home.

"We live above the office. It's nothing but we call it home."

The apartment surprised us. Small, yes, but well planned and filled with tasteful furniture and a charming burgundy-and-cream theme.

"What is your story about, Daphne?"

Looking through the old family photographs, I replied I still wasn't sure. "The characters will lead me. I want to create strong characters, based on what is real."

"Then you'd love the story of my grandmother, Adelaide. I hope you brought a pen and notebook?"

Upon our return to Thornleigh, I raced straight up to my room to write. An idea kept buzzing through my mind and I was anxious to get it on paper. I didn't always trust my memory.

"Are you coming to dinner at all?"

Jeanne. Her stomach persistently rumbled.

"Yes. I'm nearly finished. A whole chapter. I can't believe it."

My excitement failed to illicit a smile from Jeanne. When she was hungry, she was hungry, and nothing else mattered.

"All right," I conceded. "I'll put it aside and continue later."

She beamed. "I wonder what we'll have for dinner tonight? Nelly cooks so wondrously."

"Yes, she does." Nelly, I thought. I have to talk to Nelly.

After dinner, a chance presented itself. Ellen wanted a blackberry pie for tomorrow's afternoon tea.

"Nelly, I visited Mevagissey today where your grandmother lived. It's lovely and Mrs. Morgan from the pastry shop said to say hello. She remembers you as a little girl."

"Dear me," Nelly reflected. "Is she still alive?"

"Alive and working. Her pasties are famous."

Nelly's eyes rounded. "And she won't share the recipe?"

"No. And I *did* ask." I paused and offered to help put away the fine china. "While I was in the shop, something came to mind. I remember Mr. Grimshaw speaking of the pasties. He loved them. Are you sure he didn't have anything to eat? Could someone have brought him a pasty from the village?"

"It's possible . . . but I doubt it. Lots goin' on that day. Who knows what madness struck."

I could see Nelly resented the idea of anyone bringing in pasties into *her* house and offering them to guests.

"That nice sergeant came back today . . . he asked after ye." Nelly winked. "Nice lad. Had a cup of tea."

"Oh?" I raised my brows. "Ellen didn't mention the police calling. What did they want?"

"Funny. The sergeant was askin' the same thing as you and went to speak to all the maids again. Nothin' came of it that I know."

"It had to be from one of the guests." I spoke aloud, deep in thought. "They delivered the death-dealing food. I say food and not drink, don't you? It doesn't stand to reason somebody bringing him a drink unless it's hundred-year-old whiskey or some sort—" I broke off. Why hadn't I thought of that before? "Nelly . . . do you remember if there were any empty glasses used by Mr. Grimshaw on the day?"

She sighed. "As if I'd remember! I had me hands full . . . there were a hundred things goin' on. Things goin' back and forward from the kitchen. You'd best to ask Olivia."

"Thank you. I will."

Nelly frowned at me. "Where's all this leadin' though? You'd best to leave police business to the police."

"Yes, I know. You're right. Good night, Nelly."

Of course, I'd do exactly the opposite. Whiskey. Mr. Grimshaw liked whiskey and he might have indulged in a nip on the day in celebration. Nobody would think anything of it. Our maids at Cannon Hall often cleared and replaced my father's port glasses daily. It was so ordinary.

Ordinary enough to have been overlooked?

"Here is our defense."

Ellen shoved the newspaper before me, almost knocking my cup of tea. Pushing the teacup and saucer away, I proceeded to read aloud the following:

TRAGIC LOVE by Jeffrey Leighton

Last month we were all shocked to hear of the untimely death of American millionaire Mr. Teddy Grimshaw on his wedding day.

Since this tragic event, startling controversial claims have arisen from Mr. Grimshaw's former wife, Cynthia, who is pursuing a legal case against her husband's will.

Cynthia maintains her ex-husband's bride Ellen Hamilton (the main beneficiary of his will) is responsible for his death.

"There is little doubt Mr. Grimshaw died unexpectedly and we are investigating all leads," police say, but they are unwilling to confirm if Mrs. Ellen Grimshaw is a suspect.

"Her claims are outrageous," Ellen replies, agreeing to an exclusive interview at her home Thornleigh in Cornwall.

"She received a lucrative divorce settlement but instead of investing it wisely, she has spent a large portion of it and seeks more by using her daughter as a pawn."

I mentioned the late Mr. Grimshaw's will at this stage.

"Yes, I knew of the details in the will and the reasons behind my husband's decision. It is not true Rosalie Grimshaw was left nothing. She received twenty thousand pounds and forty percent of shares in a company. My husband intended that she work for the company."

"Do you think it's a fair settlement? Cynthia claims the will is a forgery," I asked.

"She claims a lot of things which aren't true. For instance, it was she who committed adultery and broke up her marriage, not my husband's alleged affair with me. I met Mr. Grimshaw in France during the war. He was injured, and had been recently divorced. We fell in love and planned to marry after the war. However, forces worked against us and in a cruel twist of fate my letters never reached him."

"What do you think happened to the letters?"

"They were destroyed."

"You believe his family had a hand in sabotaging your relationship?"

"Yes, I do, but that is past now. We found each other again."

"And you have a daughter by him? One he only recently claimed?"

"Yes . . . things were difficult after the war. When I didn't hear from him, I thought he had abandoned us."

"And on the other side of the ocean, he was thinking the same?"

"Yes . . . I'm sorry. I wish to stop now."

Mr. Teddy Grimshaw married Ellen Hamilton at her family estate Thornleigh on June 6. Together they have a daughter Charlotte. Ellen maintains her innocence in her husband's death.

"It's good," I said at the end.

"I feel I can show my face again. Your mother telephoned today. She's organizing a dinner party but she didn't want me to feel impelled to go if I am not up to it."

"You should go. It will stop people talking, too, if you are out in society."

"Yes, I know." Ellen hung her head. "I'm fighting *her* game."

"She won't be accepted if you're in town," I reminded. "She's an outsider with few connections. Wait. I have an idea. My friend Sir Marcus is back in town. Shall I get him to host a soiree? He knows all the right people."

"Sir Marcus." Ellen's brow fluttered. "The one your mother wishes you to marry?"

"Yes." I groaned. "It's the title she's after. Imagine. *Lady* Daphne. It doesn't suit me."

"I think it does. Even better still *Lady Daphne Browning.*"

I admitted I liked the sound of it and my heart became heavy thinking of him in Germany. Was it safe? What did he hope to achieve?

"Come." Ellen squeezed my hand. "You're in need of some cheering up and so am I. Charlotte is safe with Jeanne and Nanny Brickley. Let's go for one of our old rambles through the woods."

A good walk was exactly what I needed and we waved to Harry as we headed out. The fineness of the day darkened upon reaching the woodland. It didn't quite threaten rain yet. I estimated we had an hour or so.

"Life's strange, isn't it?" Ellen whispered. "Things could have turned out so differently. I was a young woman and you were a girl. What aspirations we had! What happened?"

"The war."

"Ah, yes, the war." She bit her lip. "Do you think there'll be another one?"

I shivered. I didn't want to think about it. I didn't want to acknowledge the love of my life working in dangerous Germany. I shivered again. If anything happened to him I didn't know what I'd do. I couldn't live without him. I choked back a sob just imagining him dead.

"Here. Take my coat. You're cold."

Without waiting, Ellen draped her fine ivory cashmere over my shoulders.

"Thank you," I replied and we resumed our walking and reminiscing through the woods. As we drew closer to the tree where we'd carved our initials as children, I thought I heard something. A twig breaking.

I looked around. There was nothing there.

"It's probably just a small animal—"

Then the shot fired.

Startled by pain in my shoulder, I collapsed to my knees. Blood seeped onto the cashmere. I closed my eyes and winced. I felt sick and weak.

And then darkness.

CHAPTER NINETEEN

"She's lucky. The bullet missed the collarbone and went out the other side."

"Oh, look. She's waking."

"Yes. I've left something for the pain, Mrs. du Maurier. A little laudanum will help her sleep, too."

"Is it too early to move her? We'd like her take her home to Cannon Hall," my father said.

"A slow and steady journey will do no harm."

I opened my eyes. Familiar faces loomed above me, tender and concerned. "Home," I murmured. "I don't want to go home."

"Just for a little while," pacified my mother, caressing my hand. "Don't worry. Ellen's coming, too."

"Ellen." I started and seized by pain, fell into the pillows. My head thundered and my throat was dry. I felt as if I'd collided with a motorcar shoulder first. Under the sheets, I examined my limbs. They all appeared to be intact and in good working order. "How long . . . ?" I winced, touching the sling holding my left arm.

"Have you been abed?" My father's jolly smile did little to appease me. "Two days. Sleeping like a log. Good for healing."

"This is serious." My mother sent him a glare.

"It's deadly serious," my father replied. "Where's that fellow meant to protect her?"

"He was hired to protect Charlotte." Ellen came into the room, looking as if she hadn't slept in days. "I should have listened to the major. I should have engaged another man to . . . to—"

"There, there." My mother embraced her. "Daphne's fine."

"But don't you see? Daphne was wearing *my* coat. That bullet was meant for me."

I saw my father halt with this news. He'd been conversing with the doctor over some need for eye drops. "What's this about a coat?"

"It was just before the attack. Daphne was cold and I gave her my coat. It's one I often wear."

Gazing at my father, my mother frowned before taking my hand in hers.

"You both must come to Cannon Hall," my father decreed. "I'll get a man to look into it. Where's this fellow you hired for Charlotte? I'd like to speak to him. And Harry, too. He's handy to have around."

I heard a knock at the door.

"Is she all right?"

It was Alicia Brickley, Charlotte at her side. Bursting past them, Jeanne carried a tray into the room.

"Tea and cucumber sandwiches," Jeanne announced. "Nelly's worried. She's been talking to herself all morning."

Touched by their concern, I couldn't help wishing the major was there. If not at Thornleigh, then at least in the country. A trifle piqued, I sipped my tea and ate the sandwiches. I longed for sympathy and not just any sympathy. I longed for *his* sympathy. Having my parents paw at me wasn't the same.

"We should let the major know." Ellen seemed to understand. "The attack could be important."

On saying this, her glance flew to Charlotte. If they were prepared to strike Ellen, were they prepared to strike a child?

158

Which left one question.

Who?

I experienced an overwhelming sadness when the gates to Thornleigh closed. How long until our return? I confess to a love affair with the stately old mansion; I didn't want to part from it.

Ellen looked wistful, too, staring back at the house.

"Mama." Charlotte nudged her mother's hand. "Can we go on a sea holiday now? I want to see Grandmama."

Raising haunted eyes to me, Ellen tried to put on a brave face. "Maybe we will, darling. Winter's coming."

Her words faded against the rhythmic hum of the Bentley. In the front seat, Harry adjusted the speed. He knew his cars very well, and no doubt enjoyed driving the fleet Ellen had inherited.

We spoke little on the journey. I, on the best of occasions, refrained from the chitchat I despised, the kind with no meaning or intention, and Alicia Brickley preferred the silence. Ellen sat alone with her thoughts, attempting to amuse the child with a book.

My parents and Jeanne arrived ahead of us. To my disappointment, Angela wasn't at home. She'd gone to our riverside house in Fowey to write.

Envy burned heavy against my cheeks. I planned to spend all these days composing my novel at Thornleigh and researching the area. And now a faceless villain interrupted those plans, keeping us in London.

"You may stay as long as you wish, dear Ellen," my mother said as we entered Cannon Hall.

I greeted the dismal mansion of my childhood with a tight smile. The light wasn't good and the too-familiar surroundings failed to inspire me.

"I long for a seaside holiday, too," I whispered to Charlotte as we climbed the stairs.

Alicia turned at this comment. She had an odd expression on her face. I couldn't quite make it out.

"The room will do nicely," Ellen pronounced from inside. "And Alicia, you're next door. You can help Charlotte unpack?"

Alicia nodded and resumed her duties with quiet servitude. Since Uncle Teddy's death, she seemed even more devoted to Charlotte and cared little for her own independence. I wondered how long she intended to stay on as Charlotte's nanny. Five thousand pounds was a fortune; she might well head on a seaside holiday herself.

Retiring to my room and under Mother's orders, I drank the sleeping tonic and curled up in bed. My left shoulder throbbed. To focus away from the pain, I closed my eyes and imagined the novel I wished to write.

Some hours later, I joined my father in his study.

"You look pale," he said, looking up from his desk. "Come and see this new play I'm working on."

Still in my robe and slippers, I slipped gratefully into the great armchair by the fire and yawned.

"I trust my audience won't yawn," my father joked and proceeded to read some of the play. "*The Gaunt Stranger,* by Edgar Wallace—"

"Edgar Wallace." I blinked. "Don't I know that name?"

"You should do. He came for dinner last year."

"The novelist." I hung my head low. "I remember. He's so lucky. Published and a great success. His life is so interesting . . . a reporter in the Boer War, correspondent for the *Daily Mail;* how can I possibly join his rank?"

Joining me by the fireplace, my father tipped his spectacles on the tip of his nose. "Finish the book, Daphne. I have someone who'll look at it if you do."

"Really? Who?"

"Finish the book then we'll see. No promises."

Excited and inspired, I'd have run upstairs to write but forced myself to listen to my father talk about his play.

"Here's the rundown of the story: the killer is known as 'the ringer.' He's a master of disguise who continually baffles the police. Young Detective-Inspector Alan Wembury takes over the Deptford police division and is hoping to marry Mary Lenley who has just become Meister's secretary (Maurice Meister, a lawyer mixed up with the ringer). News comes that the ringer, who had been traced to Australia and reported dead, has returned to London. Meister is his next victim, for he left his sister in Meister's charge and her body was found floating in the Thames. Soon a gaunt stranger is stalking the frightened lawyer who seeks police protection. Wembury has a hard task complicated by the fact that Mary's brother, ruined by association with criminals, is jailed for robbery—and Meister knows more than he will admit. Also, the unpopular Inspector Bliss from America is working along his own lines to solve the case. Who *is* the ringer?"

"It's intriguing," I said at length, a little dismayed by the theme. Was a gaunt stranger stalking Ellen, and in turn, any who accompanied her? "Who is the ringer?"

Grinning, my father put the pages aside. "Ah, you'll have to watch the play to find out. Why not take that Jack fellow?"

"He's gone to Germany."

"Oh, yes. To secure his inheritance, no doubt."

"Father . . . what do you know of the company Salinghurst?"

"Owned by that old stick Salinghurst and his sons. Needed to raise cash. Sold off most of it to Grimshaw and Rutland."

"Rutland?" I blinked. "The *earl* of Rutland?"

"The very same."

"But Ellen didn't mention him at the shareholders' meeting. She said the other party was a Mr. Prichard."

"Ah, the erstwhile Mr. Prichard. A Jewish moneylender. Probably put up the money and Rutland loaned his title. Nothing extraordinary there."

"But why would Scotland Yard want Ellen to attend these meetings? They must suspect someone. That's why they sent the major to Germany."

"Great Scott! Everyone's leavin' Britannia for Germany these days. I daresay they're after J.G. Jack Grimshaw. He's a shady fellow."

I stared at him aghast. "If you think he's shady, why would you want me to go out with him?"

"Because he's a charming chameleon. He'd make a good actor."

I began to feel ill. "Oh, no . . . you didn't ask him to audition, did you?"

My father grinned. "He can do accents, too. I merely suggested it may be a line of work for him."

"And how did he take that? I don't think he's the kind to like work."

"Ah, but acting is *fun* work. There's the difference."

Obviously, the two of them had had several discussions. I asked my father where.

"At the club, where else?"

"Did he say anything about his uncle's will?"

"He mentioned it once or twice. I advised him to secure his interest. He admitted he had no head for business but that his cousin did."

"What of Rosalie Grimshaw? Did he mention her?"

"No. Not a word."

I glanced down into my lap. "The two are lovers, you know."

To my disappointment, my father elicited no shock and I recalled my own girlish infatuation with my cousin Geoffrey.

"Geoffrey's in town, by the way. He's called here a couple of times," my father said, reading my mind.

"Oh." My face turned a deeper shade. Two years ago, I mightn't have been able to face Geoffrey. I had once thought myself hopelessly in love with him.

"Does it bother you to see him?" my father probed.

I shrugged. "Mother needn't strike him off the receiving list, if that is what you mean."

"You once said you'd never see him again."

"That was a long time ago. I was a child, really."

"And now you are a young woman in love with another man."

I sensed my face turning scarlet.

"I looked into Browning. It'd make a good match."

"Not against Lady Lara Fane. She, I think, is determined to have him."

Grinning, my father searched his desk for something to nibble on. "You've never backed off from a challenge, Daph, m'girl. What's stopping you now?"

"I don't know." I heaved a weary sigh. The warmth of the fire, the security of being home, and my close dance with death sent a furor of emotions warring within me. I missed him. I wished he was here.

"I telegraphed the major," my father murmured. "I asked him of his intentions."

"Oh, no, you didn't! How embarrassing . . . I'll *die* of mortification."

"No, you won't." Tearing a strip out of his pocket, he read what I needed most to hear. " 'Intentions honorable. Stop. Coming home. Stop.' "

Elated beyond words, I forgot about the pain in my shoulder for at least a minute or two. I just wanted to hug his telegram to me.

"*Gerald.* Is that you down there?"

My mother's voice found its own way into our sanctuary.

"Yes, dear. We're turning out the lights now."

"I don't feel at all tired," I confessed.

"Nor do I," winked my father, helping me out of my chair. "But we'll both be in trouble if we don't go up."

"May I read the rest of this play *The Ringer*?"

"Of course you can but that's not the title. It's . . ." At the door, my father paused to smile, his eyes gleaming with a new idea. "You've done it! *The Ringer.* Yes, that's much better. Shorter, catchy. You've got a gift, m'girl. Don't let anyone ever tell you different."

"Thank you, Papa." I reached up to kiss him on the cheek, and later that night I dreamt of my book with my name emblazoned on the cover and a title, a title with no name. Yet.

Since I was the last to bed, I was the last to wake.

"Daphne, you've missed breakfast. I'll send to the kitchen. I want a fresh cup of tea anyhow. My, my, you won't believe what's in this morning's paper."

Yawning, I glanced at the serious faces before me.

"Ellen doesn't know," my father began.

"She sent up for breakfast this morning," my mother informed.

"I knocked on her door," Jeanne relayed. "Charlotte answered and said her mother was still sleeping."

"It's very awkward . . ."

"And *unexpected*—"

"What is? What's happened?"

The three faces all lowered their eyes at once.

"It's Cynthia Grimshaw," my mother blurted out.

"She's dead."

CHAPTER TWENTY

"At least Ellen won't have to worry about the court case now." My father, adding sugar into his tea, smiled.

"Your quip, Gerald, is in bad taste," my mother said. "They say she was found dead at the bottom of the staircase."

"With her neck broken," my father put in.

I reached for the paper. I could scarcely believe it. Ellen's nemesis dead. When? How?

"It happened sometime yesterday afternoon. She died quickly. An accident, it seems."

The newspaper revealed few details. On first impression, it appeared Mrs. Grimshaw misjudged a step and tumbled to her death.

" 'A hotel maid discovered her a few minutes afterward.' " I read from the paper. " 'The police are investigating possibilities . . .' "

Possibilities. What could have induced Mrs. Grimshaw out of her luxury hotel suite in the middle of the afternoon? "How was she dressed?" I wondered aloud.

"Daphne." My mother's stern frown arrested me. "I don't like you mixed up in any of this affair."

"Ellen is my friend." I shrugged. "It's only natural I am curious."

"Two deaths." She shivered. "So close together . . ."

" 'A curse upon thee house,' " my father dramatized, to her horror.

She was scandalized. It was a good thing, I thought, that she didn't know of my true involvement in the Padthaway case, or last winter's peril at Somner House. On both occasions, I couldn't help conducting my own investigation. I did so for inspiration and future characterizations. People and their motivations interested me.

"She wasn't popular," my mother went on. "I heard from Mrs. Pinkerton the previous week. The Americans' greed for money sent her making all kinds of mistakes. Do you know she actually *called* at Langton House? She was turned away at the door, of course. As if the duchess would acknowledge her!"

"You never can tell," my father added, somewhat amused by this incident. "She had all the papers lined up to print her grievances."

"Grievances." My mother's mouth turned down in disgust. "Anyone can see it is pure jealousy which drove her over here in the first place."

"She was worried about the money. Allegedly, her *daughter's* money."

"I wonder if the daughter will continue to fight the case," my mother reflected as Alicia Brickley swept down the stairs and into the room.

Giving us a curt look, my father hid the paper behind his back. "Morning. Is Mrs. Grimshaw up and about yet?"

"Yes. She sent me down to fetch some tea."

"Oh, good. Very good."

"Is she not feeling well?" my mother inquired.

"A bad night's sleep," Alicia obliged. "But she said she'll come down after some morning tea."

"I see. Well, tell her I should like to see her in my study when she is ready."

Concern flickered over Alicia's fine features. "Is everything all right, Mr. du Maurier?"

"Everything's perfectly all right," he assured her. "Do be sure to take up some of these little lemon biscuits."

"And the scones are delicious." Jeanne grinned. "It's Cook's own jam recipe."

"Thank you." Alicia selected a plate. "I'll return for the tea."

"We do have maids to do that, you know," my father called up after her.

"I know." She smiled, pausing on the stairs. "I'm so used to it now, it's become second habit. Really, I don't mind."

"I'd drop the tray if I had to carry it upstairs," Jeanne announced.

"If you went slowly and took care you wouldn't," I replied.

"Maybe you should have told her, Gerald. She's still part of their family. She has a right to know. It would be dreadful if she found out by some other means . . ."

"They have no paper or telephone in their rooms, dear. They'll hear of it first from my lips."

"I feel sorry for the daughter," my mother confessed. "All alone in a different country and with both parents dead. Who is she to turn to?"

"Her cousin," I said, omitting the word "lover" from my lips though it was poised there. "Jack Grimshaw."

"But he's in Germany, isn't he? What of that other nice boy . . . Fairchild or something? Megan's quite keen on him. Apparently, he has been calling on her. Did you know, Daphne?"

No. I didn't know. "But I like Mr. Fairchild. I can't see that Megan's parents would approve."

"They do want her to aim somewhat higher," my mother agreed. "And Mr. Fairchild's financial situation is unstable. He's forced to become a businessman."

"A terrible destiny." My father smarted. "And what do you think I do, dear?"

"Oh, Gerald, but you're a gentleman—"

"*And* a businessman."

"—but you don't have to work. You work because you like to."

"I like to earn money."

At this brash declaration, my mother recoiled in horror. To her dismay, however, my father refused to redeem himself. "It's true we all need money. And we all like money. I don't know why it ain't etiquette to feign ignorance of the fact."

" 'Ain't,' " my mother cringed. "You ought to work on your grammar, Gerald."

"Nonsense, m'dear. I am *in* character."

Lingering outside the study, I imagined a hooded gaunt stranger entering the Claridge Hotel. *The stranger proceeds up the stairs, luring his prey out of her rooms. At the top of the staircase there is a struggle. Mrs. Grimshaw plunges to her death . . .*

Why? The great question. And who?

An accident? From memory, one would have to be terribly clumsy, or intoxicated, to fall to death on the Claridge's carpeted stairs.

Ellen blinked twice. "Dead? She's dead?"

"Yes," my father confirmed. "On the floor at Claridge's."

Clearly shocked, Ellen reached out for the newspaper report. Shaking, she read down the page. "Did she fall or was she pushed?"

"I daresay that's the question the police will be asking. Ellen, m'dear, I do advise saying nothing to the papers at present. They will try to trap you."

"You wish me to remain housebound for a few days?"

"I think it's wise," I said, wincing at a sharp pain in my shoulder.

"Best they try and hound our house rather than yours," my father added.

"But I had nothing to do with her death, Uncle Gerald . . . I hated the woman, it's true, but I certainly didn't go to Claridge's, sneak up the stairs, and push her to her death."

Listening to Ellen, I suddenly developed the urge to take tea at Claridge's. To make my outing seem normal, I telephoned Megan and asked her to join me. To my mother I said: "Megan wants to see me. I think she has some news."

"Oh, *news*."

My mother loved news.

"What kind of news? Did she say?"

"No." I smiled. "But I suspect it has something to do with a certain gentleman."

"How interesting . . ."

"It's a secret. Please don't say anything to her mother."

"Of course I wouldn't dream of breaking a confidence if you choose to trust me." Her gaze turned wistful. "Daphne, sometimes I wish you'd trust me. Who better than a mother to wish the best for her daughter?"

I said I didn't know what precipitated this outburst.

"Oh." She sighed. "You trust your father more than me. He says Major Browning is coming home to see you."

"I'm sure he has business to attend to as well," I added, my face flushing a vibrant red.

"But he's an engaged man, Daphne. It's getting quite embarrassing. Yesterday, Lady Holbrook asked after you. She said she heard you dined *alone* with the major . . . is this true?"

I turned a deeper shade of scarlet. "Yes, it's true . . . I really must go to the bathroom now—"

"*Sit down*, Daphne. I wish to have a word."

Oh dear. I knew what having "a word" entailed. A lengthy lecture.

"Lady Holbrook is a friend of Countess Rutland. News has also reached the countess's ears of your association with her daughter's fiancé."

"I don't see what the big fuss is all about—"

"Big fuss! You're putting yourself out there as a girl who facilitates broken engagements."

"Nonsense." I stopped short, breaking into a grin. "The engagement is off?"

"The major broke it before he left for Germany. He quoted *you* as the reason."

It was time to set matters straight. I was innocent. I'd done nothing wrong. After hearing my side of the story, my mother's face softened.

"Oh, my! I am soon to have an *engaged* daughter! How exciting. And we must let the world know about the faux engagement. I don't want your reputation injured—"

"I'm sorry, Mama. I can't do that."

"Can't? What do you mean, can't? We must. Otherwise, you're bringing reproach on our name."

"Mother," I sighed, "we're not living in the Dark Ages. Besides, broken engagements do happen."

"Not in my day."

"I'm sure it's not as bad as you imagine. You know since the war things have changed."

"You're wrong, Daphne. People like the countess never forget. The stain will remain with us. We won't be accepted," she choked, "we won't . . . and what of the major's family? I'm certain his mother feels the same as I do."

Her words hit hard. An uneasiness curled in my stomach. What did his mother think? It pained me to acknowledge the fact that she might oppose. Whereas before her son's entanglement with Lady Lara she may have been glad to welcome me into the family. Our name was not as illustrious as the Rutlands, true, but we had a respectable name and a fair place in society. I could see, however, how a little malicious gossip from the countess could malign our chances in certain circles and thus hurt my mother.

I did not care for these kinds of matters but my mother did and so it affected me whether I liked it or not.

I slipped out of the house after luncheon and took a cab to Claridge's. Megan was waiting in the hotel foyer.

"Why *here*?" she whispered. "That woman died here. She was Dean's aunty at one time. Funny, isn't it?"

"Have you heard from him?"

"Yes, he's coming home. He's worried about Rosalie. Her mother's controlled her life for so long he thinks she'll be lost. And she's in a foreign country, too. She has no one but Dean and Jack."

"Jack," I murmured. "What do you think of him?"

"Sleazy and charming; a toxic combination. Shall we get a table?"

"Yes, let's do."

I'd forgotten the niceties of having afternoon tea at a fancy hotel. It was one of London's saving graces, I thought, admiring the highly polished floor and luxurious interior. Busy at this time of year, I wasn't sure whether we'd secure a place in the tearoom.

"Ah, Miss Kellaway, yes, I am able to fit you in. Will the middle table do?"

"They know me." Megan's triumphant whisper turned into a smile as we snatched the last table to the dismay of others in the queue. "It's one advantage, Father's name."

"It's more than that. You're a famous socialite. You're in the papers all the time."

"Well," she grinned, removing her gloves, "I'll be in the papers less now that I'm engaged. Yes, it's true!" She flashed a ring before me. "We're engaged! We're announcing it when Dean returns from Germany."

I stared at her, aghast. "Your parents accepted him just like that?"

"Mother didn't like it, but Father was quite impressed with Dean's ethics. 'He has a mind for business, m'girl,' he said to me. 'I'm certain he'll take care of you.' And what's more he isn't entirely homeless. He half-owns a house in Boston so we're going there after the wedding."

"When will that be?"

"Oh, who knows, a year or so away. Dean wants to make sure this company is running well before he leaves it to the hands of a manager. He can't trust Jack."

"No," I agreed, "or Rosalie. Have you had much to do with either?"

"A little. Parties and that kind of thing." Her gaze lowered in a covert fashion. "I think they're lovers, or were lovers. Last time I saw them together they had a great row, Jack and Rosalie. I think he was pressing her to marry him but she's not interested. Jack's probably after her money."

"Undoubtedly."

"And what of you, my dear?" Her eyes twinkled, inspecting my hand. "No ring yet but I wager it won't be long."

I flushed. "What have you heard?"

"More what I've *seen* than what I've heard." She clicked her tongue. "You naughty, naughty, girl. *Stealing* another's fiancé . . ."

"It wasn't like that," I assured her. "And Mother's fuming about it. She believes the Rutlands will make it difficult for us."

"Possibly," Megan confirmed. "Whatever went on there, I can tell you Lady Lara wanted your Major Browning at any cost. I can't blame her. He is *devilishly* handsome," she sighed, "but not as handsome as my Mr. Fairchild. Mrs. Fairchild! Ha! How positively proper that sounds. He hasn't a title but he has a good heart and I love him the more and more I get to know him. Is that how it is with you and the major?"

I didn't answer straight away. What I felt for the major was an intensely private thing. I couldn't explain the feeling into words. Somehow, my love for him went beyond words. Yet I scarcely knew him.

"I suppose you need to spend more time with him," Megan began helpfully. "Dean and I have been thrown together so much I feel I've known him my whole life! Even Mother is warming to him now. He brings her flowers every time he calls. He's so gentlemanly and I *love* his accent. It's the twang and the drawl."

"Does his mother know of your engagement?"

"Yes. He telephoned her before he left Germany. She's thrilled."

I hung my head. "I have yet to meet the major's parents."

"I'm sure they'll love you."

"It's not so easy. I have a prejudice against me from the start, having to compete with the illustrious Lady Lara. His parents will think him a fool."

"The Rutlands aren't always what they seem. Don't be afraid of them. My father says the earl is mixed up in some kind of nasty business. I don't know what that means exactly but—"

Megan went on but I had since tuned out. *The earl of Rutland mixed up in some kind of nasty business.*

Dare she mean the Salinghurst shares?

And a reason for wanting Teddy Grimshaw dead?

CHAPTER TWENTY-ONE

"Where shall we begin?"

"The stairs. Let's go up the stairs. Did you find out which room?"

Megan gave me a furtive nod. "Four twenty-seven. The maître d'. They don't usually give the numbers out but I know him. The police haven't finished with the room."

"Naturally." There, we paused outside the hotel room number 427. No doubt it had a lavish interior but I couldn't help but wonder, what clues remained inside? What of Mrs. Grimshaw's maid? Her daughter? From last reports, Rosalie rented her own apartment on the east side of the city.

"I'd say Mrs. Grimshaw's maid is with Rosalie," I said to Megan, moving a little to the left of the room. "She must have been lured out of her room and met her assailant on the top of the stairs."

"Or," Megan suggested, "they had an argument *inside* the hotel room and carried it out to the stairs where she fell to her death."

"*Pushed* to her death, I think. Or maybe we are both wrong and she'd had a little too much champagne and tripped?"

"It does happen," Megan agreed. "But for her neck to snap, she must have fallen with some force. It doesn't add up to an accident, does it?"

"No," I agreed. "I wonder if the police met the same conclusion."

"Hello?" said a timid voice. "Can I help ye?"

A maid carrying fresh towels in a prim white uniform curtsied. Since a faint suspicion registered in her eyes, I wondered if she'd been ordered to keep watch outside Mrs. Grimshaw's room. I decided to take a risk. "Hello, there. I am looking for Miss Rosalie. Is she here?"

"No, miss." She frowned, curious as to who I was.

"Such a tragedy," I went on, using blithe babble to lower her defenses. "Though, Aunty Cynthia wasn't much liked, was she?"

The maid's eyes brightened. "Ye're family, are ye?"

"Yes, I am . . . family." I paused, shaking my head. "Who found her?"

"One of the other maids." She glanced toward the stairwell and shivered. "It's the first guest to have died 'ere . . ."

"Accidents happen . . . were you on duty when she fell? Did you see anyone or hear anything?"

Looking about, perhaps for her disapproving superior, she thought about the wisdom of answering my question. "I don't know anything, miss."

"But did Aunty receive any visitors that day? Do you know if someone came to the hotel?"

She shook her head. "Madam threw a cup at one of the maids, that's all I know."

"A cup? She did have a temper . . . do you know which maid she threw the cup at? I'd like to speak to her."

"No, miss, I don't know which one. I only heard it from Emmy, an undermaid."

"Emmy," Megan echoed. "Where can we find Emmy?"

"She don't work today, miss."

"I really must speak to her," I said. "I'd like to apologize for my aunt and maybe learn something about her last movements. It's important to me."

"Well," she paused after a time, "I've got to be gettin' back to work.

Ye can look for Emmy on the portside where she lives. The March-man building."

"I don't think this is the best part of town to be in. . . ."

I didn't have to look at Megan's anxious face. Her voice trembled as she uttered the very words on my lips.

"Perhaps we took a wrong turn?"

We'd come to the end of a lane. Old derelict buildings stared down at us and from one of those windows echoed a chilling sound. Tensing, I seized Megan's hand. Above us, the young men continued to whoop and whistle and worse, spill out onto the street in a leering line.

"What ye doin' here, fancy pieces? Don't see much of ye in these parts."

"Ah, fine!" One of them touched Megan's lace shawl.

Cringing, she stepped back into the arms of another.

"My pretty! I 'ave ye now!"

Screaming, Megan clutched her handbag to her breast. "Stay away!"

"Let her go," I interposed, terrified but hiding it. "I'm here to see Emmy. Which is the Marchman building?"

The lads glanced at each other. I hoped, *prayed,* one of them recognized the name.

"Emmy? She's my sister," one spoke up. "What do ye want with her?"

He was not to be easily persuaded. "My business is personal. Please, I'll give five pence to anyone who is willing to take us to Emmy."

At the look on their faces, I questioned my action.

"Oh, dear," Megan gushed a second later when several fights broke out.

"Let's run," I whispered to Megan and we set off during the

distraction. Emmy's brother ran hard on our heels and puffing, finally caught us.

"I won't hurt ye!" He stopped, catching his breath. "Sorry for me friends."

He was an unruly lad, to be sure, but I admired his moral strength.

"If ye follow me, I'll take ye to Emmy. She went to the markets, should be home by now tho'."

We weren't far off our destination. Three blocks south and the Marchman building rose up above a busy street filled with noisy vendors. Pulling my hat down, I squeezed Megan's hand. The entire incident had frightened her and she wanted to catch the first taxi out of there.

Up a set of grimy stairs, we followed Emmy's brother into a roomy apartment filled with screaming children. Two sets of families, and they all stared at us in utter disbelief as we came through to the kitchen.

With her back to us, Emmy jumped when her brother smacked her bottom. "Friends to see ye."

"Friends?" Her brow furrowing, she gaped at us.

"We've come from Claridge's, Emmy," I said. "I'm sorry to hear a cup was thrown at you. I'm connected to the family and offer my apologies."

Eyes widening, she examined our clothes.

"I need to know if you saw or heard anything in or near that room on that day. What happened, Emmy?"

Sighing, she rolled her eyes. "I've had me fair share of these fine madams. This one, though, this one was really bad. From when I saw her come, I says to meself 'this one's trouble.' And trouble she was. Nothing was ever right. She complained about everythin'. And temper! She was always throwin' things around. And all the time I heard her she were complain' about money."

"Money." I paused, glancing at Megan. "Do you think somebody was trying to blackmail her?"

"I dunno, miss. Maybe. She were involved in some court case where she reckoned she'd get more money."

"Did she have any visitors that day?"

Emmy thought hard. "None that I saw but one of the other maids heard voices in Madam's room. It weren't the sound of her daughter's voice, but it was female."

"Did the voice sound young or old?"

Emmy shrugged. "Couldn't say. Ye could just make out there were someone in there talking to her."

"Were the voices heated or raised?"

"No, miss. But afterward, Madam rings for tea. So I take her tea. And she says it weren't hot enough. She threw the cup at me. I left the room and next thing I know Madam is lying dead at the bottom of the stairs."

"How horrible for you, Emmy."

"I've told all this to the policemen." She frowned. "Did they question you, too?"

"Not yet," I answered truthfully.

"I don't think she were murdered," Emmy said, escorting us downstairs to catch a cab. "I think she just tripped and fell. There's a raised bit in the carpet there. I've snagged on it before. I told the police that."

"Thank you, Emmy. You've been very helpful."

Before we got into the cab, she waved her hand. "What's ye name, miss?"

I hesitated. I didn't want to give her my real name should she quote it to the police. "Rebecca Simmons," I said on inspiration, liking it. I made a note of it. The name sounded perfect for a character.

I returned to find my mother in great distress.

"Two cancellations. *Two*. And on the flimsiest excuses. They must be friends of the Rutlands. It's a snub, a very direct snub."

"The Rutlands aren't the most important people in England, Mama," Angela soothed, the eldest of us three girls and more sympathetic to such a social catastrophe.

"They have influence. I didn't think Lady Holbrook would cave to their pressure."

"I don't like Lady Holbrook," I said, thinking of the long-pointed-nose woman.

"Daphne." Angela frowned. "That's hardly helpful."

"I have a set dinner for sixteen," our mother lamented, "and now I have seven empty places. *Seven.* Who can I get on short notice? Everyone is busy or otherwise engaged."

Angela and Jeanne thought hard.

"What about the Darlingtons?"

"Or the Cartwrights?"

Shaking her head, my mother waved her objection. "The Darlingtons don't mix with the Harrods and the Cartwrights," she shivered, "and not altogether whom one invites to a small dinner party."

I sat on the couch, detesting these kinds of affairs. I liked dinner parties, if interesting conversations carried their course with interesting people. However, designing a dinner party to *impress* left me not wanting to attend at all. They only spoke of what people had and who they knew and what people those people knew and so forth.

"Daphne can invite Megan and her fiancé," Angela prodded.

"He'll mix well with Ellen," Jeanne put in. "And out of all the Grimshaws, he's the nicest."

"We ought to include Alicia, too," I said, "if you are inviting Mr. Fairchild. It's only right as she is his cousin."

"But she's a *nanny*." My mother was not convinced. "Even if she has means not to be one, she has chosen that profession."

"It's more about her connection with the child, Mama," Angela advised. "And things might change in the next year or so. Who knows, perhaps Nanny Brickley will make a grand match and then you'll be sorry you didn't include her."

"True," my mother acquiesced. "But that fills only three or four places at most. Who else can we get?"

Having heard enough, I left the room to make a telephone call. Two days, three hours, twenty-six minutes and *still* I hadn't heard from him. Surely, he'd made it back to his hotel by now.

"George Hotel. May I help you?"

"Yes, hello." I cleared my voice. "I'd like to be connected to Major Browning's room, please."

"Do you know the number?"

"No. No, I don't."

"Wait a moment, please."

I waited there in the hall, speaking as softly as I could manage. I didn't want anyone to catch me or to hear our exchange. Such may smack of desperation but I had to know. I had to know he was safe.

"Yes, madam, we have a Major Browning in two forty-one. I'll connect you."

"Thank you."

I began to feel a little hot. Leaning into the corner, my fingers anxiously wound around the telephone cord. *Please pick up. Please pick up.*

"Browning here."

His voice! I heard his voice. Closing my eyes, I whispered: "Tommy, it's me."

"Daphne?"

"Yes . . ."

"How's my girl?"

He sounded the same. Slightly amused, tired. "I'm good. I've been worried. I didn't hear from you."

"Miss Impatient. I was going to call on you this afternoon. Are you free tonight for dinner?"

I bit my lip. "I wish I was. Mother's got a dinner party and she's short already. If I beg out . . ."

"How many is she short?"

"Six at the moment. I'm going to ask Megan and Dean Fairchild.

They probably already have plans but I'll try. Everyone is busy, it seems. Oh, Tommy, I'm sorry I can't get out of this—"

"Don't worry. I want to see you. I'll come for dinner, if your mother will have me," he added with a sardonic pleasure.

"Oh, perfect!" I hugged the phone with glee. "You don't know anyone else, do you? We had late cancellations from Lady Holbrook and friends, loyal to your Lady Lara. Apparently, I am the girl who felicitates broken engagements."

The phone went quiet and I thought I heard him curse under his breath.

"How many more do you need?"

"Another two, if possible."

"Leave it with me, darling . . ."

We hung up then and I put the receiver down and sighed against the wall. He was home and he wanted to see me. I was a little piqued about the intimate dinner I was missing out on but he was as graceful as ever. If I put myself in his shoes, the last thing I'd want to do is go to dinner with prospective in-laws after coming home tired from a mission in Germany.

I went in to report to Mother.

I swallowed, unable to contain my excitement. "Major Browning is coming and he'll bring two. So there, you should have your sixteen."

I turned to sweep upstairs, in a rush to find something to wear.

"Oh, excellent work, Daphne. You'll make a fine hostess one day," my mother called out.

I smiled.

It was the first time in my life I actually felt useful in the sense of being a lady.

CHAPTER TWENTY-TWO

I stood in front of my wardrobe. I had *nothing* to wear.

Ellen discovered me thus. "What are you doing?"

"I can't find anything. I imagined the velvet but it's a trifle too tight."

Grinning, Ellen stepped forward to inspect my wardrobe. "You're not comparing yourself to that Lady Lara, are you?"

"Yes," I moaned, miserable. "She's so elegant. I'm not. I don't know what I am or what my style is. Awkward, I suppose."

"The only awkwardness I've seen in you is when you look at Major Browning," she teased, looking better than she had in days. "Why don't you survey my wardrobe? It's a fortuitous thing my maid packed for me otherwise I'd have nothing to wear, either. Come. Hop to. We have much to do."

Going into the guest room, we passed Charlotte and Alicia at their lesson.

"I hope you're joining us tonight," I said to Alicia. "My mother expects you."

"Yes." She smiled, quietly turning the page of the book Charlotte was reading aloud. "But I'm afraid I have nothing suitable to wear."

Since she was taller and thinner than me, I offered her my velvet dress. "It's emerald green and the length won't matter. I'll bring it back for you to try on."

Her doe-brown eyes widened. "Nobody's ever done anything so kind for me before. Thank you, Daphne."

"She's so odd, I can't make her out," Ellen murmured to me, shutting the door. "Teddy's left her a small fortune but she seems to want to remain in service. Why? Doesn't she desire a husband and children of her own?"

"Have you asked her?"

"One doesn't ask Alicia Brickley anything. Teddy used to call her Alicia Prickly. And I know some of the cousins call her the same. She is prickly when it comes to her private life."

"I think she likes cousin Dean and he's engaged now."

"Oh, how sad. He's the best of the bunch. And fancy, Jack will be here tonight. I don't know whether I quite trust him."

"Father's invited him early for a drink. Perhaps we ought to eavesdrop?"

We both burst out laughing and Charlotte rushed in.

"What is it, Mummy? What's so funny?"

"Oh, nothing, petal. Aunty Daphne and I were just laughing at this silly feather."

I picked up the diamond feather comb and slipped it in my hair.

"It looks pretty. Are you going to wear it to dinner?"

"No." I looked away, horrified. "They always slip out of my hair."

"This dress is the ticket." Pulling out the apricot cashmere and lace, Ellen spread it over her bed. "And I've diamond stud earrings and a bracelet to match. Quick. Do try it on so we can attend to that mop of your hair."

"It is a mop," I lamented, slipping on the dress, delighted that it fit me. Moving to the mirror, I liked how the material accentuated the small curves I possessed and enhanced my bosom. I'd never have a *large* bosom like Lady Lara and this I must accept. However, I reflected, she couldn't run as well as I, could she?

"My cream shoes will go nicely with that, if they fit."

Alas, they did not fit. "Never mind, black will do. I'll wear a black-and-silver headband too."

Like two schoolgirls, we played dress-up and Charlotte and Alicia followed. As I predicted, she looked fabulous in my emerald-green dress. We also persuaded her to leave her spectacles behind. "The major might bring a friend," I teased and she turned away, downcast.

"You have heard Dean is engaged?" Ellen broached the subject.

"Yes," she replied, keeping her gaze lowered.

"Come, now," Ellen prodded, "there's plenty of fish in the sea."

"I wasn't interested in him *that* way," came the sharp retort and Ellen and I shared a glance.

"I told you," she whispered later, "it's Alicia Prickly."

Abandoning the mirror, I hurried downstairs, careful to avoid the servants. I didn't want any of them reporting to Mother that Miss Daphne had gone down early.

Seeing a hat and coat in the hall, I gathered Mr. Grimshaw had arrived. I heard his low American drawl emanate from my father's study.

". . . she's up and steaming ahead. With any luck, we'll control the market again."

"With cheap German imports. Salinghurst won't have a chance."

"That's what Uncle Ted had in mind when he bought into Salinghurst. A foot in the door. They can't budge without his say-so."

"He was a clever man," my father said. "I've no head for such things."

"You could invest with us, Sir Gerald. My cousin will upbraid me for propositioning you on a dinner date, but I'm what they call the black sheep of the family."

"So I've heard . . ."

"I can promise you full returns. Let's say an initial investment, five thousand pounds?"

I nearly choked. Five thousand pounds!

"Daphne du Maurier! Get away from that door at once!"

Caught by none other than my mother sailing down the stairs, I crept away like a naughty child, hoping my father or Jack Grimshaw hadn't heard her. How embarrassing if they had. I mistrusted Jack Grimshaw enough without him having a handle over me.

The door opened and Jack stood there, smirking, his hands in his pockets. "Miss Daphne. What a pleasure."

So he knew I'd been listening. "How was your trip to Germany, Mr. Grimshaw?"

"Oh, no. A short trip and we're back to *formalities,* are we? I seem to remember you promising to come with me to a play. Are you still keen? Shall we say tomorrow evening?"

I swallowed, watching the maid answer the bell at the door. Heart pounding, I sensed him before he entered. Major Browning.

"Daphne?" asked Jack Grimshaw.

My face had a habit of betraying itself. "Oh." I smiled, my gaze anxious to meet the caller as the door opened.

The major's dark eyes sought mine. Neglecting to answer Mr. Grimshaw, I went straight to him, wishing him to sweep me up in his arms.

Instead, since eyes were upon us, he swept my hand to his lips. "How fare thee shoulder?"

I could have melted under the tender regard of his face. "I-I can't feel it at the moment," I stammered. "Today's the first day without the sling."

"You look beautiful." He stood back to appraise me before turning to greet my parents and Mr. Grimshaw.

Covering for my faux pas, the major engaged in a discussion of Germany. Following my mother to the drawing room, I strained my ears to hear what was being said. Exchanges, pleasantries, neutral observations; however, I detected a caution between Jack Grimshaw and my major.

Within a short sequence, the remainder of my parents' guests arrived and we journeyed into the dinner party fray. I longed to have a private talk with the major but my mother had strategically placed him down the other end of the table with two of his late-arrival colleagues from Scotland Yard.

"I hear the stairs are slippery at Claridge's." My father couldn't help himself. "What are they saying? Accident or murder?"

"We don't know yet," Inspector Pailing answered. "But we're appealing to the public for information. The deceased received a visitor in her chambers just prior to the time of her death. We wish to speak with this visitor."

"Oh?" My mother shared a concerned glance with Ellen. "Do you know anything about the visitor?"

"Only that she's a woman, Mrs. du Maurier."

"A woman? How do you know?"

"A maid overheard voices in the room."

"Perhaps it was fancy? A busy hotel . . ."

"No, Mrs. du Maurier. The maid is very certain, but she's frightened."

"Frightened? Why, pray?"

"Because two young women came to see her giving false names. They were asking about the murder."

My mother put her spoon down and I sank farther into my seat. Down the far end of the table, I felt the major censuring me with those too-shrewd eyes.

"Inspector Pailing believes the young women may have murdered the woman and seek to silence the maid," Major Browning informed, keeping a steady gaze on me.

I sank even lower, blaming the wine for my face turning a shade too pink.

"Does anyone know what the two young women look like?" Ellen asked.

"The description is well-bred and between twenty to thirty. May

I ask where you were, Mrs. Grimshaw, between three and four on the twenty-second?"

Ellen's brow furrowed but her eyes never wavered. "I was here with Charlotte."

"You never left the house?"

"No, Inspector. We'd just come to town. I was still unpacking."

"No murderers here, Inspector," my father joked. "Isn't it more likely the silly woman just tripped? If she was in a temper and missed her step?"

"She was enraged about something," the inspector said. "But I don't think we'll ever find out about what." Wiping his face with his napkin, the inspector bowed his head. "Forgive me, Mrs. du Maurier. This is a social call. Not a business one."

Normal conversation ensued, helped by the main course and my father's excellent choice in wine.

"What do you think happened?" I asked Jack Grimshaw across the table. He'd spent the first two courses completely engaged with the pretty daughter of Mr. and Mrs. Harrod. No doubt he'd heard she had an ample dowry.

"To Aunty Cynthia?" He raised his glass in tribute. "I believe she met with an unfortunate accident."

"Does Rosalie think the same?"

He paused, his thick lips curling in consideration. "I cannot speak for my cousin. She is still in shock."

"We called on her today." Megan joined our tête-à-tête. "It's true she's overwrought." Lowering her voice to a whisper so Ellen couldn't hear, she added, "She says somebody got rid of her mother because of the court case but I don't think that's true. From what Dean says, they didn't have a chance, anyway. Phew! How scary was that before with that inspector! I didn't tell Dean. He doesn't know."

"Hmm." I nodded to circumvent Jack Grimshaw's interest in our whispers. "Will Rosalie go home to America now?"

"Not until after the hearing," Jack answered, reserving a smug salute to Ellen.

Before Ellen felt the full thrust of his comment, I steered the conversation to safe grounds, leaving Jack Grimshaw to Angela, Jeanne, and the pretty Harrod girl.

"We haven't really had a good chat yet, have we?" He approached me after supper, lighting a cigarette. "You support murderers."

Searching for the major, I found him imprisoned between my father and Mr. Harrod. He was only a few feet away yet at this moment it felt like miles. "I'm not sure what you mean, Mr. Grimshaw. Is it a private joke at my expense?"

"Oh, it's no joke. There's two dead bodies . . . and one murderer, I say." His gaze swept across the room to Ellen. "Who do you think benefits from both deaths? Your friend Ellen Hamilton. Oh, I've looked into the Hamiltons. Illustrious family but with no money for their precious Thornleigh."

"Are you suggesting Ellen murders to fund Thornleigh?"

To me, my voice sounded sharp, and Jack chuckled, perhaps to disguise it from others.

"I'm not suggesting. I know something's amiss here and something's at play."

"How was Germany?" I attempted to change the subject.

"Fruitful . . . even with hounds around."

I followed his glance to Major Browning. "The police are there for protection and to prevent crime, are they not?"

"Your police are too nosy. They should concern themselves with catching murderers."

"Fraud and embezzlement are also crimes," I reminded him, gaily smiling to whoever looked our way. "They can lead a person . . . to murder."

His eyes danced. "You are a bold piece, aren't you? Do you know what sometimes happens to bold pieces?"

"I've no idea." I smiled back.

"They pay a price for their interference . . . and next time it may not be a shoulder wound."

CHAPTER TWENTY-THREE

"He *actually* said that?"

"Yes. Yes, he did. I can't believe it. He tried to kill me. Or he tried to kill Ellen and instead nearly killed me—"

"Calm down . . . calm down."

Leading me by the hand, Major Browning pulled me into the corridor. "What did you say to provoke him?"

"Me?" I gasped. "I'm innocent here and *he's* a murderer. He's so smug and looks like a murderer—"

"Looking like a murderer doesn't mean he is one," he murmured as he roped me into his protective embrace. "Daphne, Daphne, you must stop reading novels. Real life is not so dramatic."

"It is," I begged to differ. "Remember Padthaway and Somner House?"

He paused. "Hmm, you have a point. Danger seems to follow you, or do you follow danger? I've warned you before to stay out of police business. That is their job. Let them do the investigating."

I sighed. "Maybe I'd do what you say but that would have been *before* somebody tried to shoot me. It puts a different complexion on matters, a bullet, you know. What if it hit me in the head? I'd be dead and I'd never see you again."

Tears sprang from my eyes and I buried my face into his coat. "I'm sorry . . . I'll probably ruin this . . . and you look so nice."

He laughed against my hair. "Darling girl . . . darling *silly* girl, it was you who went to see the maid, wasn't it?"

I nodded. I couldn't have lied to him and if I had, I'm sure he would have intercepted it.

"The police are drawing a description, you know."

"Oh, dear." I shook my head. "I should have worn a disguise! Next time . . ."

"No. There'll be no next time. I want your word on it, Daphne."

He sounded so authoritative.

"Do you have any idea what it was like to be in another country when you were injured?"

"But he tried to shoot me! Jack Grimshaw. What are you going to do about it?"

"What do you suggest? Call him out? He'd just deny what he said. No, no. We're watching him. He'll make a mistake soon."

"Maybe he killed Cynthia so he has full control over Rosalie?"

"We had better return before we are missed." He put a finger to my lips. "But not before . . ."

His mouth caught mine and any objections faded away against the rhythm of his heart. Clinging to him there in the corridor, I failed to see the shadow approaching until it was too late.

It was my father.

"Daphne. Major. My study at once."

Wary of the stern manner of the usually jovial Sir Gerald, the major kept my hand captive in his.

"I wish to ask for your daughter's hand in marriage, sir," he began the moment the door closed.

"Yes, yes."

Retreating to his desk, my father surveyed us both. "Sit down, both of you. I have a few questions to ask and I'm looking for honest answers.

"What, sir, is your connection with the Rutlands?"

"Business, sir."

"What kind of business?"

"I cannot say, sir."

"This is to do with Rutland, isn't it? That wily old dog, never trusted him. You were asked to watch the family?"

"Since the earl's health has deteriorated, he's made the mistake of leaving his fortune in the wrong hands. I can say no more."

"Very well. And part of your business with them was your engagement to Lady Lara?"

"Yes, sir."

"And she was a willing partisan in this?"

"It went two ways. She wanted the engagement for other reasons."

"What reasons?"

"To please her father."

"And perhaps herself? What is your relationship with the family?"

"They are friends of my parents. Lady Lara and I grew up together, for want of a better term. I regard her like a sister."

"But she may not regard you as a brother," my father observed. "She has a handsome dowry, too. I cannot compete with that."

"I'm not asking you to do so, sir."

"You choose Daphne over Lady Lara then?"

"There was never any choice, sir."

"What do you see in my daughter? Do you love her?"

Turning to me, the major enclosed my hands in his again, a charming little protective thing he liked to do with me, I noticed. Warmed by love and support and his humility in allowing my father to interrogate him, I waited for his proposal.

"Daphne," his voice matured to a sincere timbre, "since I met you, I cannot imagine life without you. Headstrong, intelligent, and sometimes foolishly inquisitive, you are the storm to my sea, beautiful, wild, and intoxicating. Each day is an adventure with you and if you will take me, I'd like to share life's journey with you as your husband."

My mouth raced to say yes; I wanted to burst out with joy and tears, so happy those words made me, I knew I'd cherish them forever. It was a beautiful proposal, perfected when he slid down to one knee and searched my face, waiting, willing my acceptance.

Staring into his eyes, and showing a faint uncertainty there by my silence, I caressed his hand with my hands before jumping into his arms.

"I take it that's a yes then." My father chuckled, adding caution by shaking his head and looking for a cigar. "We had better post the engagement in the paper to stop these wagging tongues. Your mother will be pleased. Why don't you go and tell her the news, Daphne? I promise I won't monopolize your major."

My major.

How well that sounded. "Lady Daphne Browning," I murmured, preparing to announce my engagement to the world.

As expected, I whispered the news to my mother and she announced it. Acute relief, I thought, rather than natural elation.

"How fantastic," Megan gushed, embracing me hard. "Engaged in the same year! When is your wedding?"

"Not for some time," my mother answered, and my sisters came to congratulate me.

Inspecting my hand, Angela gave me a sly smile. "No ring? Does he need to get it back from Lady Lara?"

"Don't bother about her," Jeanne put in, "she's just jealous. You're going to be the first one to marry amongst us. Where is he? I like him as a brother."

The Harrods expressed their congratulations next, followed by Jack Grimshaw.

"What a pity." He lingered over my hand, his dark eyes intense and glowing. "I don't suspect we'll have our date now?"

"I never agreed to a date, Mr. Grimshaw," I replied. "And are you not otherwise engaged to your cousin? I saw you in the woods together."

The truth blurted out. I knew why. Armed with the major behind me, I felt invincible, able to take on the world.

"You must always be careful in the woods," he said in return. "You never know who lurks about."

I paused, asking him frankly what I had shied away from earlier. "Did you try to kill Ellen for Rosalie's sake?"

Chuckling, he downed the remainder of his wine. "You are overly imaginative, my dear. Tell me, can you see me as a villain in one of your books? I fancy I'd make quite a good villain."

"No, a great one," I assured him, knowing I'd get nothing from him unless he were to offer it.

After that encounter, I raced upstairs to see Ellen. Complaining of a headache, she'd retired and I found her reading a book to Charlotte.

"She should have been asleep hours ago . . . hearing the noise downstairs startled her. She wanted to join us."

"I know what it's like." I groaned with Charlotte. "I used to sit on the steps and watch my parents' parties. I liked watching the grand ladies and handsome men."

"Is Uncle Jack here? Uncle Dean? Can I see them, Mummy?"

"No, my dear. It's bedtime now. We'll see them another day."

Charlotte smiled as Ellen bent down to kiss her forehead.

"Mummy," she said when we were at the door, "will I get to see my sister now that that woman's dead?"

"From the mouths of babes," I quoted, following Ellen into her room. I had planned to celebrate my engagement news and relay my encounter with Jack Grimshaw, but after Charlotte's words, I couldn't.

"It's natural she wants to see her sister . . . I'm not sure if the influence is good for her, though. And this is depending upon whether Miss Rosalie wishes to see Charlotte at all. We have the court case still pending as well. Oh, Daphne, I must confess to a huge relief in knowing she's dead. She's made the world a better place for leaving it."

"What will you do?"

"Return to Thornleigh. It's like a massive cloud hanging over our heads has disappeared. I'm even going to cut Farnton. We don't need him anymore."

"I'm not sure that's wise, Ellen . . ."

"Oh, nonsense. There was a danger when that woman was alive. She'd do anything to harm us but I don't think Rosalie will continue in her stead."

"But what if those threats were from somebody else? One of Teddy's disgruntled business companions?"

"We haven't received anything lately. In any case, I'm selling the Salinghurst shares. I want no part of it."

"Have you informed the Yard?"

"Yes. Dean's already approached me to buy them. I know Teddy would want to keep it in the family, so I'll sell to Dean."

"You're selling to Jack Grimshaw, too," I reminded her. "I think he did it, Ellen. I think he killed your husband."

Sinking farther into the pillows on her bed, a soft cry escaped her lips. "Do you know what the papers are saying about me, now? That I'm a murderer. Oh, Daphne, I'm afraid. I was nowhere near that hotel but I lied to the police. I wasn't here. I took Charlotte to the park that afternoon. The police know that I lied but they haven't come back yet. I'm afraid they'll come for me and say I did it."

I paused stroking her back. Over the years, we'd formed our friendship through letters. Those heartfelt letters, exposing and declaring all our inner fears and secrets, consoling our losses, celebrating our successes . . . had I missed something? I'd never known her to lie before.

How well did I really know Ellen? Had she become a character to me and not a real person?

I forced myself to swallow the truth. I'd waited eagerly for those letters to arrive. I savored every word. It was like living someone else's life in all its intricate detail and emotion.

But deception lurked. I sensed her fear now.

CHAPTER TWENTY-FOUR

"I am happy for you, Daph," Angela said early the next morning, sneaking into my room without invitation.

Yawning, I half-opened an eyelid. "It's all right. I didn't expect you to blow a trumpet. Go back to bed, Ange."

"No." She planted herself on the edge of my bed. "I'm sorry. I should have shown more sisterly jubilation. It was unfair of me."

Maybe she was jealous? I tried to open my eyes but I was so tired, they insisted on sticking together. "It doesn't matter," I assured her. "I won't take offense."

"But this is one of these moments I feel like I've failed. I'm your sister. We've shared a great deal together. I don't know what overcame me . . . perhaps jealousy because I've missed my chance."

Struggling to keep my eyes open, I propped myself up to see a single tear fall down her cheek.

"You haven't missed your chance."

"I have," she choked, "I-I have . . ."

"You said you didn't want to marry."

"I know and now he's married with a child on the way. Oh, Daphne, I spurned him and sent him packing. Why did I? For some foolish reason that he wasn't good enough in my parents' eyes and I could do better? Ha! I'll end an old maid on the shelf."

"You're still young." I sighed. "Remember Dorothy? She married when she was thirty-six. And look at Ellen. She loved and lost and then loved again."

"And lost again." Angela lowered her head, miserable. "I won't make a splendid match. I've always known that and I rejected a good man. You're lucky, Daphne. You've got a great catch, a handsome, charming man, and I know you'll be happy."

Forcing myself awake, I scanned her face, looking for clues. "Is it my eventual going away that concerns you?"

"Yes and no." She sighed. "I suppose I never expected my younger sister to set up house before me . . . establish herself in society, that sort of thing."

"I'm not getting married tomorrow." I grinned. "Mother insists on a two-year engagement. I say one."

A twinkle returned to Angela's blue eyes. "I'd not wait for a man like that. Speaking of which, your engagement announcement is sure to cause a stir."

"The only person I wish to rattle is Lady Lara," I confessed, recalling the hard, determined look in that too-perfect face. "I fear she'll always be a thorn in my side."

"Then tread carefully, sister. You are too naive in such matters."

Was I? Chewing on my lip, I abandoned my bed for the mirror. The face that stared back at me did appear young and innocent, I thought: porcelain skin, neat, clear features, a tiny snub nose, and a mouth too eager. Faint shadows drifted over deep-set eyes, secretive eyes, and I wasn't sure what lurked in those mysterious depths.

I set down to write a few pages before breakfast. I was very excited about the concept for my novel. I'd wanted to write a family saga since the Padthaway case, but I couldn't settle upon characters or a location. Now I had both: Cornwall and Janet. My Janet was middle-class, from a working family, I decided.

Reviewing what I'd written earlier at Thornleigh, I suppressed a groan. Those few chapters gave me a glimpse into Janet's world but I had to force myself to agree it wasn't the place to begin.

Scrapping the chapters by shoving them in my notebook for future reference, I glanced at a fresh page and began:

Janet Coombe stood high on the hill above Plyn, looking down upon the harbor. Although the sun was already high in the heavens, the little town was still wrapped in an early morning mist. It clung to Plyn like a thin pale blanket, lending to the place a faint whisper of unreality as if the whole had been blessed by the touch of ghostly fingers . . .

"Daphne! Major Browning is here."

Oh dear. I hadn't even brushed my hair. Making haste to the bathroom, I discovered I looked worse than I initially thought. After combing out the knots to look less like a bird's nest, I tucked my hair behind my ears and washed my face.

Still in my dressing gown, I hunted through my wardrobe for a pretty day dress. Drat. I couldn't find one of those, either. I must pay more attention to my wardrobe as my mother warned me.

Going into Angela's room, I borrowed a dress of hers, a cream base with red frills. There, I checked my image in the mirror, pleased with the result.

My heart started beating faster the moment I heard his voice. The low timbre suggested his entertaining the women and enjoying it. For a moment, I paused outside the door. I don't know what overcame me but I felt afraid. I didn't want to go inside; I didn't want them all looking at me.

Of course I must. He was my fiancé. Taking a deep breath, I pushed open the door.

"Daphne darling." He leapt to his feet, taking my hand and sweeping me into the room.

Gazing up at his handsome confidence, my love for him deepened. He knew I had these occasional bouts of flagging self-esteem. And he'd come to my rescue, a real modern-day knight in shining armor.

"How lovely you look in my dress." Angela grinned, eager to make up for last night's icy reaction. "Keep it. It looks better on you than me."

"I have just the hat to go with that dress." Ellen beamed, happy to be going home to Thornleigh. "Charlotte, race upstairs and tell Nanny to leave out the red hat. Daphne must put it on for her outing."

"My outing?"

"I have gained permission to take you for a stroll in the park," the major drawled. "Forgive the early morning intrusion, ladies."

"Oh, you may come anytime," my mother assured him, sending him a winsome smile before a motherly embrace. "You are like family now."

"Thank you."

Once outside, I burst out laughing. "I've never seen her so happy. I'll never understand all the bother about daughters getting married."

"Maybe you'll understand when you have a daughter of your own."

I stopped. I hadn't imagined having children until then even though it was the natural progression of life.

"You do want children, don't you?"

He was amused by my hesitation.

"Or do you wish to pursue your career as a novelist?"

On arriving at Hyde Park, I smiled at the sunny day. "Both. Some consider their books babies, you know."

"The less noisy kind."

Offering his arm while I adjusted my hat, he chose a path for us. He looked so tall and handsome, I felt proud to accompany him and prouder still to belong to him.

The day was splendid, the sunshine spreading over us like a warm woollen blanket. Many seized the initiative to bask in it, walking, sitting, running, reading books under trees, playing with children on the green and by ponds, or strutting the path like we, a newly engaged couple.

"Mrs. Edgecombe." The major tipped his hat, passing a plump lady of austere character. "She's a friend of the Rutlands," he whispered.

"That explains her austerity. I hope you warned your family?"

"I did that before I left Germany."

"Oh no! They must think—"

"That you're extraordinary. My future wife *is* extraordinary and they'll see for themselves in a moment."

I held my breath. "What did you say?"

"Don't bite your nails nervously." He tucked my hand under his arm. "We are walking toward them."

"You scoundrel," I whispered under my breath, trusting I looked as I should meeting his parents for the first time.

They waved at us from ahead. I swallowed and smiled, accepting his mother's embrace.

"Why, Tommy, she's lovely. Younger than I expected."

"I look younger than I am," I replied, shaking hands with his father.

"Tommy's told us all about you." His mother pulled me aside to inspect the flowers by the lake. "And Susanna speaks well of you."

"That's kind of you," I replied. "I'm afraid we've attracted some unpleasant remarks for his breaking with the Rutlands—"

"Now, now, you're not to think we'd rather see him wed to Lady Lara. We want our boy to be happy. He mentioned you long ago and I wondered."

"Oh, indeed?"

"Yes . . . he sent us a postcard from Cornwall. He said he was on a fishing trip and that he'd found 'a rare fish from the sea with ancient eyes.' Later, he spoke of a girl with a penchant for writing and getting herself into trouble. 'She needs looking after,' he said and I knew then that you were special. He never spoke of the other girls like that and especially not Lady Lara. Theirs has been a very *public* romance."

"You knew it was a farce?"

A serene smile touched her lips. "I guessed. It's a sense intrinsic to mothers."

We walked a little way with them. They said they were rarely in town and invited me to stay a weekend at their home.

"There, that wasn't so awful, was it?" the major teased later, steering me down a prettyish kind of wilderness. "The humble wayside flower has a charm all of its own."

"It does," I agreed, grinning, "and am I really like a storm?"

"You certainly have stormy eyes when you're angry."

"And foolishly inquisitive?"

"I trust you have learned caution after your shoulder wound."

"I have." Linking my hands around his neck, I pinched him on the ear. "Where's your sympathetic concern?"

"It's here." He removed my hand to his heart.

"A ring!" I gasped, ripping open the box. "Oh, it's lovely . . ."

"It's a family heirloom. The reason we met my parents today is because of the ring. They offered to bring it. Does it fit?"

I examined it under the sunshine. Old gold, a scrolling pattern entwined with rubies and diamonds.

"It belonged to my great-great-grandmother. I thought you'd prefer something antique?"

"How well you know me. I love it! It's perfect."

Inspecting my hand, he frowned. "Even if a little big? We'll have it resized."

Walking back arm in arm, proud to show off my ring to any passerby, I told him of my intentions in regards to Ellen.

"Go back to Thornleigh? Are you mad?"

"Ellen's sold her shares. There's no reason for her to stay on in London and she's keen to resume the renovations. She asked me to go home with her, only for another month or so."

His brows knitted together as I explained that I must go. "I've started my novel. I have a feeling about this one but I need to do some more research. I've decided to set it in a fishing village instead of a grand estate. What do you think?"

He laughed, tucking my hand under his arm. "You're impossible. I had envisaged going out with you every night. Enjoy the town and so forth."

"You know I prefer the country. You could come? Ellen wouldn't mind—"

"Before you race ahead and scheme, my precious, remember I've work to do and I need to do it here."

Hailing a cab home, we climbed in and sat close together. I leaned my head against his chest, thanking him for the wondrous day and for my ring.

"Darling, go to Cornwall if you want. You must go, if it's good for your writing."

"There's less distractions there." I smiled up at him. "It's the quiet I love. I hope we live there one day."

He was amused. "What do you have in mind? Grand estate or modest fishing village?"

"Either." I laughed back. "As long as we are there, overlooking a harbor. Can you imagine? Looking at the sheet of white water daily, the jetties, the moored ships, the gray roofs, and clustering cottages—"

"All right, Miss Writer. It's an agreement."

CHAPTER TWENTY-FIVE

I had promised him to stay out of trouble. That meant screwing up my page of murder suspects and the notes I'd made about those suspects.

It was a difficult thing to do. Though the police put Teddy Grimshaw's death down to "unknown," doubt still lingered in the air.

"I never want to go back to London." Ellen shivered. "Those ruthless newspaper people. Hounding the door every day. I hope they won't follow us to Thornleigh."

So did I. Nothing sabotaged quiet inspiration time like noisy cockney reporters.

"I can't wait to show Uncle Harry my bird," Charlotte said when we reached the gates.

I offered to open the gates. The drive from London went too quickly for my liking. I so would have loved to stop for lunch, but Ellen was determined to get back. She was not the most confident of drivers.

As it happened, the usually splendid drive gazing at the passing scenery became a nightmare. Charlotte's bird, sitting on a gilded cage on her lap, squawked the whole time, dissatisfied upon being confined behind bars.

Grinding my teeth, I pushed open the gates and the car went through. "I'll walk the rest of the way." I waved to Ellen.

We'd left the good weather in London. A light shower drifted from a deepening gray sky. More rain. Suddenly, I ached for the warm sunshine with my major.

Bearing down the long winding path with its foreboding ancient trees and ghostly branches, I questioned the wisdom of my decision. The doubt lingered only a moment for there, through the rustling leaves stood Thornleigh, proud and old and beautiful.

Approaching the place, I understood Ellen's passion for it. It was her home and filled with memories.

"I'm going to mount our family portrait up there." She pointed upon entry, Harry carting in the package for her. Waylaid by Charlotte and the bird, he put the portrait down.

"His name is Harry, too," Charlotte informed him with a parental gravity.

"Well, hello, Harry. Nice to meet ye."

"How is everything?" Ellen asked. "Did you contact the builders while I was away?"

"Yes. They said they'll start after a first payment. I have the bill in my office."

Ellen nodded. "Good. I'll see you later then. Oh, Harry. Ask Nelly to set another place at dinner. Nanny will be joining us from now on. She is, after all, family."

"I know certain people of my acquaintance would frown at such a thing," Ellen said to me later, "me having nannies and estate managers to dinner, but we've all suffered the anguish of loss. Alicia lost her father and Teddy took her up. She's quite determined to stay on as a governess. I warned her doing so she's less likely to meet men cooped up here down in the country."

"What about her mother? Doesn't she want to go home eventually?"

"She doesn't get on with her mother. It's exactly like me. Remember how hard my parents were on me?"

I recalled what Alicia had said about her parents.

I spent the rainy afternoon in the library. Convinced I was starting my novel at the right place, I drafted out the first chapter.

Rereading what I'd written, I was pleased with my effort. As the time grew close to wash and change for dinner, I wished I'd stayed in London. Dining with Ellen, Harry, Alicia, and Charlotte came in a miserable second to an evening out with my fiancé.

I smiled whenever I glanced down at my ring, though. I'd insisted on taking it with me. There was time to resize it later.

"Don't lose it," Ellen warned me over dinner. "You'd be in a sorry state then."

"The Pendarrons called while you were gone," Harry informed after a mild tête-à-tête with Alicia. "They are having the annual masked ball. Everybody who's anybody is invited."

Feverish with excitement, I dropped my fork. The Pendarron ball was famous. My mother had always craved an invitation but had never made the list.

"The household of Thornleigh is invited," Harry went on.

"They honored us with a personal invitation?" Ellen gasped.

"You are relations," Harry reminded, smiling.

"A cousin of a cousin of a cousin. They didn't invite us in previous years because my parents never went. I always begged them to go but I was either too young, in the war, or in the black books."

"Her ladyship also passed on her sympathies," Harry murmured. "She asked after Charlotte, too."

"Oh Mummy, can I go? Can I go?"

"You're too young, dearest."

"But I'm not too young. Really, I'm not."

"They have an age limit at these kind of things."

"I shall stay home with her," Alicia said.

She blinked away, seemingly immune to the thrill of a ball. Didn't every girl long to go to one? Perhaps she'd had a bad experience and dreaded the idea?

After dinner, we retired to a sitting room for tea. Declining an invitation to join us, Harry returned to his office.

"The tradesmen are coming back during the week. If you keep away from the west wing, Daphne, they shouldn't disturb you."

"When I'm writing, I don't hear the outside world. Jeanne was calling me the other day and I vow I didn't hear her until she was standing right over me."

"How is your writing going?"

This question came from Alicia, peering over the book she was reading to Charlotte. Surprised by this rare show of interest, I said a little about the story. "I can't say too much otherwise I won't write it."

"How liberating it must be," she reflected, "to conjure up a world and people and have them do exactly your bidding."

"That's why I love it. The power to create."

"Daphne's going to be famous." Ellen grinned. "You'd best seek her company now while she's unknown."

"I've never sought other people's good opinions," Alicia replied, her voice smooth as silk yet laced with acrimony.

"You should hear what poor Alicia put up with in Boston," Ellen said, shaking her head. "It's a cutthroat society."

"Only certain families," Alicia advised.

"They didn't accept your father, did they?" I remembered.

"No." She put the book aside as Charlotte amused herself by the fire.

"You loved him? You were close to him?"

"Yes."

I nodded, sympathetic to her plight. "And your cousins? Did you spend much time with them growing up?"

"We were invited to the annual Christmas gathering and I went on vacation with my cousins whenever they felt a duty to me. That was once every two years."

I felt sorry for her. "Your cousin Sophie is nice . . ."

A faint smile touched her lips. "You omitted the others. I admire how you English adhere to social etiquette when you really want to say how horrid my other cousins are." She sighed. "You are right. Amy was nicer a few years back but then she became pretty and started getting attention and it went to her head. Rosalie, well, you know the story with Rosalie. She's her mother's protégé."

"Alicia did write her a note of condolence," Ellen murmured. "They had the funeral on Thursday."

"I suppose I should have attended the funeral." Alicia wrinkled her nose. "But Dean carried my note and flowers for me. I was never really part of the family."

"And since your inheritance, you are hated," Ellen added. "Emotions are rife at funerals. I advised her not to go."

"I'd rather stay here," Alicia said. "This is my home now."

Ellen's face softened toward her. "You are part of our family now . . . you're always welcome. Charlotte loves you."

"Thank you." Alicia turned away to hide the tears in her eyes. "It's very kind of you. And I like it here. I like England."

Going to bed, I reviewed my first impressions of Alicia Brickley. I had mistaken her character. Sullenness for reservedness, furtiveness for candor. Candor with those whom she trusted. She trusted Teddy Grimshaw. She trusted Ellen.

She was an interesting person.

And devoted to her adopted family.

But could such devotion invite danger?

"The muse has left me." I sounded sullen on the telephone to Tommy. "It's strange calling you Tommy . . . I shall always think of you as the major."

"I trust you are not interfering in any ensuing investigation?"

"No . . ."

"But something bothers you?"

"Yes. It's Ellen. I'm worried about her. She lied to the police, you know. She was resting that day Cynthia was killed but she forgot to mention she took Charlotte to the park. It's not a big thing but I can see worry lines in her face. The police can't frame her, can they?"

"The daughter is making all kinds of statements. She says her mother was murdered."

"Murdered by Ellen?"

"Yes. A hired killer."

I swallowed. "Still no word on the other woman who was in the hotel room?"

"The lead is cold. Unless two charming young women own up to a foolish antic?"

I felt very ill all of a sudden and twisted in the hallway, staring up the grand staircase. "Some things are better left out. I can see now why Ellen refrained from mentioning the visit to the park that day."

"She did have the child with her," the major murmured. "If it comes to it, the child can testify in her favor."

I breathed a sigh of relief. "That's good news."

"But as for you, young lady . . ."

"I am incorrigible. I can't help myself. Everything I see I want to capture with words. Oh, guess what? We're invited to the Pendarron ball. It's on the thirtieth. Do say you can make it. Come down for the weekend."

"I'll try. I can't promise anything."

"How's your work going? I know you can't discuss it with me, but are you all right? Did Ellen do the wrong thing in selling those shares?"

"No, it was a very clever move and one I imagine Teddy Grimshaw planned to do himself."

"What do you mean?"

"Buying into that company to direct its ventures, ventures which make his competitor company profitable. I put my money on Dean Fairchild. Gildersberg is destined for success."

"Is that fair practice?"

"Absolutely not. That's why we're involved."

"Will the boys get into trouble for it?"

"Since the shares changed hands from Teddy to his widow and now to his nephews, it's going to be hard to prove it. If Teddy were alive, certainly, he'd find himself in hot water."

My eyes widened and I lowered my voice to a whisper. "Do you think he committed suicide?"

"It's possible. A death on a wedding day is out of the ordinary."

"And he died to protect Ellen . . . and his money . . . have you conveyed these suspicions to the police?"

"Yes, but they won't visit Ellen until they have proof. There is no need to cause her further grief. Teddy Grimshaw is dead. He won't rise from the grave . . . although, I think that is maybe what he originally intended."

"Do you mean to fake his death?"

"Yes. You must admit, it's a good plot."

I was astonished by this piece of news. Of course, it was supposition. What proof was there unless Teddy Grimshaw showed up from the grave?

I hung up the receiver to take a long walk. My head ached with images of the wedding, the guests, the emotions, the terror of finding the groom lying dead . . . had he intended to live? Had he taken too much potion and, instead of faking his death, accidentally killed himself?

I felt immeasurably saddened and steered toward his grave under the tree. The place looked so peaceful I wondered whose body lay beneath it. Teddy Grimshaw was an extremely wealthy man. He could have paid off people to achieve a fake death.

I counted the months since the day.

Running my fingers over the headstone, I whispered: "What happened to you? What happened?"

"Are ye mad, miss?"

I jumped at the voice.

There was old Haines, the grave digger. He came out from behind the tree.

"I'm fine. I don't usually talk to myself." What brought him to the gravesite? "Don't you wonder, too, what happened?"

He guarded the grave like a soldier. "An accident, miss, that's what happened."

" 'An accident,' " I echoed, looking down at the grave. "Strange for a man on his wedding day . . . you don't think he was murdered?"

He blinked, and I sensed he knew something he didn't want to tell me.

"My Mary says accidents befall us all . . . it's in the good book. Even rich fellows die. Money can't buy life."

"And how is your Mary? Nelly says she's been feeling poorly lately."

A shadow passed over his face. "She took a cough last winter. Spends most days indoors now."

"Oh, that's sad. It's such a beautiful season. Perhaps I'll stop by later and bring the outdoors to her?"

Haines was surprised. "That's awful kind of ye, miss."

After giving me directions to their cottage, he bid me good-bye and left the site, whistling away to himself. He lived on the estate and occasionally helped out with grounds work.

One fact remained clear. Grave diggers did not return to the site unless there was a reason.

But what reason?

CHAPTER TWENTY-SIX

I wasted no time in making good my word.

Filling a basket of flowers from the Thornleigh gardens and taking great pleasure in the collection: pure white snowflakes, arum lilies, and traditional Cornish anemones, I set off in the early hours of the afternoon.

The house was very quiet when I went down, ghostly almost. Slipping out the servants' entrance through Nelly's kitchen (who insisted I carry a tonic and half of a freshly made date cake to Mary), I followed the line of trees to the dirt path.

Ten minutes later, I ambled down to the cluster of farming cottages gracing the eastern part of the estate. I paused to appreciate the scene greeting my eyes. Grass, green and luxurious, like a thick carpet clothed the grounds where fattened cows grazed, chickens roamed free, and children played while curious sheep looked on from the hillside.

Stepping into this real-life painting, I located Mary's cottage without any difficulty. The first on the right, Haines had said.

Relieved to see no sign of him, I knocked on the door and was bidden entry.

"Oh, Miss Daphne. He said you'd come and so ye have."

Confined to a wheelchair, Mary Haines was a short, large woman with ginger-gray hair and a lively face. It was only when she coughed that the wheeze betrayed her ill-health for otherwise she talked on and on about village affairs and how she missed the use of her legs.

Devouring the cake, she gave her own rendition of the recent tragic events.

"That poor girl. As if she hadn't suffered enough and then he dies on their weddin' day! Folk say it ain't a good sign."

"Surely they don't believe Miss Ellen is guilty?"

"No! Not of murderin' her husband, though that's what his other side say, don't they? Oh, I've been readin' the papers. I keep up with it all. Looks like the daughter's goin' ahead with her claim. Wants more money. Followin' in her mother's footsteps. I 'spose it can't be helped, can it?"

"Mrs. Haines, what do you mean?"

Wiping crumbs off her chin, she gave me a toothless grin. "Death. Death at Thornleigh. This is the second funny one. Things come in threes."

Her words chilled me and I hastily gulped my tea. "Are you talking of Mr. Xavier? But he died during the war . . ."

"No, not him. Lady Gertrude. Ellen's mother. It was all hush-hush at the time but I always found it odd, her dyin' so quickly. She weren't a nice woman; it was more her than Mr. Hamilton in threatenin' to disown poor Miss Ellen. Fancy such hardness with the war and losin' Mr. Xavier and all."

"Is that why I found your husband at Teddy Grimshaw's grave, Mrs. Haines?"

She nodded. "My Jem's a good man. Ever loyal to the Hamiltons."

"But this is the second grave he's dug with a funny death. Ellen's mother died of an overdose, didn't she? Self-administered?"

"Humph. She the last kind to take herself off. If she'd had her way, she'd have plagued Miss Ellen's life forever. She were one of those kinds who never die. They just stay old and ill and cranky. She'd have made Miss Ellen's life a misery."

"But nothing was said at the time? If anyone suspected, they should have told the police."

"Oh, it was them crazy war days. Everybody was actin' out of sorts. Probably why they never picked it up."

I stared at her, beginning to feel very uneasy. "Picked up what, Mrs. Haines?"

Her eyes widened, and she looked at me as if I were daft. "The murder, Miss Daphne."

"The murder of Lady Gertrude."

"Hello, Mother. Can you please post down my letter cache? You'll find it in my third drawer and the key is in the pocket of my gray coat in the closet."

"Letters?" my mother echoed, her voice sounding distant on the telephone. "Why do you want them for?"

"Inspiration," I lied. "I need them for my book."

A little white lie, I justified. I had intended to get them out while we were in London but the days slipped away. It was something I did every once in a while. Read through old letters. I loved it. It was insight into my life at the time, and into the lives of those who had written me.

In particular, I now burned to find the letters from the time when Ellen's mother died. It seemed a blur looking back; there was so much tragedy.

Mary Haines's gnarly voice persisted in my ear. *Lady Gertrude. It was all hush-hush at the time but I always found it odd, her dyin' so quickly. She were one of those kinds who never die . . .*

Murder, Mary Haines said. She had mentioned no suspects but for the veiled insinuation. Who else stood to benefit from the old cantankerous woman's death? Ellen. And Ellen alone.

I refused to believe it. Though she despised how her parents had treated her, she wasn't the kind to murder. Ellen was the sort who would have allowed her mother to make her life a misery, fetching and carrying, always grateful that her mother had accepted her back and she and Charlotte had a place to live.

"Look, Daphne. Andrew has bought an old church spire. We're going to mount it on the new roof."

Eyes brightening, Ellen went on to say what a bargain it had been and that the spire survived a bombing during the war. "It'll look marvellous on the tower, don't you think? And we'll see it from miles away."

Sharing her excitement, I agreed to go and view the piece.

It was larger than I expected. Seven and a half meters high, its stone fretwork imitated the grand medieval masonry spires back in fashion with the Gothic revival. I reached out to touch a piece of the stonework, admiring the intricate artistry.

"Thank you, Andrew." Ellen nodded to the builder and he covered the piece. "It'll take a few men to lift it. The work is dangerous but Andrew assures me it can be done."

"He's a smart builder."

We were standing out in the front lawn. Keen to start work, Andrew and his men had descended upon the place like ants.

"Two years to restore her," Ellen said to me on the way to breakfast. "Then Thornleigh will be the most magnificent mansion this side of England. It's been the dream of the Hamiltons for as long as I can remember."

I thought it was a good thing for her to focus on after the death of her husband.

"Daphne," she paused, "do you think it's wrong of me to resume works? I don't have a choice, really. Andrew wrote a report for Teddy. Without the proper repairs to the roof and certain parts of the house, it will decay. I can't let that happen . . . not when I can prevent it."

Collapsing in a parlor chair as we entered the house, she hid her face from me. "I know what they'll write next. That I'm not grieving him . . . but I am, in my own way. It was our dream together to restore Thornleigh." A little smile tempered her lips. "I remember when Teddy first saw the place. He had no idea I came from a family grander than his. I never told him, you see. What was the point? We met during the war. Who we were didn't matter then. A prince could marry a pauper and nobody would look sideways."

"When did he find out?"

"When he came back to London. Do you remember? I wrote you about it. 'I'll take you to my country home,' I told him. 'Where I spent my childhood.'"

"Had he not asked about your family before?"

"Oh, yes, and I just made the usual reply: ailing parents at home. Brother Xavier in the war like us. If I mentioned the town, he didn't remember for on the drive, he thought I was directing him to Penzance."

"Penzance?"

"He's American." She smiled. *The Pirates of Penzance?* It's famous. Well, they wouldn't know Fowey and Truro and Newquay, would they?"

"Was he shocked when he saw Thornleigh?"

A mischievous glint danced through her eyes. "His reaction was priceless. Oh, you should have seen it! I kind of led him to believe we lived in a small community, which we do, but he was prepared for a tiny cottage."

"Did he guess when you entered the estate?"

"No. Even then he thought I lived *on* the estate in a humble dwelling."

"How long did you make him wait?"

"Until he stopped the car and I handed him the key. 'Here, darling,' I said. 'Our home. I hope you like it.' He was astounded, to say the least. Not many could render Teddy Grimshaw silent but I did that day."

"He must have wondered why you remained silent?"

"Yes and I told him. I was pregnant, my parents had practically disowned me, and all my letters to him went missing. I thought he had abandoned me. Why mention I belonged to a grand English mansion and a noble family? All of that didn't matter. Though," she reflected, "I did relish when he later informed his relations of my family and my inheritance. Here they thought he was marrying some young penniless woman making a claim on him!"

I recalled the Americans arriving at Thornleigh and admiring it. Who wouldn't admire it? It was magnificent.

"So, you see, even though he'd spent his whole life making money, all he wanted to do was to restore Thornleigh. He loved the history of the place. He was determined to make his mark here, but somebody cruelly stole that from him. Someone who benefited from his death."

"Some say *you* benefited from his death."

"Though Thornleigh needed attention, the estate is worth a fortune. Of course, my last resort would be to sell but I made ends meet. My mother hated it when I came back and worked from the sweat of my hands growing and selling vegetables. Who cares if we dirtied our hands? But she cared. She *hated* it. She once came out in her nightgown and ordered me to stop. *'Stop mixing with that class! I forbid it!'* She didn't understand. There was no money after Papa died. We all expected Xavier to come back a hero and rescue us."

"If your mother had lived, would she have accepted Teddy Grimshaw?"

"Who knows," she rolled her eyes, "but she would have appreciated his millions. Her father was a duke; she knew how important money is to families like us."

Since she wanted to talk, I couldn't help myself. "Ellen, what happened the night your mother died? I know you wrote me of it, that night, how horrid it was, and how scared you were . . ."

"Scared?" She seemed surprised. "I think I was *shocked* more than anything. Mother was always fastidious with her medicines. The doctor prescribed her laudanum to help her sleep. She always insisted on mixing it herself."

"Who found her?"

"Edith, her maid."

"And you called for the doctor?"

"Yes . . . but he was late in coming. In those days doctors were scarce. He looked Mother over, inspected the bottle, and concluded she had taken a fatal dosage."

"What was her mood like the previous day?"

"The same. Grumpy. She yelled at Charlotte for making too much noise. Ordered poor Edith around; nothing unusual."

"Why didn't you insist on an investigation?"

Meeting my candid gaze, she lifted her shoulders. "Frankly, I was relieved she died. I may sound heartless but she was an unlovable woman. The only one she ever cared for was Xavier and when he died, the world stopped for her. Maybe she decided to end her life that night and join him. I don't know. She left no note."

I nodded, and suggested we better have breakfast before we missed out. "You are aware," I said on the way in, "that some people still think your mother was murdered. That it was an odd death?"

Her eyes arrested mine. "Who have you been talking to?"

I didn't want to betray Mary Haines so I made up a story of overhearing maids talk.

"Servants," Ellen dismissed, "they're always fanciful. When Teddy died, they were the first to scream murder! Murder. I don't think he was murdered now. It's curious. I have a strong feeling about it."

I waited for her to explain, but since Alicia and Charlotte were in the breakfast room, the conversation changed.

I buttered my toast and ate it with a smile; however, the gnarly face of Mary Haines rose up to haunt me. *It's death. Death at Thornleigh.*

And things come in threes . . .

CHAPTER TWENTY-SEVEN

"There's a shipbuilder's family in Polruan. I read about them in the evening post."

"Great. I'll make a trip there. I might visit Angela, too . . . she's at our house in Fowey. That is, if I have time. I might get sidetracked."

"Undoubtedly."

Tommy's voice was full of tender humor.

Receiving a phone call from the major had seen me climb down from my self-appointed office in the library in record time. Opting to take the call in the study instead of the main hall, I arrived, naturally, a little breathless.

"How many pages have you written this week?"

I gulped down a swallow. "Not many, but I did finish a chapter and a few character sketches." *I have been too busy playing the role of inspector.* "How's London? Work? Are you able to come to the ball?"

He breathed a long sigh. "London is *moyenne*; work even more *moyenne,* and yes, I can make it to the ball. The Pendarrons are in town, by the way. I've seen them at several places."

"So you've been busy working and going to parties?" I summed up, missing him beyond words and wishing I was there. "What else is new?"

"In fact, I do have a piece of news you will find interesting. Jack and Rosalie have run away together. Or so it's assumed."

"Run away?" I echoed, dumbfounded. "I thought she'd palmed him off?"

"I don't know about that but young Grimshaw is in the hot seat. He's been selling information to Salinghurst through Rutland. It appears he's been working for the other side for some time."

I was shocked. "Against his own cousin and against his own shares?"

"He's not interested in the shares. He wants the easy way: no work. I spoke to Fairchild. He's kept Grimshaw on a tight leash but not tight enough, it seems."

"What will Dean do?"

"Oh, he's already paid him out. They had a huge row. Jack left town with a black eye."

"And Rosalie went with him? Why?"

I couldn't wait to let Ellen know. This time of day she was usually in the morning room so I hurried up there, skidding to an abrupt halt when I heard raised voices.

". . . what else do you expect me to say?"

Ellen's voice.

"I had . . . maybe I was stupid."

Harry. *Harry?*

"My husband is not dead a year. I can't even think of remarrying yet."

"Did you ever love me, Ellen? I have to know . . . did you ever?"

"Love you? Harry, you *know* I love you. But not in the way you now say you'd like. I love you like a brother. You've been a brother to me in every way and I am so grateful—"

"Grateful? I don't want *your gratitude.*"

Thumping footsteps ensued and I slid into the nearest room before Harry sauntered past, a grim look on his face.

When I went to Ellen, she was seated at her desk, holding her face in her hands. "Oh, Daphne . . . it's you. Thank goodness, it's you. You will never guess what just happened—"

I approached her. "I heard a little. Harry fell in love with you. Is that so extraordinary? You've done everything together for years."

"I know," she cried. "He was there at Charlotte's birth . . . he was there when my parents died . . . he was there when I found Teddy again. He's always helped me but have I returned the favor? I never once thought our friendship would be marred this way . . . I thought, I thought he thought of me, too, like a sister. He has no family. He often joked we were a family and now I think of it, he meant not in the brotherly way. He's been waiting all these years. Why didn't he speak up when Teddy came back into my life?"

I sat down. Having witnessed the anguish in Harry's voice and seeing the forlorn look on his face gave me some kind of idea. "Because he knew you were still holding a candle for Teddy all these years. If he had spoken to you then, you would have ignored him. He obviously put such feelings aside but when Teddy died and he sees you now alone and vulnerable, naturally he thought . . ."

"He'd just step into Teddy's empty shoes," Ellen finished miserably.

I saw the conflict in her face. She worried over losing Harry. "What will he do?"

"I shall try and talk to him later. He loves Thornleigh. I can't imagine he'd give the place up because we had a row."

"Speaking of rows, I have some news for you."

Her mouth gaped open when I told her of the major's news. "I'm not surprised. Jack's a chameleon. Good on Dean. He's well rid of him."

"He's fled in disgrace . . . and he's taken Rosalie with him."

"Willingly or unwillingly?"

"Nobody knows but they are both missing. Unless she is elsewhere? But everyone in London thinks she's with Jack."

"Where can they be going? France? The only money they have

is—" She broke off, suddenly afraid. "They wouldn't come here, would they?"

"And beg charity?"

"Not charity, but a threat. Don't you see? Since that woman's death, the notes have stopped. She must have been sending them and she sent the chocolates and she tried to shoot me and her daughter means to follow suit."

"But how can they possibly harm you? You are protected here."

"Oh." She turned very pale. "Are they able to track them? I'd feel so much better knowing they went to a different country. I can't explain it. It's an ill-feeling I have, a premonition."

I laid my hand on her shoulder. If I were in her shoes, I'd probably feel the same. When one's security is threatened, desperation and fear trouble the mind. There's no antidote for it. I didn't want to say that, of course; all I could do was suggest she rehire the man the major recommended.

"Yes, I'll do that. You were right. It was silly of me to let him go. I don't know what I was thinking . . ."

I was thinking back, too, to the various notes I'd seen, and to the poisoned chocolates. With Cynthia Grimshaw dead, we'd never learn the truth unless Rosalie knew of it. But even if she knew what her mother had been doing, she'd not confess to it.

Unless there was some way of trapping the truth out of her. Returning to the library, I opened a new page of my notebook and wrote the name *Rosalie.* The *R* had a nice slant to it. I liked names beginning with *R*.

So I wrote *R* and a question.

R. What is your secret?

"Miss du Maurier? May I have a word?"

"Yes, Inspector. Nice to see you. And Sergeant Heath? Good to see you, too."

The young sergeant grinned while shaking my hand. "It's always a pleasure to visit Thornleigh with such charming guests in residence."

Inspector James frowned at this comment, looking over his sergeant as if he'd committed a cardinal sin.

"Miss du Maurier, shall we take a walk? Heath, why don't you go and inform the staff to keep watch. Start with the cook."

The sergeant's grin widened. "Excellent, sir. Will do so, sir."

"He's a good lad," the inspector said, watching him go. "He's been pressing me to return here so when I received Lady Ellen's call late yesterday afternoon, I thought a day out of the office."

Strolling through the lovely gardens, I remarked on the fine day.

"Fine, yes. But what lies beneath, Miss Daphne?" He paused, and glanced up at the huge mansion, taking in every detail with his shrewd eyes. "How is your shoulder? Healing well?"

"I hardly feel it anymore. The slight wince here and there."

Taking out his leaf pad, he flicked through it. "Reviewing one's notes is quite revealing, don't you agree?"

I watched him with great interest. "What are you looking for?"

"An inconsistency. Maybe small, maybe great. Something is wrong with this whole case. Or I should say *cases*. For I have two dead bodies. Are they linked? Ah," he paused, squinting in the morning glare to read his scribble, "here it is. Lady Ellen. She failed to mention the other death threats until later. Why do you think she'd do this when her daughter is at risk?"

"Because her fiancé Teddy Grimshaw asked it of her. After he died, that's when she came forward about them."

"But there's something in the silence. It's telling me something. I can't quite put my finger on it. Can you help me out, Miss Daphne?"

"Me?" A half laugh escaped my lips. "I'm no inspector!"

"But you are perceptive and you are a friend of Lady Ellen. You are here. You have seen and heard things. You, I think, have the key to this riddle."

"Me?" I echoed again.

His frank gaze scrutinized me. "Who do you think did these murders?"

I was taken aback by his brutality. "I-I, er, don't know."

"You have an idea then? What is it?"

"They are not linked. There are two killers out there."

"What makes you think so?"

"A simple deduction of character and motivation, sir."

"It seems a woman killed Cynthia and the same woman could have killed her husband on her wedding day: your friend, Ellen Hamilton."

"No." I put my hand up to stop him. "No, it's not possible."

"But everything is possible, Miss du Maurier, particularly when an estate as grand as this one is at the center of it."

Thornleigh. I glanced over the house, feeling a strong connection to it. "I don't think it's fair, Inspector, to blame a house for these deaths. Ellen didn't do it; I'd bet my life on it."

"What do you think happened then?"

"I think Teddy Grimshaw has taken his secret to his grave. I think he had a secret. And that secret explains why he didn't involve the police in the death threats. He didn't want an investigation which might lead back to him and his business dealings."

"You are talking of *unscrupulous* business dealings?"

"It's only a guess. And I guessed it because after finding Ellen and Charlotte, it doesn't stand to reason that he'd willingly jeopardize them unless he stood to lose everything."

"So you think he killed himself?"

"Yes. Yes, I think I do."

"Have you told his widow this theory of yours?"

"Certainly not. It would only upset her."

"Then let me say my theory now. The moment Ellen discovered Teddy Grimshaw was in town, she made a plan to catch him. Do you know that year she approached two estate sellers? Oh yes, it's true. She didn't have the money to keep Thornleigh and as a matter of estate law, she couldn't sell off one acre or sell one painting. It was either keep it whole or sell it whole."

I stared at him, not believing a word. Ellen would have told me if things were so bad. Surely. "If it's true, you're only accusing her of marrying him for money."

"Money supplies motivation to marry as it does to kill. It is simple. She married him for his money and then she killed him on the day of his wedding. She knew of his heart condition. She slipped the hemlock into his wine and he died of a heart attack that very night, leaving her a very rich widow."

"You're missing a vital clue, Inspector. Such may have been that way if a certain emotion wasn't involved."

"What emotion?"

I paused. "Love. Ellen has always loved Teddy which is why she never married. Admittedly, when she read the notice of his being in London, she naturally looked him up. He needed to know he had another daughter, a daughter he knew nothing about because Ellen's letters never reached him."

"It is clear then. She married him for *revenge*. Steal his money and kill him."

"Then why make plans? Why buy three tickets on a cruise ship for America if she planned to kill him?"

"Such plans are merely a deterrent, an alibi. She planned it cleverly. Fill the house with wedding guests. Nobody suspecting the bride . . ."

"Ellen wasn't alone once during those twenty-four hours." As I said the fact, I recalled her ashen face when she admitted to omitting that she was at the park when Cynthia Grimshaw was killed.

Leafing through his notepad again, he had to concede the fact.

"You have to agree that somebody is trying to kill Ellen. I was wearing her coat. That same somebody tried to poison her. For a killer, she's very vulnerable."

"Perhaps somebody knows she is guilty and is blackmailing her?"

I smiled. We were at loggerheads, I on one side of the fence and he on the other. "Or maybe somebody wants the police to think she is guilty in order to miss the real killer?"

"Humph." On seeing his sergeant approaching, he offered his hand. "You have an interesting mind, Miss Daphne."

"Thank you, Inspector." I accepted his handshake. "I enjoyed our repartee, too."

CHAPTER TWENTY-EIGHT

"There's post for you, miss. On the tray in the hall."

"Thank you, Olivia. Is Nelly in?"

"Yes, miss. But she's due to leave in half an hour."

"I'd better catch her then."

Slipping the letters in my skirt pocket, I hastened down to the kitchen where a scrumptious evening meal baked away. "Oh Nelly, it smells wonderful."

"It's new-season lamb," she said proudly, removing her apron.

"But it's *how* you've cooked it."

"Slow," she affirmed, "and I do a nice mix of rosemary from the garden, mint, and basil for sweetness. I also rub a little honey and salt on the meat and add garlic to the sauce."

"But no hemlock?" I joked, savoring the delicious aromas.

"Humph! Poisons don't come from my kitchen, I'll hav' ye know. That's what I keep tellin' that nice young sergeant. He was here to-day. Came to see me special-like."

"Oh?" I leaned across the bench, interested. "What did he ask you?"

"About that day again. He said something was botherin' him. It were the same thing that you asked me about, that missing glass? I thought about what you said the last time and it's a bit of a blur since it were a crazy day, the craziest of my time, but I remember the maid Olivia nearly tippin' over a tray. I've said to her again and again to be careful, 'specially with the crystal glasses."

"Crystal glasses." I tapped my lip, deep in thought. "So there *was* one empty glass returned from Mr. Grimshaw's room?"

"Yes," Nelly confirmed. "Olivia owned up to it. She didn't tell me at first for she thought she'd get in trouble. Ridiculous child! The man weren't even dead yet, and I'd be takin' a spoon to her if she didn't clear the dishes from the rooms."

I pieced all this information together, leaving Nelly to her work. Going back to the crime scene, Teddy's room, I envisaged the elements of that day. Teddy dressed in his wedding attire, jacket-less, pouring himself a glass before the ceremony. Since no poison had been found in any of the decanters at the time, the hemlock must have been dropped in the glass between when he poured it and when he drank it.

Since everybody denied going to Mr. Grimshaw's room that afternoon, other than Olivia the maid who came later to clear any dishes, how did the poison get into Teddy Grimshaw's glass?

Someone had gone there.

Someone had gone there and lied about it.

The question remained:

Who?

I carried my letters to my room.

The larger package postmarked London contained all my correspondence with Ellen, neatly stacked and tied with red ribbons. Putting that one aside, I eagerly opened the other.

It was from Megan Kellaway.

> *Dear Daphne,*
> *How I miss you! I can't believe how busy I am being*
> *an engaged woman. With Mother hounding me on*

one end to start organizing my trousseau, and Dean on the other insisting we go to every function we're invited to, there is scarcely time to write.

What are you doing down there in the country? I've bumped into the major a few times and he says you're working on your book. My dear friend, writing books is for old women. Young women like us need to stay close to our men.

In saying such, I am obliged to tell you that the major has been seen out with Lady Lara Fane. I saw them with my own eyes this morning at the Egyptian exhibition at the museum. I was about to go up and rouse on him on your behalf but Dean held me back. My dearest Dean, he's so proper! I do love him so . . .

Falling out of my hands, the letter floated to the floor. I didn't want to read any more. Red fury consumed me. I felt my face. It was burning hot. How could he? How could he humiliate me this way?

I twisted the ring on my finger. It was still too large.

Tearing to my feet, I paced the full length of my room. If I had a car, I would jump in it and drive straight to London. But I did not have a car. And it would take me an age to travel back there from here.

Lady Lara must be laughing to herself. *The poor major has no escort. His fiancée fancies herself a novelist! A novelist, pray. What has she published? I vow she won't even finish the book . . .*

Now I was livid. My heart thumped so loud it hurt. Why had he failed to mention he'd seen her? Why had he omitted her name from our conversation?

Though tempted, I refused to make a telephone call. Pride forbade it. My mother always said I had too much pride. *Pride goeth before the fall.*

Scratching those words down on paper in big black letters, I stared at them. Mocking, they stared back, growing larger until they obscured the whole page.

Watery tears kept sprinkling the page, without my permission. "Oh, wretchedness," I muttered. "Wretchedness."

Crunching up the messy page and throwing it in the wastepaper basket, I forced myself to think. Think, think. Think about the *book,* not about *him. Him and her.*

Seeing the paper ball perched perilously on the edge of the basket, I seized it and looked at the mess I'd created. The page reminded me of those death threats Ellen and Teddy had received.

The notes.

There's a clue there, I thought, trying to recall the wording of each one. Two had said: *Pay £10,000 or you, your woman, and child die,* and giving instructions to place the money at the grave of Ernest Gildersberg. The other, accompanying the box of chocolates said *DIE.*

"Ellen, those other notes you destroyed, do you remember the wording of them?"

Reclining in the sun by the pond, Ellen lowered her sunglasses.

"You should have kept them."

She wrinkled her nose. "I know I should have, but they were profane."

"What did they say? Why were they more upsetting than the others?"

She shuddered. "I don't know . . . they were more directed at me and Charlotte. Like, 'Let the Bitch Die,' and so forth."

"Did the police think they were from the same source?"

"Yes. Both had the same theme: Die. *Die. Die. Die.* Somebody wanted us all dead."

Sitting down on the grass, I began to pluck a few blades out. I wished I could see all the notes together. The police held the others, and I didn't want to show myself a busybody by asking to see them. However, Inspector James had come to speak to me, hadn't he?

I decided I would make a telephone call . . . to Inspector James.

"Miss Daphne? Is everything all right there?" the inspector asked.

"Yes, for the time being, but I just thought of something which might be important." After summarizing my reason, I added, "the ones Ellen destroyed carried emotion. Such as might have been sent by a woman."

"You mean Cynthia Grimshaw?"

"Yes, while the others appear more directed at Teddy Grimshaw, perhaps by a business associate he wronged. Didn't that note say money was to be placed at the grave of Ernest Gildersberg?"

"We've considered that. The family of Ernest Gildersberg have no notion of having written them. He left behind a widow and two daughters, and a cousin or two unconnected to the business."

"So who do you think wrote the notes and why?"

After releasing a low chuckle, he sighed. "That's a lead we're still investigating."

The line went dead.

Incensed by his flippancy, I suppressed a sudden desire to go fishing and catch a large fish. I'd love to dump such a fish right on the inspector's desk.

I ordered a cup of tea instead.

Tea always had a calming effect on me. And still upset with Major Browning, whom I'd normally share my find with, I wrote a concise summary:

Death 1   *Teddy Grimshaw, died heart attack / hemlock poison*
Death 2   *Cynthia Grimshaw, died broken neck / fall down hotel*
   stairs
Death 3   *?*

I paused. Should I write Ellen's mother, Lady Gertrude, as Death 3? Leaving it blank, for I instinctively felt there would be another death, I continued on with the suspects:

Suspect 1   Rosalie Grimshaw / Jack Grimshaw (received money from death)

Suspect 2   Unknown business enemies (received nothing from death?)

Suspect 3   Ellen Hamilton / Alicia Brickley (received money from death)

Perusing the page again, I tapped my finger on Suspect 2. I had written received nothing from death, but perhaps that wasn't true. Perhaps in some way this killer, in a business sense, had benefited by the death of Teddy Grimshaw.

Recalling the initial investigation, my work with the major over the pile of paperwork, I added a name to unknown.

Salinghurst.

Major shareholder?

Rutland, the earl of Rutland.

Lady Lara's father.

"How's the play going?"

"Excellent. I've tickets for you, Ellen, and Alicia to attend the premiere, oh, and your major will be there, of course. I said you'd be coming up. You wouldn't say no to an old father."

I groaned inside. I didn't want to sound mulish and suggest Lady Lara accompany him rather than his *fiancée* who was away down in the country. "Where did you see him?"

"At the club. We had a drink together."

"He's often there, isn't he?"

"And everywhere else. I had no idea he is so well connected. Well done, Daphne."

Except the engagement's off. "Megan wrote me. She said she's run into him, too, a few times, *with* Lady Lara Fane."

"Oh, don't read into that sort of thing. They were childhood friends."

"Others may read into it."

"You're the only one who counts so give the old boy the benefit of the doubt, won't you? Don't go using your torrid imagination and paint him a chameleon."

I smiled. "I've been using that word quite a bit, too, lately. It's from your play. How's the title? Will it stay *The Ringer*?"

"Yes, and I've got the best cast. I'll see you there. Two nights' time."

I hung up the receiver.

The last thing I wanted to do—go to London. I wanted to hide down here in the country. Write my book. Write *a* book to the finish, publish it, and throw it in Lady Lara's face.

To my dismay, Ellen liked the idea.

"It's only for a night. It was kind of your father to invite us and kind of Jeanne to offer to babysit Charlotte."

"Mummy, why can't I go to the play?"

"You're too young, darling."

"Why does Nanny have to go? She can stay with me."

"No, nannies sometimes need a night out. You mustn't monopolize her, or she won't want to live with us."

"Oh, she's no trouble," Alicia assured Ellen. "I'd rather stay with her in any case. I've never cared much for plays or opera."

I asked her why.

"I only went once or twice," she said. "And both times I simply made up a number. Nobody wanted me along."

"You speak of your cousins?"

"Yes . . . Rosalie and Amy, mostly."

"You accompanied your parents?"

"My mother." She spat the word with dislike. "My father preferred to stay at home. He worked long days and often went away so when he was at home, he preferred to stay home."

"Your mother now cares for your grandmother? Have you heard from her?"

"No. She didn't approve of my going to London to work for Uncle Teddy. 'Work,' she said. 'And bring further reproach on our name?' You see, our family, even if we were poor, we had to be poor quietly."

Fascinated by this insight into harsh Boston society, I asked her more questions on the drive to London. Not daring to ask Harry to drive us after their argument, Ellen commanded the front seat while we girls relaxed in the back.

"I'll never go back, ever."

She caressed Charlotte's hair, her long, slim fingers encouraging the curls.

"Here I am my own person. Over there I am simply an appendage nobody wanted."

Frowning, Ellen shook her head. "Oh, my dear, I'm sure that's not true. Not all of your family are that bad."

A coldness touched Alicia's eyes. "Yes, they are. They have hearts of ice."

"Well," Ellen grinned, "we'll endeavor to find you a nice young man here and you can marry and triumph over them. Fancy landing a *title*? Smear *that* in their faces."

The merest smile came to Alicia Brickley's lips and for once she allowed herself to ponder such a dream.

CHAPTER TWENTY-NINE

By the time we reached London, we'd convinced Alicia to go to the play.

"I really don't mind staying behind," she persisted as we began to embellish what attractions belonged to us.

Still in mourning, Ellen chose safety in black. I dared to wear a deep oceanic blue drop-waisted number, adorning it with various-length pearl necklaces. Charming in the color salmon, Mother complemented Angela's demure cream and lace.

Jeanne and Charlotte, having great fun watching us make these elaborate preparations, thought Alicia should borrow my green velvet again, since it became her so well.

"Keep it," I said as we piled into the motorcars.

Her eyes widened. "Are you sure?"

"Of course I am." I glanced at her face, free of spectacles and her lips reddened with Angela's rouge lipstick.

"Thank you." She smiled back at me. "It's kind of you."

I raised a brow, wondering what she intended to do with her five thousand pounds. She appeared such a shy, retiring figure I imagined it to sit earning interest in a bank. If she didn't marry, as Ellen predicted, she'd grow old and take the odd seaside holiday.

Speaking of marriage, I shot out my hand to view my engagement ring. Still too large, I had slipped it over my satin gloves. I was certain Lady Lara would be there tonight and I intended to stick it right under her little nose.

As arranged, my father met us in his office. He promptly put out his cigarette and came to greet us.

"Ah, you ladies look ravishing . . . enough to steal the limelight—eh?"

"We shall behave like withering flowers in the background, Papa," Angela vowed as my mother went to correct my father's necktie.

"Thank you for inviting me, Sir Gerald." Alicia bowed, and my father popped in his theatrical eyeglass.

"Who's this—eh? Another lily of the pond. Daphne, your friend? Angela, your friend?"

"It's Nanny Brickley." Ellen saved Alicia from further embarrassment.

"No! My word, is it? Can it be?" Adjusting his eyeglass, he glowered like an old rogue. "Ever thought of the theater, my girl? You have the looks for it."

I don't think Alicia had ever received a greater compliment. Having grown up in the shadow of her rich and beautiful cousins, despised and barely tolerated, she'd never have dreamed of making an impression far across the seas.

"Gerald," my mother stepped in, "don't tease her. Is everything ready?"

Peeking behind the curtain, my father surveyed the thronging crowd. "Daphne, I spy your major. Come here and see."

I did as I was bid. A sea of faces, smiling, laughing, greeting, talking. All attired in their finest, the heightening babble expanded as new arrivals entered the hall. I caught my breath. Major Browning led the group, tall and debonair in a black suit. The ladies admired his charm while the men admired his conversation. He commanded both sexes and could fit into any crowd.

"Why don't you go down?" My father pushed the small of my back. "Surprise him."

"I have no wish to intrude," I replied. "I suppose you invited him to our box?"

"Yes, of course I did."

"And did he accept?"

"No. He already had tickets."

I lifted a brow at the plural use. "Tickets for how many?"

"Can't remember. Go on. Go and see him. Don't hide yourself up here."

While the others made their way to their seats, I snuck out into the corridor. The crush dampened my spirits. Suddenly claustrophobic and nervous, I waited behind the shadow of a plant, confident nobody would notice me there.

"Daphne, isn't it? Gerald's daughter?"

I turned at the melodious voice to see a young man around my age, his raven-black hair combed to one side and spectacularly good-looking. He grinned.

"Escaping the crush or people?"

"Both," I said.

"Are you afraid?" His eyes danced with amusement.

"I suppose I am. You're an actor, aren't you?"

"An actor of Shakespearian tragedy, at the moment," he presented, flashing white teeth.

"Do you work for my father?"

"I hope to. I'm interested in trying new roles and he's an eye for direction."

I knew his ilk. Eager young actors with ambition. "You hope to go to America?"

"No, I hope to stay here. Produce my own, like your father."

The crush had dwindled to an odd straggler or two searching for their seats. "I must go. It was nice to meet you, Mr. . . . ?"

"Olivier. Laurence Olivier."

As I made my way to our box, I thought I must mention his name to Papa. His cavalier demeanor reminded me of Major Browning. I wondered where his seats were and who he'd brought to my father's theater.

"Here." Ellen shoved her spyglass to me. "I found him. He's over there on the left."

My heart fluttered. Was he with *her*? Squinting through the glass, I smiled with relief to see him sitting with two male friends. However, three rows behind him I also discovered Lady Lara Fane. She was accompanied by a male friend but I caught the odd fleeting glance to the major when he responded to the play.

As expected, *The Ringer* was a great success. The mystery kept one's interest and as I watched the various scenes unfolding, I couldn't help but apply it to the case at hand. A master of disguise, the villain masquerades as anything to get near his prey. His prey? His very own partner, the one closest to him. Why? For revenge, revenge because his partner killed his sister.

"It was originally called *The Gaunt Stranger.*" My father beamed on his first audience appraisal. "Daphne came up with *The Ringer.*"

"She has a way with words."

My heart stopped.

Crouching under the door, Major Browning joined us without ceremony. I flushed. I felt like an idiot. Why hadn't I called him to say I'd be in town? It was immature of me and decidedly feline.

My shame echoed in my mother's face. "Tommy, how delightful. Didn't Gerald invite you to our box?"

Thank goodness she'd not said, *Didn't Daphne invite you to our box?*

"Yes, he did, but I was already committed."

His eyes bore into mine and my face turned scarlet.

"Daphne, care for some fresh air?"

"Y-yes." I leapt to my feet.

He said nothing to me until we were outside. Once down the main corridor, we ran into the general mill, the major breaking off to shake hands with an old friend of his. While I stood there stupidly, suppressing the urge to bite my nails, Lady Lara brushed by me.

"Oh, sorry, I didn't see you . . ."

I am certain you did. "Oh, hello." I smiled through my teeth. "Enjoy the play?"

She looked beautiful. Bathed in a feminine pale mauve gracing her figure, she stood over me, tall and graceful with red lips and manicured hair. "Yes . . . I didn't see you with Tommy."

She was assessing me, wanting to know the reason why we'd not sat together. Curious hope flickered in those long-lashed aristocratic eyes.

"You came alone?" I asked. It was my best attempt at an insult.

"Oh, no." She laughed. "Tommy gave me the tickets. We attached ourselves to his trio."

Her mouth curled on the word *attached.*

Before I could inquire as to the "we," the major usurped our dangerous tête-à-tête. He steered the conversation toward the play and said how proud he was of his future father-in-law.

Her eyes seethed behind their demure congratulations.

"She is why I didn't call you," I said to the major as our feet touched the street. "I have friends, you know, friends who care about me. When they see my fiancé spending time with his ex-fiancée, it gives cause for comment—"

"Lara." He laughed. "She's just like a sister to me . . . how can I convince you?"

"She's too beautiful to be anyone's 'sister.'"

"Do you think I'd really want to marry someone like her? She'd make my life a misery. I've known her all my life and while she's beautiful, yes, she's also selfish and superficial."

I lowered my lashes. "I should have telephoned you. We're only here for a night."

"Then we must make the most of it. Have you dined?"

"My mother's organized a supper party back at the house. Can you come? Bring your friends." I grinned. "I'm sure we can find some cozy corner . . ."

Sharing a cab with the major and his two friends, Ellen and I reached home about nine-thirty. In preparation for our arrival and the subsequent party, every window emanated a deep yellow glow. I loved old houses lit up at night.

Having indulged in a sweet champagne punch at my father's premiere, I slipped out of the motorcar a little light-headed. Thankfully, the major prevented my foot from making a dramatic plunge into a ditch.

"And here is your shawl."

Draping it across my shoulders, he lowered his lips to mine. "Shall we go in? I'm famished."

I was, too. I realized I'd hadn't eaten anything since lunch.

Among the first to arrive at the house, and, as daughter of the house, I gave the order for the kitchen to start serving. Shepherding everyone into the designated room, I flicked on the gramophone and listened to the first accordion ballad my mother had selected. Adjusting the volume, I watched with a smile how music relaxed one's guests. We might have been in a French cafe.

Seeing that everyone had a glass in hand, I handed mine to the major to look for Ellen. After helping me settle the increasing number of guests, she said she'd sneak a peek at Charlotte and then return. Since her husband's death, it was the first night she was actually enjoying herself and the entertainment. Being in London, without the responsibility of Thornleigh, its renovations, and the recent quarrel with Harry, made this trip all the more appealing to her.

Hurrying up the stairs, I heard a door slam.

Ellen charged out, a sleepy Jeanne crawling at her feet. "Daphne, quick! Call the police!"

I halted at her panic-stricken face. "What is it? What's happened?"

"It's Charlotte. She's missing."

CHAPTER THIRTY

"Missing?"

"I don't know anything." Jeanne wept into my mother's arms. "Last time I looked she was asleep like me. I went back to bed. Where could she have gone?"

Suddenly, my father's successful party turned to one of morbid concern.

"I think it's a good idea if everybody left." My father nodded to Major Browning and he began escorting the masses outside.

"Now, Ellen. Didn't you mention that Charlotte sleepwalks? Daphne used to sleepwalk. One night she went walking outside. As you can imagine, Muriel was in a panic but we found her. I'll send Tim and William out to look. Rest assured they'll search every nook and cranny. She can't have gone far."

Still waiting for the police, Jeanne was questioned again.

"I don't know the exact time, Papa," she wailed. "I swear I heard nothing, not even a peep from her. We had our dinner, I read her a story or two, and then she fell asleep. I stayed with her for a while and then I went to my own bed. I woke up once to check her and then I went back to bed."

After a gentle coaxing of the facts, my mother established Charlotte had gone missing between nine and ten o'clock.

"It's my fault." Alicia shook her head. "I shouldn't have left her. She was in *my* care."

"No, it's mine," Ellen cried. "I'm her mother. It's *my* responsibility to ensure her safety and now she's gone . . . kidnapped, murdered, or worse."

"Now, now, Ellen m'dear, don't go jumping to conclusions." My father reined her into his solid embrace. "We're doing all we can to retrieve her."

"But don't you see? She's not just *any* child. She's Charlotte Grimshaw, a great heiress in her own right."

"When was the last time she sleepwalked?"

"Two months ago?" Ellen conferred with Alicia.

"Six week ago," Alicia said. "The night she had the bad dream. She walked out of her room and into mine."

"We've summoned all the household staff," my mother said. "Someone must have seen her."

Still waiting for the police, my father began the interviews.

"No, sir, we seen nothin'. Not since they went to bed."

"Who walked through the front hall between nine and ten o'clock?"

Seven faces stared at him.

"All of us, sir." The butler spoke. "Except Mrs. Ireson."

The cook. Yes, well she didn't leave the kitchen often.

"And did any of you see Miss Jeanne go into Charlotte's room like she says?"

"No, sir. Most of us were down here, you see, helpin' with the party."

My father looked grave. The same look registered in the police inspector's face when he finally arrived at eleven.

"Sorry, we've had a murder hereabouts. It's been busy. If you say, Mrs. Grimshaw, your daughter sleepwalks, then there's little we can do. Sir Gerald has already sent out his men to look for her. I'm sorry. We're understaffed and murders take precedence over missing people. She'll show up."

"You *hope* she'll show up," Ellen shrieked. "You don't understand. I don't think she's been sleepwalking. Someone's taken her. They said they'll strike and they have! Oh, I never should have left her, not even for a moment!"

Squeezing my hand, the major glanced down at me. "I'll join the search." And to my appealing gaze, he smiled. "No, you can't come."

I protested, asking my father if I could go with him. Obtaining permission, I hooked my hand in his.

"I'll come." Alicia jumped to her feet.

"Me too," Ellen said, glaring at the inspector. "It seems in this town one can't rely on the police."

"Or perhaps it's the people who are the problem and not the police, madam."

Pausing at the door, Ellen turned. "What are you insinuating, sir?"

"Only that misfortune has occurred to two people close to you. Your husband . . . and now your daughter—"

"Are you daring to say I had anything to do with it?"

"You say 'it,' madam. What is it?"

Seething, Ellen shook her head. "I won't waste my time. Good day, Inspector."

"Good night, madam."

"I can't believe the gall of that creature," Ellen railed once we were on the street and into a hired cab. She gulped. "They still think I'm guilty, don't they? That woman's poison did it. Everybody believes I murdered my husband."

"No, they don't," I soothed, but what she said was true.

"I know you didn't do anything to hurt Uncle Teddy," Alicia spoke out, quietly, keeping strict lookout for Charlotte.

"Thank you." Ellen seized her hand. "You've been so good to me."

"It's an unsolved case," the major explained. "Naturally, the police feel the pressure when they have no answers. Don't take it personally, their assumptions, Ellen."

"And you, Major? Do you believe I'm a murderess? That I murdered my husband on our wedding day out of spite?"

"Spite? I believe you mean for his money?"

"Oh, yes. Of course. Forgive me. My mind is all over the place . . ."

In the deep shadow of the taxicab, I examined Ellen's fine profile. Her shrivelled nerves had suffered an attack from a police inspector who should have known better. However, why had she reacted so strangely?

It was a curious reaction and one I felt uncomfortable attributing to my innocent friend.

Innocent? I reckon she's as guilty as sin. She didn't have to see her fiancé on the day of his death. She merely had to ensure he drank or ate the poison. Who better than she knew he had a bad heart? That a small amount ingested into his system would achieve a so-called natural cardiac arrest.

Tearing out the typewritten page, I read it over. "What shall we call you? Inspector Pessimist?"

Scrapping the page, I threw it in the wastepaper basket and resumed Janet's world. However, the quiet seaside village of Polruan seemed as far from me as the moon. Unable to concentrate during this infernal waiting period, I rejoined the group downstairs.

"It's been too long," Ellen was saying. "*Someone's* taken her. I just hope it's money they want."

"Charlotte might turn out like Oliver," Angela tried. "She's smart and adventurous. She could walk in through that door any minute."

Alicia suspected the worst. Fear framing her face, she endeavored to read her book. Besieged with guilt, I imagined what kind of torment went through her mind. She hadn't wanted to go to the play. She was happy to stay at home with Charlotte. And if she had, Charlotte might still be here.

Poor Jeanne. I felt sorry for her, too. She hadn't stopped crying and apologizing, from one to the other. Eventually, Angela took her out.

While they were gone, the butler delivered a note to my father. I caught the exchange on my way back from the bathroom.

". . . are you sure? What age?"

"About ten, sir. He was too fast for us. I'm sorry, sir."

"That's all right, Stamford." My father sighed, picking up the neat little letter. "This can only have bad news, but bad news is better than no news—eh?"

"I agree, Papa." Going to him, I anxiously hung on his sleeve. After last night's search ended in nothing, the major promised to continue it today. He said he knew someone familiar with parts of London criminals inhabited. "What does it say?"

Grim, my father bore the note to Ellen. "Shall I read it?"

"Yes," Ellen whispered, looking like a ghost.

" 'Mrs. Grimshaw, I have your child. If you want her back alive, it will cost you ten thousand pounds. The longer you delay, the higher the price. Deliver the money to post office box number five-four-two in the name of Hillier. When I get confirmation of its arrival, I will release your daughter by the ticket office at Victoria Station.' "

"There's no name? No signature?"

"No . . . and the writing is in black capitals, probably not even by the hand of the kidnapper, though I am no policeman."

"We had better telephone them," my mother murmured.

"I'd much rather Inspector James," Ellen said. "Can't we ask him to come?"

"It's not his jurisdiction."

Sinking into a chair, Ellen lifted a weary hand to her forehead. "I'll have to see about the money . . ."

"The police will probably advise otherwise," my father said.

"How can you not try with a child?" my mother retorted.

"What assurance does she have though, if she goes ahead?"

Crying softly, Ellen answered us through her tears. "None."

True to my father's prediction, the police suggested no negotiation.

"I'm sorry. I just can't. I've got the money ready and I know Teddy would have done the same. Major Browning?" Moving across the room, Ellen handed him the package. "Can you deliver this for me?"

From the other side of the room, I saw the indentation in his jaw-line. His mouth tightening, I knew he didn't approve of Ellen's choice, but he accepted the package. "There is no guarantee this will bring back your daughter," he did warn and my father echoed the major's sentiments, volunteering to accompany the major on the mission.

The two men left and I watched them go, my father and my future husband. They were strong men, handsome and charismatic, and I loved them more than anything in this world. What if something should happen to one of them?

I dared not think about it.

CHAPTER THIRTY-ONE

"We've looked everywhere, Mrs. Grimshaw. No child has been found with her description."

Glassy-eyed, Ellen nodded. We'd all joined the hunt for Charlotte at Victoria Station and now as darkness expanded over the city, it was time to admit defeat. Taking Ellen in her arms, Mother led her to a waiting car, intending to put her to bed with a sedative.

At the mention of sedative, an uneasy feeling crawled up my spine. Lady Gertrude, Ellen's mother, had died of a misapplied sedative. Since Charlotte's disappearance, I trusted no one. And once again those chilling words of Mrs. Haines's echoed through my head: *Death comes in threes.*

Who would be the third?

"Thornleigh," I said to myself. "Thornleigh has the answer to this riddle . . ."

We had to go back.

Driving home with Ellen, I talked her out of a sedative and instead went to Father's study for brandy. Pouring a glass out of the decanter, I sniffed it. The pungent odor assailed my nostrils. It smelled normal. It smelled safe.

As I stood there inspecting the golden liquid, I thought of Teddy

Grimshaw. He'd have thought nothing of it, sipping his death-dealing potion just prior to death. Would I suffer a similar fate?

What the inspector said of Ellen appeared true. She was at the center of all of this. Someone had tried to kill her twice and those around her were at risk. Having been at risk twice before, I hesitated before sipping the brandy.

"Daphne? What are you doing there in the dark?"

Yawning, my father scratched his belly. "Fancy a drink, do you? Then pour one for both of us."

"I'll pour three," I said. "I have to take one to Ellen. I'd rather her have it than a sedative. Remember her mother died of a sedative."

"Ah, the abominable Lady Gertrude."

"What do you remember of her?"

"Nothing much," my father admitted. "Only saw her once or twice. What are you doing with those glasses?"

"Inspecting them. What if they are poisoned?"

"Nonsense, my girl! You're allowing all of this business to play on your mind."

"But you must acknowledge we are exposed to danger."

"Poor Ellen. Someone's out for her and it ain't Cynthia Grimshaw."

"They are after Teddy Grimshaw's widow."

"Give me the drink. I'll test it."

My father wasn't a patient man. Squeezing my eyes closed, I heard him slurp the first centimeter.

"It's safe." He chuckled. "You may tell Ellen I am now her cup bearer." He laughed again, and after I'd delivered Ellen her nightcap, I rejoined him.

"How is she?"

"Not good. She can't stop blaming herself. What would you do if I went missing?"

"Dear me, I don't know. I'd go mad I suppose."

"Would you have paid the ransom?"

After a deep sigh, he raised his glass to me. "It's a question any parent will answer yes to."

"But I'm not asking any parent. I'm asking you."

He delayed, and eventually his gaze connected with mine. "In this case, I'd have waited."

"Why?"

"Because of the note and how it's written. 'The longer you delay the price goes up.' He did not intend to release her at all. At least, not yet."

"He wants more money?"

"Invariably. It's a game and we are not equipped to play it."

"If she hadn't paid, she'd get another demand?"

"Yes, and that note might have given us another clue."

"Is it worth a child's life? Playing a game like this?"

"Well, I don't envy the police who have to deal with such creatures."

Nor did I and I felt sudden sympathy for the police around the world.

Going upstairs, I knocked softly at Ellen's door. There was no answer so I moved on, intending to go to bed. Yawning on my way in, I groaned. I really should check that she was all right. I hoped she was fast asleep for sleep gave her a brief escape from this nightmare.

Turning the doorknob, I looked inside. It was dark and quiet. Tiptoeing closer to the bed, I swallowed.

The bed was empty.

"There's only one place she could have gone," I said to my parents, waking them up in a frenzy.

"She could be on the streets anywhere." Hauling himself out of bed, my father put on his nightrobe and slippers.

"I'd do the same." My mother sighed. "I couldn't rest, either. I'd keep searching all night. Why didn't we think of it?"

I followed my father downstairs.

A deathly silence greeted us. "I don't suppose anybody heard anything?"

"Let's not wake the servants." My father yawned.

"Where shall we start looking?"

"You think she's gone to that post office and not searching the streets, like your mother says?"

"Yes, I do. Can we take the car?"

I persuaded him to go out. Both of us left in our nightgowns.

"This is a waste of time," my father said, driving down darkened streets where the only activity was the dull flicker of a night lantern. "She could be anywhere."

"Let's check the post office first. If she's not there, she's at Victoria Station."

"I'm not even sure how to get to this post office, as the major drove yesterday. I do know how to get to Victoria Station."

"Then let's try there. We have to try, Papa. We can't leave her out here alone."

My father's face turned solemn. "That might be what the blackmailer is hoping. Perhaps he's using the child as bait."

"But isn't he after the money?"

"Not if it's personal. That fellow Jack Grimshaw. He's Rosalie's lover, isn't he? The two of them are probably working together."

A sickening reality curled in my stomach. Who else needed money more than they did? Who else could have such a grudge against Ellen and Charlotte?

With her mother dead, Rosalie Grimshaw seemed the most likely suspect. Was she the type of person to kidnap her own sister?

With Jack Grimshaw handling the particulars, maybe. My father and I discussed this possibility in the dead of the night.

Having never seen London in these wee hours, I appreciated the ghostly buildings, the glowing street lanterns, the empty streets, the busy promise of tomorrow.

"Grimshaw's burned his chances this side of the ocean," my

father acknowledged. "Wily fellow. I'm glad I chose not to invest with him."

"He'd have stolen the money and run. Easy money is what he wants."

"And if he's on the outer, kidnapping is a way to easy money."

Driving into the umbrella of Victoria Station, my uneasiness increased. There was no one in sight and such a place invited danger. Switching off the engine, we came to a slow stop.

"I should have brought my pistol," my father joked, getting out of the motorcar.

"You should have." Catching my breath, I walked on with him, expecting to run into a criminal at any moment. Worse, Jack Grimshaw, lurking behind some column, armed, and holding Ellen for ransom.

I hoped she had the sense to conceal herself. An eerie feeling consumed me as we approached the deserted ticket office.

"No one's here. Let's go home, Daphne."

I nodded, turning back once more. "She has to be here, though. Living in hope for Charlotte's return."

I looked again. I fancied I heard a whimper far down the hall. "Maybe we should go down there?"

My voice sounded small and intrepid. I wished my father had brought a pistol. I wished the major was here with us. I'd probably get a lecture later this morning but I didn't care.

Clutching my father's arm, we proceeded across the hall. Drawing closer, I felt my father tense. Each step became slower. I'd never seen my father so afraid before and my heart pounded. Pallor crept into my face. Are we walking into a trap? Our death?

Another whimper.

Faint, and that of a female.

I halted. "Ellen?"

The whimper vanished.

"Ellen?"

Then a voice out of the darkness. "Daphne?"

I shut my eyes, smiling.

We found her crouched in a corner, crying.

"Excuse me, sir. This arrived for you."

It was midday. Seated at the breakfast table sipping a coffee, I glanced at the maid. I'd expected her to announce the arrival of Major Browning. But no, simply delivering the mail to my father.

Opening the envelope with his butter knife, my father blanched. "Outrageous!"

His outburst rustled my mother's teacup. Swooping to steady it, I examined his face. "It's about Charlotte, isn't it?"

My father nodded, grave. "He wants more money."

"Oh no." Putting aside her tea, my mother looked over his shoulder. "What does he say this time, Gerald? Why has he addressed it to you?"

"Because Ellen is staying under my roof. He wants full attention. He's a sadist."

"May I see the note?"

It was similar to the first demand and with the same neat black handwriting. "I think you're right, Papa. These two are different from the other threats. The kidnapper is not the person who tried to kill Ellen."

"If not him, then who?" my mother cried.

"I'll telephone the police." Heading toward the door, my father paused. "Keep the news from Ellen for the minute, if you will."

When he left, my mother and I faced each other.

"It's so dreadful, all of this business and it doesn't help to have that inspector on the case. How dare he insinuate Ellen being a murderess!"

"I daresay he explores all possibilities."

"What a pity they never caught Teddy Grimshaw's killer. If they had, this might have never happened."

"It still would have happened."

Shaking her head, my mother gave me her look of disapproval. "You romance things too much, Daphne. We are not living in a novel."

Crossing my arms, I thought a novel much tamer than life at the moment.

However, one didn't disagree with Lady Muriel du Maurier.

CHAPTER THIRTY-TWO

"I'm still not sure this is the best way . . ."

"You have the power to respond here," Inspector James replied. "Remember, you tried the other way and failed. Trust me. I have experience in these matters."

"But what if he gets angry and harms Charlotte?"

"He won't harm her. She's too valuable. If she wasn't a great heiress, then perhaps I'd advise you otherwise. But she is, and it's her value that keeps her alive."

"Thank you, Inspector. Your assurance gives me confidence."

Hanging up the telephone, Ellen sought my hand. Hers shook as she asked if I'd heard everything.

"Yes. I agree with him."

Staring hard at me and Major Browning, she nodded. "Then let it be done. Request him to come to Thornleigh to get his money. He's to bring Charlotte to her father's grave and that is where we shall make the exchange."

"The gravesite?" Lifting his eyebrows, my father muttered under his breath. "Not a good idea. Too isolated."

"It's a place that will appeal," the major countermanded. "We need to lure him out face to face. This person doesn't like face-to-face. That's why he used the post office box to communicate."

Upon hearing this, I began biting my nails again.

"Daphne!"

I should have expected my mother to catch me.

"Let her chew away."

After hearing the major's fond assessment of my bad habit, she left me alone at it. Chewing my nails helped me think. I conjured up my characters this way, mulling over their personalities and their motivations.

I was glad to go back to Thornleigh. The drive kept one occupied. Ellen and I each stared out of the window while Alicia Brickley conversed with Major Browning in the front.

I tuned in to some of their conversation.

"My uncle was a clever man but something unsettled him before his death. I saw him at his desk one day rubbing his chin. He only ever rubbed his chin when he couldn't solve a riddle."

"He was worried about the threats against Ellen and Charlotte."

"No . . . actually I don't think he was. He was a rich man. He'd dealt with threats before. It was something else that bothered him."

"To do with his business?"

"Yes."

"Something he couldn't solve? A riddle?"

She nodded and I admired the nape of her neck. She held herself well, Alicia Brickley. Tall, graceful, reserved. A perfect secretary. A perfect nanny.

Anybody too perfect bothered me.

Keeping my suspicions to myself, for I didn't know exactly what I suspected Alicia of doing, I turned my attention to the scenery I loved so much. Wild roses crawled up the walls of passing cottages. I dreamed of living here. Here in the heart of Cornwall.

A dusky pink tinged my cheeks. Now, as an *engaged* woman, I could begin hunting for a house. Somewhere deep within this country. I dreaded the thought of having to spend my first married years in London.

In truth, I dreamed of living in a place as grand and as ancient as

Thornleigh. I envied Ellen. She'd been born into it, a lucky birth placing her in one of England's great families.

Alas, I was a du Maurier. My father was well-to-do and we owned Cannon Hall and our house Ferryside in Fowey. But Cannon Hall and Ferryside were not Thornleigh.

It wasn't the grandeur of the place, I decided, once we entered the gates and began the drive which sent a tingling excitement running up my arm. It was the history. The generations who'd lived here and died here. How Thornleigh, the great mansion, played a part throughout our nation's history.

Walking inside, I experienced a sense of peace. Holding hands with my major increased the sensation. It was like coming home.

"Forgive me," Ellen said after giving curt instructions to her staff for our accommodation. "I'm going to my room."

Alicia sailed straight after her, picking up the handbag she'd dropped on the floor.

"That leaves you and me." The major's seductive murmur caressed my ear. "*Un*chaperoned."

"It's probably why Ellen has put us in different parts of the house. You're in her husband's room. It's a great compliment."

"I don't know whether I like the idea of sleeping in a room where the man spent his final moments."

I pulled back, laughing at this sudden and unusual reticence. "Oh, come. Nothing will happen to *you*." But after saying so, I shivered at the thought. Could I sleep in a dead person's room?

"Then, I'll see you for lunch." His lips brushed my forehead. "Perhaps after we may take a stroll across the grounds?"

I said I'd love to and headed up the staircase. Olivia, the maid, carried my bag for me. Since Ellen hadn't yet informed the staff of her daughter's disappearance, everybody assumed Miss Charlotte had stayed behind in London. But why had Alicia come back?

Normally timid, Olivia asked me about Miss Charlotte.

"Oh, I expect your mistress intends to make an announcement later."

Nodding, Olivia walked on, a puzzled look on her face.

"I know you are all concerned and there is a good reason for it. Please prepare the others. I believe Miss Ellen will make the announcement before luncheon."

"Oh, dear. It's that bad, then?"

"It's that bad," I echoed, lingering at the door of my room while Olivia placed my bag on my bed.

"Shall I unpack for you, Miss Daphne?"

"Yes, do," I said, wanting to keep her a little longer.

She couldn't help herself. "Has something happened to Miss Charlotte? Is she sick?"

"She's . . . er—unavoidably detained."

Not sure what I meant by that expression, Olivia continued to hang up my clothes. "Olivia, why didn't you say you cleared a glass from Mr. Grimshaw's room?"

Tensing, she turned scarlet.

"You were worried someone might think you did it?"

"But I didn't, miss! I only carried it. I didn't know what was in it."

"I believe you, Olivia, but can you just stop and go over the details with me? I think the police might have missed a vital clue."

"A clue, miss?"

"Yes, a clue Sergeant Heath is working on. That's why he keeps coming back here, as much as he enjoys Nelly's cakes."

A fresh shot of fear plagued her eyes.

"When you went to collect the dishes, you heard Mr. Grimshaw. He wasn't alone, was he?"

I maintained my direct gaze. Eyes locked with hers, she began to wilt.

"No, he weren't alone. He was with his daughter, Miss Rosalie."

"Why didn't you tell this to the police?"

"Because Mr. Grimshaw said not to. 'Olivia,' he said. 'I want what you saw here to remain a secret between me and you. Do you understand?' 'Yes, sir,' I says, and left with the cup."

"But after Mr. Grimshaw was murdered, didn't you think this was important?"

"I thought she'd tell the police how it was. That Miss Rosalie. Didn't she?"

"No, she did not. She claimed she did not see her father before the ceremony."

"Oh. Well, she lied then."

"Yes, she lied. What did you hear, Olivia?"

She gulped. "I don't want no trouble. I don't want to lose my job here."

"You won't lose your job," I assured her. "I won't mention any of this to Miss Ellen or the police. It stays between me and you, just like Mr. Grimshaw said."

Wrinkling her nose, she sifted through her memory. "I was making my rounds as normal. The house was full of noise and people. When I came close to Mr. Grimshaw's room, I heard something. At first, I thought he were talkin' to himself and I was about to knock when Miss Rosalie said her piece."

"What exactly did you hear?'

She sighed, trying to recall. "It started with Mr. Grimshaw asking if her mother sent her. He kept asking and she kept asking about the will. Mr. Grimshaw said he'd made a new will and there were big changes in it. Miss Rosalie wanted to know what the changes were. Mr. Grimshaw said it weren't the time or place, right now before his weddin'."

"How did she respond to that?"

"She kept on at him, refusin' to leave until she knew, so he told her."

"What did he say?"

"He said the bulk of the money were going to Ellen and Charlotte and that he'd left her an inheritance. 'There's some money,' he said, 'but it won't last unless you work. I'm making you a partner in a business with your cousins. Work is the best antidote for a lazy and idle life.' "

"That must have shocked her, Miss Rosalie."

Olivia's eyes rounded. "Oh, it did. She ranted and raved at him. She said it weren't fair and it was *her* money. 'If you want money,' her father says, 'you'll have to work for it. Work will do you good, Rosalie. It will give you a proper respect for it, something your mother's never taught you.'"

"What happened then?"

"She called him mean and said she hated Miss Ellen and Charlotte. 'You've always wanted a sister,' Mr. Grimshaw told her. 'You have a choice. If you want some kind of relationship with Charlotte and your stepmother, stop doing what your mother tells you to do and make your own decision. Your mother is only using you as a tool. She's heartless and ruthless.' 'No, she isn't,' Miss Rosalie cries, 'she's protecting me.' 'Protecting you?' Mr. Grimshaw laughed. 'She only cares about the money. Always has. If she cared about you—'"

"Then what happened?'

"Miss Rosalie ran out the room and just missed me. I went inside to collect the cup and Mr. Grimshaw made me promise not to repeat what I'd seen."

"Oh, Olivia." I sat down. "This is very important. You should have told the police."

"It'd make her look like she poisoned him, wouldn't it?"

"Maybe, but I don't think she did . . . the nature of that argument was unplanned and spur of the moment. Poison is not spur-of-the-moment. It has to be carefully planned." I raised my face up to the frightened Olivia. "You have my word. I'll keep my promise. Mr. Grimshaw must have had his reasons for not wanting that argument publicized and it will stand. We owe the dead this one small mercy."

CHAPTER THIRTY-THREE

Vastly relieved, Olivia finished arranging my wardrobe.

Listening to her singing an old nursery rhyme, I reclined back on the bed and pictured the scene she'd described again.

"You won't say nothin', miss, will ye? Miss Ellen'll have my neck if she finds out."

"Your job," I corrected, giving her my solemn oath. As the words slipped out of my mouth, I wished I could publish this news. Poor Ellen had been labeled a murderess. If the truth became known that Miss Rosalie saw her father shortly before he died, she'd find herself arrested for his murder.

People and the police wanted a quick solution. The truth didn't always matter.

It mattered to me.

Selecting a new summer dress to wear to luncheon, I spent a little time at my vanity. Curling my hair, applying color to my lips, and trimming my bitten nails, I approved the result and left my room.

I met Ellen in the hall. She'd summoned the entire household. Looking at all the anxious faces, for a summoning usually meant something good or something bad, I watched the shock register at the news of Miss Charlotte.

"I'd appreciate if you could keep this news to yourselves as long as possible," Ellen said, her face drawn and thin from the strain. "The police are doing all they can to recover her. You will see them here in a protective role because quite frankly we are under attack. They were after my husband, they were after me, and now they've taken our daughter. I ask you all to be on your guard and report anything out of the ordinary. Thank you for your time."

Thus dismissed, the staff began filing out of the hall and I caught Olivia's brief look of terror. She raised her eyes up to me and I read the question there. Miss Rosalie. Could Miss Rosalie have kidnapped Charlotte?

I hated to admit the likelihood.

So did Ellen.

"You did well," I said to her as we walked down the corridor.

"I hate it. Harry usually addresses the staff but he's gone to visit his mother in Brighton. I've sent for him to come back." Choking back a sob, her eyes flooded with tears. "They must have taken her . . . Rosalie and Jack. Who else? They're missing. They want quick money. They won't wait until the outcome of a court case which probably won't rule in her favor. So you see, they had to act . . . and act they have."

I hesitated before I spoke. "Ellen, do you really believe Rosalie murdered Teddy?"

"No," her eyes flashed, "but they were up to no good, she and her mother. Some of those notes, the personal ones against Charlotte and me had to have come from a woman. She obviously thrived on blackmail. That was her business and in the end, it turned around on her."

Keeping my promise to Olivia, I sealed my lips together. Ellen knew as I did that Rosalie didn't kill her father. She didn't have time to plan it. Still, I began to open my mouth and promptly shut it again.

"Ah, there you are."

Lounging at the table, Major Browning swept to his feet as we ladies entered the dining room. Alicia was already there and also rose to her feet.

"Thank heavens that's over." Ellen sighed, collapsing into a chair. "Dear bless Nelly's heart. She'd made my favorite soup."

"Pea and ham," the major remarked. "It is remarkable."

"It's more of a ladies' lunch," Ellen apologized. "But we have roast beef for supper. Charlotte loves roast beef. Oh, dear. Forgive me." Crying into her napkin, she struggled to regain her composure. "It's nerves, I suppose. I don't know how I'm going to wait until tomorrow. It seems a lifetime away and the minutes drag and drag and drag."

"Try to rest," the major suggested. "You'll need your strength. Charlotte needs your strength."

"But what if this isn't the right way? I'm torn, Tommy. May I call you Tommy? Inspector James will have his men in the woods, but I have to make the exchange alone as promised. But who goes first? Money or Charlotte? Will she be there? Will they give her up?"

"Pretend you are exchanging a book instead of a precious child. You both hand over at the same time. Remember, we're right there with you."

"I'm coming, too," I said.

"No, you are not. You were lucky last time. One doesn't tempt fate twice."

Gazing into his determined face, I surrendered, this once, to the man I loved. I must credit my limitations. I was not trained to deal with clandestine villains.

After lunch, as promised, the major and I strolled through the gardens of Thornleigh. He was as fond of long walks as I was and we often stopped to admire the flowers, or a rusty old gate, or ivy strangling a wall, or the progression of Thornleigh's renovations. Raising our heads to see the new spire gracing the tower, I talked of my love affair with grand houses. "However," I grinned, "it is nothing to what I feel for you."

"What a compliment. I am compared to a pile of stone. That's what they are at the end of the day, Daphne. Inanimate stone. Lifeless. Heartless."

We were sitting on the left flank's stone bench and my fingers, entwined with his, scratched the surface. The stone felt cool to touch, especially against the heat of his hand. Sudden warmth tingled inside me. I thought of the lovers I'd seen in the woods, Jack and Rosalie. Dare I picture myself in such an embrace?

"What are you thinking?"

"Wanton thoughts." I stopped to smile up at him. "I hope we don't have a long engagement."

"Nor do I," he murmured, kissing my hair. "You're too much trouble on your own."

"I can't help it. My imagination is the culprit, except in this case I have not imagined Jack and Rosalie in the woods together. That's what I was just thinking about, daring to imagine you and I there."

Laughing, he roped his arm around me. "Why don't we go there now?"

"I'd rather an open field, a bed of wildflowers by the ocean."

"My wicked girl."

Hearing the tenderness in his voice, I swallowed. "I have been wicked. I found out something earlier. Something I've kept to myself."

His amused face became serious. "What have you discovered this time?"

"It isn't much but it might be. Olivia the maid. She saw Rosalie in her father's room before the ceremony. Mr. Grimshaw made Olivia promise not to say anything because they were arguing over his will and the money."

Pulling away, every fiber in his body became tense. "Don't you realize what this means for Ellen?"

"Complete exoneration." I nodded. "But think about it for a moment. From what Olivia says, it was an argument of rising emotion. If she intended to kill her father, she wouldn't have bothered to argue with him, would she?"

"Perhaps to argue *was* her intention. When she failed to get any results, she decides to murder him."

"By a gun or a knife in passionate anger, yes. But not by poison. And while Rosalie was in her father's room, Olivia came to clear the empty glass. He must have drunk it just before his daughter arrived."

"Or during. I'm surprised you didn't run straight to Ellen with the news."

"I was tempted," I confessed, "and I feel terrible about it but Olivia is terrified of losing her job and you and I both know Rosalie did not kill her father. If the information comes out, Inspector James will seek to arrest her. A closed case looks good on his record."

"You underestimate the man. He is foremost an inspector and on the side of the truth."

"Sergeant Heath keeps coming back to see Nelly. It's only a matter of time before he finds out. If Olivia forgot about the glass, she forgot other things. Once confronted, she'll confess of her own volition. What is it, Tommy?"

He lifted a hand, deep in thought.

"Is it about the murder? Or the kidnapping?"

"It's Teddy Grimshaw," he said finally. "In asking the maid not to repeat the scene, he was doing more than protecting his daughter. He was protecting himself. He's orchestrated this entire affair."

"From the grave? What the devil do you mean?"

"I've been following the case for some time. This is all about big business and illegal trading. Teddy Grimshaw is guilty."

"Guilty?"

"He's a grand master and he knew how to play the game. He reaped millions from it but he made a few errors extending his empire over here."

Taken aback, I stared at him. "Your engagement to Lady Lara suited you more than her. It put you close to Rutland, didn't it?"

"Yes, and during that time I was able to steal into Rutland's office. I found evidence of Jack Grimshaw selling information to the opposition."

"You informed Dean Fairchild and put Jack Grimshaw in disgrace but what has this to do with Teddy Grimshaw? How is he guilty? He's dead."

"Fortuitously so. If he had lived, he would have paid the price for his trading practices and lost most if not all of his fortune. The government wanted his money. Grimshaw knew the only way to protect it was to die and leave it to his widow. He planned to die that day. He wanted it to look like murder. The investigation would take precedence over his fight with the government and preserve his fortune."

"That's why he didn't involve the police with the first death threats. He sent them to himself."

"Yes. He wanted the police there, ready to protect Ellen."

"Because there was another aggressor, Salinghurst and Rutland." I began to feel very ill. "I wonder if Lady Lara knows of her ailing father's antics?"

"She knows a little. You were upset hearing reports of our being seen together in London. It was part of my job to stay with her, to prize whatever information she had concerning her father and his shares in the company Salinghurst. He'd invested heavily, you see, and wasn't about to surrender his fortune to an 'American buccaneer.'"

"Poor Teddy," I whispered. "He was hemmed in by all quarters. He thought his dying would protect his fortune and his family. That day in the woods . . . and the poisoned chocolates. They were from Salinghurst?"

"Before Ellen sold the shares to Dean Fairchild, she was in danger. If they removed her, the shares would have reverted back to the company and in their control. Selling the shares saved Ellen's life."

"But our government wanted to use her as bait? Monitor their meetings and thereby placing her and Charlotte in danger?"

He shrugged. "Those were our orders. Sometimes you don't agree with them but you obey. Why do you think I placed myself at Thornleigh straight after the funeral?"

"For our protection," I answered. "And to try and seize the money."

"No," he corrected, running a finger down my face. "I came here for you."

CHAPTER THIRTY-FOUR

Walking back to Thornleigh hand in hand with the man I loved, I no longer needed to dread what could or might happen. A serene peace surrounded me, the security of being loved and loving in return.

In a daze, I returned to my room. Still tired from the journey, Tommy suggested I rest. I smiled to myself, curled up in bed with my stack of treasured letters. On the top, with a white ribbon, were his to me, everything written and preserved for all time.

After attempting sleep and having sleep desert me, I sorted out the letters, hunting for those I intended to read. Here it was . . . the account of Ellen's mother's death:

> *Dearest Daphne,*
> *I have bad news to import. I can scarcely believe it myself. My mother is dead. It happened quickly . . . overnight. I admit I'm a little in shock. You were aware of the status of our relationship so forgive the apparent lack of grief on my part. Earlier in the day, she was in the garden and yelled at Charlotte for daring to pick roses. The poor girl only intended to*

pick them for sick "Grandmama" but that is my
mother. She won't allow anybody to do anything
nice for her.

I paused here, resting the paper's edge under my chin. Lady Gertrude. The name suited the cantankerous woman.

She had her dinner in her room as usual and like always, I checked in on her before I turned in. She was grizzly, complained of little sleep and a great headache. Since she was abed, she asked me to pass her her laudanum. Carefully measuring out the spoonful, she waved me off and I kissed her cheek. "Good night, Mama," I said, never expecting they would be my last words to her.

  Oh Daphne, I feel dreadful but I am actually relieved she is dead. I'd grown weary with the daily threats of disinheritance. And her going on and on about Xavier, her precious son. I miss Xav. He would have made a great master of Thornleigh. I don't know how I'll go as mistress of Thornleigh. Am I worthy of the title?

That was the end of the letter and I burned to know what my reply had been. I hoped I had imparted some comforting words. As for Lady Gertrude, I thought her better rested in the soil of Thornleigh than tormenting my poor friend's life. I read on:

The funeral was today. Some of the looks I got! They think I've done it but I'm innocent, Daphne. She took an overdose. Perhaps in her angry mood she measured it out incorrectly? I can't mourn her, is that horrid of me? She always loved Xavier first. Xavier this, Xavier that. If I'd had a son she might have been happier. A son for Thornleigh! A son and his name should be called Xavier. Poor Charlotte. She always asked me questions about her grandparents. She thought grandparents are nice. I haven't yet told her she has another grandmother far across the seas in America. Now Mama is dead, there is no reason to keep up the pretense. I am a widow, I've put about, and yes, I am a widow at heart because I still love him, Daphne. I still love Teddy. Shall I ever see him again? Why has he not answered my letters?

Turning over that letter, I thought how far Ellen had come from those war days. I skipped two letters to another:

Sorry, I've been too busy to write! My hands, how awful they look. Gnarly. But I like working in the dirt. Our vegetables are a great success and it keeps us alive. Sadly, the house still remains closed. We live in a small part but I hope one day to open all those ghostly rooms again. I went to see the estate lawyers. They won't allow me to sell any portion of the land or household fixtures but they have granted me a sum to help with the maintenance. It covers us and the small staff we have here and we are relatively happy . . . but I still dream of Teddy.

PS . . . Charlotte turned five today. She asked about her daddy. We said a little prayer together, hoping to see him again. It isn't like him, Daphne, to not reply. Perhaps I've had the wrong address all this time?

No, you had the right address. Reading these letters, I felt immeasurably sad for Ellen. To love, to have lost, and to have loved again so briefly. Hunting for the letter where her exuberance almost transcended off the page, I found it at the bottom of the pile.

Daphne, you will never guess. Teddy is here! I've seen him. There was a clipping about him in the paper. He's come over here for business but he says he really came to search for me. He knows about Charlotte. Daphne, he says he never got my letters. When I ran off from Boston, he was on the next ship. But the next ship was two years later because of the war. He had to wait and then when he came to London, the city was such a mess, everybody searching for their lost relatives, he couldn't find me. He went to Thornleigh and got a very bad reception from my father. Funny, they never told me of his visit. I suppose at that time I was disinherited living in a little flat in London. Having an American lover show up was not the way to impress my parents. I wonder if they'd have reacted differently if he'd mentioned he was a millionaire? In any case, we are reunited and he says he loves me, has always loved me! We don't know what happened to the letters but I have a good guess. Rosalie. She didn't want her father to marry again, but it doesn't matter. We're making up for the lost years. Teddy is going to stay! He's anxious to get to know me and Charlotte. How wonderful is life.

On the back of that letter, she added a postscript:

D, can't finish the letter as I'm off to Paris! Teddy is taking us and Harry said he'd post this for me. Will write more soon, x E.

Slipping that letter back in its envelope, I collapsed onto the pillow with a sigh. Paris. I wanted to go to Paris. Some say you can live a lifetime in a few short months and Ellen certainly had. Beginning to feel sleepy with dreams of traveling with my fiancé, I turned over the envelope to place on the stack.

Icy fear gripped me when I saw it.

MISS D. DU MAURIER
CANNON HALL, CANNON PLACE
HAMPSTEAD
LONDON NW3

The same neat black capitals I'd seen elsewhere.
On the ransom note.

CHAPTER THIRTY-FIVE

Leaving my room, I headed straight for the stairs.

A morbid quiet greeted me. Midafternoons in huge houses radiated mausoleum silence. Since my discovery, the quiet appeared deadly. Heart pounding and still clutching the envelope, I hurried to Major Browning's room.

I knocked.

There was no answer.

I knocked again.

Still no answer.

Out of breath, I rested there a moment. Where could he have gone? After our walk, he had intimated enjoying a sojourn himself.

Pressing my ear against the door, I hoped for a snore or something. But there was nothing, nothing but that deathly quiet.

Ellen. I'd check her room and the morning room.

She wasn't in her room, either. Noting the tousled bed, I assumed she'd lain down for a rest and restlessness had put her on her feet again. Slipping across to Charlotte's room, I found Alicia sitting there in the rocking chair. "Have you seen Ellen? Do you know where she is?"

"No." Alicia shook her head. "What's wrong? Do we have news? News about Charlotte?"

"Maybe . . . where can I find her?"

"She stopped in here to get a photograph. I thought she'd gone back to her room."

"No, she isn't there. I'll try the morning room."

She'd risen to her feet. "Shall I come with you? Something *is* wrong, isn't it?"

"Yes," I murmured. "It's just important we find Ellen at once."

The echo of our footsteps resounded throughout the expanse. I shivered at the sound. Sinister and foreboding, I tried to still the roar of my heart. I couldn't get to Ellen quickly enough. I sensed evil at Thornleigh, it was here in the house, and I had to hurry . . .

"The door's open," Alicia remarked as we rounded the corner.

The long corridor loomed ahead. Light drifted from the morning room, casting its pale glow on the timber floor. A shadow emerged, and Alicia and I halted, lingering outside the door as Ellen and Harry talked inside.

". . . give over the money and he'll release Charlotte. I have his word."

"Harry, I ought to ask the police—"

"No police. He's very firm on it," Harry responded.

Sighing, Ellen moved across the room back to her desk. Glancing at Alicia, I signaled for us to go forward, closer to the door.

"Why were you on the train, Harry? I thought you'd gone to see your mother."

"Yes . . . lucky for you I changed my mind. A moment earlier, and I'd have missed them."

Taking a deep breath, Ellen sat down. "I knew it was them, Jack and Rosalie. I knew it. Is Charlotte safe? How did she look? Did she see you?"

"Yes . . . she saw me. She is unharmed and you'll have her in your arms by the end of this day, that is, if you play by the rules."

"Oh, how I wish Teddy were here!" Tears spilling down her face, Ellen removed a key out of her pocket.

"You aren't alone . . . you have me."

Raising her tearstained face to Harry, Ellen clutched her hands together. "Shall I go with you? I want to make sure they release her first."

"No. Let me deal with them. Stay here."

Slipping into the first room before he exited, I put my finger to my lips. Following, if mildly surprised, Alicia waited until the footsteps faded down the hall.

"I'll explain in a minute," I whispered. "Come with me."

Going into the morning room, we found Ellen loading a pistol on her desk. The firm set of her mouth intimated she intended to go after Harry.

"Don't go. Let me get the major."

Looking at the two of us, she smiled. "What do you want me to do? Just sit here and wait when my daughter is out there?"

I shut the door. "Listen for a moment. Charlotte is safe. She is safe because Harry has her."

"What? No, Harry is going to get her—"

"Look at this." Thrusting the envelope before her eyes, I took a deep breath. "You probably have never noticed Harry's writing. This is a letter you wrote me where you asked Harry to post it for you. Does this look familiar?"

Sagging to her knees, Ellen shook her head. "It can't be . . . why would Harry do such a thing? He loves Charlotte . . ."

"And he loves you, and above everything he loves Thornleigh."

"Harry," Alicia echoed under her breath. "Harry took Charlotte?"

"To return her to Ellen. To look the hero but his plan went awry."

"No, it was the other way about. Harry was coming home. He saw *them*. They had her."

"That's what he'd like you to think. You're forgetting he's doing this for you and for Thornleigh. He wants to marry you, Ellen. I know . . . because one day I overheard." I gulped. "I'm sorry. I shouldn't have eavesdropped."

"I still can't believe it," Alicia murmured. "You say Harry has her? He's had her all this time?"

"Yes. Somehow he took her from my father's house. He knew we were going there and he knew we were going to the play. What a perfect time to effect a kidnapping. The party . . . many guests . . . it was easy for him to steal inside and locate Charlotte. Charlotte trusts him, too. He might have said he was taking her to the park to see the night lights and she would have believed him—"

Ellen shot to her feet. "I have to go after them. If he's done this as you say, there's no knowing what he might do." Examining the handwriting on the envelope again, a deathly pallor crept into her cheeks.

"I'll call the police," Alicia offered, laying a comforting hand on Ellen's shoulder.

"No police." Ellen shivered. "Not until we have Charlotte back. I don't care what happens then."

"Alicia will go and get the major. He'll know what to do."

Uncertain, Alicia paused at the door. "But are you safe here?"

"We'll lock the door. Knock twice and we'll open. Do hurry!"

"I hope they get here before Harry does," Ellen said after she'd gone. "Otherwise, I'm going to have to play along with him, aren't I? I'll have to pretend I don't know what he's up to. I don't think I can do it, Daphne. I've never been good at pretending."

"Yes, you can. You're stronger than you think."

Silence enshrouded us. Tortuous minutes passed like hours. We dared not move or make a sound.

Ellen played with the pistol on her lap. "I'm not a good shot. Are you?"

Taking the weapon from her, I endeavored to recall the mechanisms. It had been some time since I'd been hunting.

"Teddy gave it to me on the night of our engagement. A strange gift, along with a ring, but now I understand it. We were in danger from the very beginning . . ."

Poised at her desk, she suddenly sat up straight. "Someone's coming . . ."

We both waited, breathless.

The footsteps reverberated along the corridor. They became quicker, shorter. Heart pounding, I stationed myself behind the chair.

The door sprang open.

"Mummy!"

Catching Charlotte in her arms, Ellen sobbed with mixed joy and relief.

"I told you I'd bring her home safe." Grinning at the door, Harry came inside, his expression turning stony when he saw me.

It wasn't the reunion he'd planned in his mind. He imagined Ellen alone and grateful to him. Since my presence prevented his romantic assurance, I remained holding the weapon behind my chair.

"Mummy, I'm so tired, I just want to go to bed."

Ellen and I exchanged a glance. So he'd drugged her to keep her distracted.

"It's all right, darling. Are you hurt?"

Letting her mother examine every inch of her, Charlotte yawned. "No, they didn't hurt me." She yawned again.

"I'll carry her."

"No thanks, Harry. I'll take her. We'll talk later?"

Seizing her child, Ellen made for the door. I caught the frantic look in her face. She wanted to get Charlotte as far away from him as possible and I was to detain him. Feeling the weight of the pistol, I naturally asked what happened.

"They've got the money. They're leaving England."

"You mean you've got the money."

Drawing the pistol, I pointed it at him.

"No," I said as he tried to reach his pockets. "I know you did it, Harry. It was your handwriting that betrayed you. Years ago, you posted a letter for Ellen. *This* letter."

Confronted with the evidence, he rolled his shoulders. "That doesn't prove anything."

"It proves something to Ellen. She's always trusted you and treated you like a friend. She's more than repaid the kindness you showed her in the early years but it wasn't enough, was it? You wanted more. You became insane with greed."

A tiny smirk flickered at the corners of his mouth. "Your imagination, Miss du Maurier, has clearly clouded your judgment."

"Ellen believes me."

"I very much doubt that. What have you been doing here all this time? Dreaming up all this nonsense? When did I become a villain in your book?"

"The day we went to Mevagissey. You said you'd do anything for Ellen."

Lounging by the door, he crossed his arms, still smiling. "I fail to see the significance."

"You wanted Ellen and you wanted Thornleigh. When did your love affair with the house begin? When did she become your mistress? I guess it was when you murdered Lady Gertrude. Getting the old woman out of the way opened many doors for you, didn't it? You had Ellen solely in your power and you had Thornleigh."

"I can see why you write novels. Your head is full of nonsense."

"Nonsense. But I am making perfect sense and that is what unsettles it. You nearly got it away with it. Admittedly, you had to pay off Jack Grimshaw and that cost you. Or, more importantly, it cost Thornleigh. You intended to give the money back to her. In your mind it was never ransom money but a loan. Tell me, did you get the idea to kidnap Charlotte from the real ransom notes?"

"I don't know what you're talking about."

"Oh, I think you do. From what the police have already established, there were two different writers. We can easily dismiss one as the raves of Cynthia Grimshaw. The second, still unknown, gave you the idea to become the third and thus turn everything—Ellen, Charlotte, and Thornleigh—back into your power."

A low chuckle escaped his lips. "There is something wrong with your brain, Miss du Maurier. You have no evidence or witnesses and your silly little letter—what will that prove? The police wouldn't waste their time to consider it."

"But we will consider it, Mr. Mainton."

The calm voice produced Inspector James.

Relief tingling my veins, I kept my finger poised on the trigger. If Harry went for his weapon, I'd have to fire.

Taking out a set of handcuffs from his pocket, Inspector James said: "We can go quietly or by force. I strongly suggest the former, Mr. Mainton."

"Mr. Mainton?"

Harry's gaze locked with mine. An arrogant coldness consumed him, and he shrugged, surrendering his pistol to Inspector James. "I have nothing to hide."

His blasé comments and manifestations of innocence echoed down the hall. Following at a discreet distance, I hunted for any signs of the major. Where *was* he?

Near the front door, Inspector James paused. "Miss du Maurier. Can you assist me? The keys are in my right pocket."

I hurried over to him. He didn't want to lower his weapon for a second and I understood why when Harry made a dash for the door.

A gunshot fired. I reeled to the floor, my hand tangled in Inspector James's pocket. Disengaging it, I ran with the inspector.

"Go back," he puffed.

"I'm fitter. I'll run after him."

"No, let him go." Stopping by a hedge, the inspector fished out a handkerchief from his pocket. "We'll catch him later. He can't go far."

I didn't want to question his intelligence but I thought Harry could go very far. He knew every square mile of this country. He could hide anywhere. "Is it true, Inspector? Is the evidence not enough to incriminate him?"

"We shall make a careful study of the writing. I think maybe he knows there is plenty here to match it."

"Because he ran, that makes him guilty about something."

"Yes and no. Sometimes one runs because of other reasons."

"Such as?"

"Protecting someone."

"Or a secret?"

"Or a secret."

"He killed Lady Gertrude. He killed Teddy Grimshaw, too. He has the biggest motivation. He wants Ellen and Thornleigh. He had to remove her mother so she could inherit. He had to remove Teddy so she was free again. I overheard him professing his love for her, you know. She rebuffed him."

He paused, his eyebrows shooting up in surprise. "When was this?"

"A few weeks ago. Her saying no might have induced him to stage the kidnapping."

"And win the widow."

"You must confess. It's a clever plan, one I never thought he'd do. He saved Ellen. He supported her."

"Yes, but if this support included the death of Lady Gertrude, it is warped. It was only a matter of time for the ugliness to manifest itself again."

Standing on the landing outside Thornleigh, I stared into the woods. "He's out there. And he's angry . . ."

"No need to worry, Miss du Maurier. We are here."

"I wish I had your confidence, Inspector."

CHAPTER THIRTY-SIX

Back inside the house, I asked for Alicia.

"She's upstairs with Miss Charlotte, miss," whispered a maid, startled by the drama of the last two hours.

"Have you seen the major at all?"

"No, miss."

Climbing the stairs, I flexed my right hand. Twisting it in the inspector's pocket left it strained.

I knocked at the door to Charlotte's room.

Low voices awaited me, and Ellen, after establishing it was me, answered. She looked tense and afraid and I updated her.

"Harry," she echoed, resuming her seat. "What monster took hold of him? He was always so good to us."

"Greed. I believe he murdered your mother, too."

"Yes," she whispered. "I know. I never wanted to admit it. We'd had a conversation that day she died . . . I remember standing by the rosebush. Mother had been particularly mean. He caught me crying and I remember saying 'I wish she was dead.' Afterward, when they laid her in the ground, I wondered if my saying it had caused it to happen. The investigation found nothing so we never spoke of Mother again, but in my heart, I suspected Harry switched her dosage. And she, unknowingly, swallowed the fatal medicine."

Listening quietly across the room, Alicia shook her head. "Her death made life easier though, didn't it?"

Ellen nodded without hesitation.

"One can't condone bad acts, but one can understand them," I said. "Alicia, did you go to the major's room?"

"Yes, but he wasn't there."

Ellen shivered. "Where is he and where is Sergeant Heath? I don't feel safe enough to leave this room."

"You stay here. I'll go down. Maybe Nelly knows where they are."

The presence of the pistol knocking against my leg lent courage to my searching the house. Inspector James promised to stay on hand, and he telephoned for more officers. Considering the size of Thornleigh and Harry's intimate knowledge of the place, there was a chance he'd come back. Maybe for money or papers or other personal effects. His intention to elude the police put danger into my step. Harry didn't like me. He didn't like my being close to Ellen. And he certainly didn't like my reading into his true character.

If I hadn't uncovered the truth he might have convinced Ellen and gradually wooed her into marriage. She'd have never known it was he who had kidnapped her daughter.

To my intense relief, I made it to the kitchen without trouble.

"Oh, my!" Nelly raised her eyes. "What a t'do. Well, I always thought he was too big for his boots and too close to Miss Ellen. It weren't right. Harry's had designs on her for some time, I'd say. He killed Mr. Grimshaw. That's why he's run off. He knows we're on to him."

I allowed a little smile to play on my lips. "Nelly, you have a fine understanding of matters. But until Harry is caught, we are under siege, for want of a better term."

"Under siege." She picked up a chopping knife. "How can I help?"

Lowering her weapon, I fought back a smile. "He's dangerous and best left to the police. Speaking of which, have you seen the major?"

"He went out with Sergeant Heath. Some tip-off, I expect. How is Miss Ellen? Is she frightened? I'll go up and sit at her door."

"That's very kind of you, but I think it's best you stay here and act normal. If Harry does come back, there's a better chance of catching him if he thinks everybody is doing their usual work. Inspector James has gone to wait in Harry's office. That's where we think he'll go."

"Bad devil he is, takin' Miss Charlotte like that. Ye see them together, ye think he loves her!"

"He loves Thornleigh more."

"It ain't natural to love a house."

Yes, but I understood such an obsession. Perhaps it was easier to love a house than a person. A house may fall into disrepair but its loyalty stayed infallible.

Not knowing what to do, I ordered afternoon tea and took it to the inspector.

"Do share a cup with me," he offered. "The writing on the envelope matches this ledger book. I ought to hire your services. You've a penchant for detection."

"Thank you."

"And what have we here?" Inspecting the items on the plate, he glowed with anticipation.

"Cherry chocolates and lemon biscuits. Nelly didn't know which you'd prefer."

"Cherry chocolates, and you, Miss du Maurier?"

"Same." I smiled and selected one. "Do you really think he'll come back here?"

"Well, he'll have a devil of a time taking off those handcuffs without a key. And he can't keep away from the house."

"But he must know we're here waiting for him."

"Yes, but if I know anything about anything, he'll risk it."

"Why are you so sure? He has the money."

"The money, Miss Daphne, is the clue. And there is one fellow who thinks himself lucky enough to escape us."

"You're speaking of Jack Grimshaw?"

Consulting his watch, the inspector gobbled down the last of the chocolates. "Right about now, we should have him. Well," he conceded, "Major Browning will have him. We received a communication pinpointing the location of Mr. Grimshaw. We've been wanting to talk to him for some time but he always manages to elude us. Not, I suspect, this time."

"Having one in custody doesn't mean they will talk. Who betrayed him?"

The inspector smirked. "Do you care to hazard a guess?"

I thought for a moment. "He's out of favor with his cousin Dean Fairchild so it's not him."

"There you are wrong. It seems Mr. Grimshaw was stealing from both sides, as Mr. Fairchild attested. Selling information is a dangerous game. Let's say the business caught up with him and his former employers wish him locked away."

"Salinghurst . . . the earl and the others."

"Yes. They say they hired Jack Grimshaw to persuade his uncle's widow to give up the shares. The term *persuasion* is used in the liberal sense. I think you follow my meaning."

"The attacks . . . in the woods and the chocolates . . ."

"We suspected but we didn't know. Now we know for sure because a woman got it out of him."

I stared at him. "Rosalie? She turned him in?"

"Precisely. It seems the little time she spent with her sister encouraged her to make a stand. Major Browning and Sergeant Heath will bring her back here."

I stood up. "I must warn Ellen . . . I must prepare her. Rosalie is not the person she is made out to be."

"No, she isn't. I have spoken to her on the telephone myself. She says she knew little of the truth. I have enlarged it for her."

"It doesn't explain who killed her mother."

The inspector sighed. "We shall never know that one, I fear. The city is too busy to bother about the case. She shall go down as unsolved." He paused, and looked at me. "Something bothers you, Miss du Maurier?"

"I don't like unsolved."

"Yet in life sometimes one doesn't know if one is good or wicked. You say you like to write books. Why not write one where we do not know if the character is good or wicked. Make the character itself unsolved. An interesting concept, don't you think?"

It was a great concept. Leaving him, I went to jot it down in my journal. I wrote: *A widow. A rich widow. Husband died mysteriously. Is she good or is she bad? Is she innocent or is she guilty?* Beside this, I added a name. *Ellen . . . , no, Rachel. Yes, Rachel.*

I convinced Ellen to come down to dinner.

Inspector James sat with us, only after posting another sergeant in Harry's office. "I wish to make it as inviting as possible for Mr. Mainton to enter the house, so we have two men on the grounds and two inside the house. Ladies, please retire to your chambers and lock the door."

"Why is Uncle Harry bad?" Charlotte asked her mother. "He's always nice to me. We were going to the seashore. He said you were meeting us there, Mummy."

Exchanging a glance with each of us, Ellen sighed. "Sometimes, darling, a person's mind becomes sick. Harry got sick."

Frowning, Charlotte considered this answer. "Can we give him some medicine to make him better, Mummy?"

"We can. That's why Inspector James is here. He'll take Harry away and make him better."

"Oh." Charlotte bestowed a beguiling smile at the inspector before returning to her mother. "But maybe Uncle Harry doesn't want to take his medicine and that's why he's run away?"

"But darling, you know what happens if you don't take your medicine. It's important Harry takes his."

"If he hates taking medicine like I do, he'll come in through the secret place."

Dropping her spoon, Ellen stared at her child. "What secret place?"

Charlotte looked away. "It's our secret, Mummy. Mine and Uncle Harry's."

Swooping to the knees, Ellen began her appeal. "Darling, you need to take me to that place. Me and Inspector James. It's really important we help Harry while we can. Where is it?"

Charlotte still wasn't sure.

"You think you're breaking a promise with me by telling us but you're not, darling. Where is this secret place?"

"I'll show you," she said at last.

Filing outside the dining room, a strange calm descended on the house. While Inspector James, Ellen, and Charlotte headed down the eastern corridor, an instinct drew me west.

The dull lights guided my footsteps. It was around the dinner hour so I imagined the servants to be at their table after serving the mistress. Not wanting to leave Charlotte's side, Alicia went along with the others and I wondered if I should have done so, too.

The uncanny quiet grew with the thickness of the summer air. It was a beautiful evening: still, warm, the only sound being my shoes on the old wooden floor. Allowing the floor to lead me, I walked on, removing my cardigan in the heat.

The west wing loomed ahead. Funny, I had always thought it the coldest part of the house. Passing the knight standing guard to the entrance, I opened the door to the ancient hall and gasped.

Fire . . . fire everywhere.

I tried to pull back but it was too late. Flames lashed out at me, surrounding me as they continued their merciless destruction of the library. Standing in the midst of this destruction, an acute sadness touched my bones watching the flames lick over all those glorious books. Irreplaceable books . . . now swept away by an infernal heat.

Heat scorching my shoes, I jumped from stone to stone. The carpet and chairs were on fire, and crackling timber began to dislodge and fall from the walls. Dodging one, I said a quick prayer. *Oh, please, please, someone, please save me . . .*

I hid my face with my cardigan. I couldn't breathe. There was no air. I felt faint and weak. I longed for and dreamed of water. Water, lots of water. The fire raged on, lashing out at me. I tried to get out of the room but I couldn't find the door. Where was the door?

In desperation, I ran to the other side to hear the splintering windows. Glass shattered all about, an incredible piercing noise, and I shut my ears. I couldn't bear to hear it.

"Daphne!"

Someone threw something wet over my head.

"Daphne, I'm here now but you're going to have to jump."

The major. I could have wept with relief. "Jump?" I echoed, not daring to look.

"Don't look down. I won't let go."

The authority in his voice transcended into an order. We didn't have time. He said to jump now. Trusting him completely, I wrapped myself in his coat, shut my eyes, and jumped.

Drawn out on the grass, his coat sizzling around me, I stared up at the house. "Oh no . . ."

Tearing the coat off me, he examined my hair, my face, my hands, my feet, indeed, every part of me. Submitting to his thorough ministrations and reading the terror in his eyes, I smiled. "You came for me . . ."

His face was black from the smoke. "Of course I came for you. You don't know how scared I was . . . driving down the hill and rounding the bend to see the orange glow in the sky. I thought, 'That's not a holocaust. That's Thornleigh!' "

"It was," I said miserably, witnessing the fire spread from one end of the house to the other. "Harry . . ."

"He's dead. I saw his body . . . or what was left of it."

I shuddered. If he couldn't have Thornleigh, then nobody else was going to have her. "The others . . . ?"

"Are safe. Come, my angel, this is the most expensive fire you'll ever see."

He took me away to a clearing near the woods but I dared not watch. I looked upon the great mansion as a person and I couldn't bear to see her suffer. Generations of history, lost. Valuables beyond price, destroyed. And home, Ellen's home, taken from her in one night.

Thornleigh, lost forever.

CHAPTER THIRTY-SEVEN

"She's destined to become a ghost. They shall come to visit her ruins..."

A week later, sitting on the balcony overlooking the river in our house at Fowey, Ellen found the strength to accept the tragedy. "I don't have the money to repair her. She'll have to sit there, a desolate ruin, uninhabited."

"I'm so sorry," Rosalie murmured, now united with Ellen and Charlotte in their grief. Having put the past aside, Rosalie had agreed to come with us to Ferryside.

"Nothing was saved." Ellen wiped a tear away. "Nothing."

"You have memories," my father reminded.

"And photographs," Charlotte pointed out. "We have photographs of Thornleigh, Mummy. We even have postcards."

We all shared a smile at that.

"Postcards," Ellen echoed. "I don't know what to do now. Thornleigh has always been my life—"

"No, Charlotte is your life," my mother said. "And now you have your stepdaughter. You have all suffered a loss. Perhaps you can rebuild something together?"

"Oh, yes, Mummy, can we go to America? Rosalie says Grandmama's house there is as big as Thornleigh."

"It's not as old," Rosalie put in, "but it has some history and Daddy grew up there."

"Oh, can we go, Mummy? *Please.*"

Gazing down at her exuberant pleading face, Ellen smiled. "Maybe."

"It's the best idea in the circumstances, Ellen dear," my father advised. "Get away from all this nonsense. When you're ready, come back. Fresh sea air is what you all need. And you've got a good guide in Rosalie. She knows the town and the people."

"And the relatives." Rosalie rolled her eyes. "I'm afraid we can't escape all of them, can we, Alicia?"

I looked at the two cousins. They'd formed an uneasy truce after the fire. Rosalie had changed since her time in England. Her mother's death opened the way for her to make her own choices and putting cousin Jack, no longer Lucky Jack, in prison further freed her.

"So we are to America *after* the ball," Alicia said later upon asking to see my room. Glancing out of the window, she added, "It's a nice view. Shall you write your book from here?"

"Yes. Well, I hope to. I have so many ideas running through my head, I don't know which book to write first!"

"You should catalogue them. Each story has its own notepad. When you get an idea, write it down but concentrate on one story at a time."

I watched her as she stood there by the window. She was young, yet she appeared ancient. "Alicia, did you ever think it would end this way?"

"End what way?"

"With Ellen and Rosalie and Charlotte. There were so many odds against them."

Still staring down at the river, a whisper of a smile touched her lips. "It was Uncle Teddy's wish to have it so."

"It seems like a miracle."

She shrugged, and turned aside, saying, "Perhaps not" as she walked out of the room. Suddenly I had my answer. She had killed Cynthia Grimshaw. She was the female voice heard by Emmy the maid at Claridge's.

Chilled, I recalled her lack of surprise when we read about the murder in the paper. Ellen had had Charlotte that afternoon . . . Alicia was free. What had been her original intention? To reason with a woman—her aunt—who barely noticed her?

I did know one thing. Characters like Alicia Brickley, intensely private, never publicized their reasons. Whatever had happened that afternoon left Rosalie free to follow her own destiny.

Alicia Brickley, a murderess.

But a murderess for the greater good?

"Keeping information, Miss du Maurier, is a serious offense."

"I wouldn't call it information exactly, Inspector James. Let's say a logical deduction."

"Yes, but you got the maid Olivia to talk. My sergeant failed to do so."

"She was frightened and I am less formidable than a police officer."

He laughed on the other end of the telephone. "Good-bye, Miss du Maurier. I hope our paths don't meet again."

"I hope they do. Good day, Inspector."

I sensed the major's proximity before he reached me. Smiling when his hand settled on my waist, I surrendered the telephone. "Jack Grimshaw will be in prison for a while . . . but that still leaves the mystery of what happened to Teddy Grimshaw."

Caressing my temple, he groaned. "Does your mind never rest?"

"Not when there's questions. Don't you wonder, too?"

"Time, my dear girl, has a way of solving mysteries. Leave it alone. I don't want your mother—or mine for that matter—arranging our engagement and wedding."

"Wedding," I murmured, slipping my hands around his neck. "That's a pleasant business, one I could—"

He stopped my mouth with a kiss. The first of many, and for once, my mind was put to rest.

EPILOGUE

I received a letter the next year, postmarked from America.

> *My dear Daphne,*
> *Thank you for your engagement invitation. Unfortu-*
> *nately, we are not returning to England just yet. Char-*
> *lotte and I have adapted very well to the climate on*
> *this side of the world. Teddy's mother has welcomed*
> *us with both arms and we make a curious little*
> *family—Charlotte, Rosalie, Alicia, and I. I am deter-*
> *mined to see the girls married off, so maybe we will*
> *be back next season.*
>
> *But as you know, there are unpleasant memories at*
> *home. Daily I think of Teddy, and today, my dear*
> *Daphne, I have word. Teddy wrote me before he died*
> *and left the letter in the care of his solicitors. He in-*
> *structed them to release it a year after his death.*
>
> *My dear Daphne, he had cancer. He found out two*
> *weeks before our wedding. "I can't allow you, my*
> *dearest darling," he wrote, "to suffer the indignity of*
> *caring for an old man or for my mistakes. I love you,*
> *Teddy." By mistakes he means that if he had lived, he*

would have lost his fortune. He took his own life, Daphne. And Alicia knew about it. She's told me everything now. How her uncle charged her to say nothing until a year after his death and how she purchased the hemlock for him to take on the day of our wedding.

We're keeping the secret. There is no sense to release this news but I thought you'd like to know . . .

Your friend always,
Ellen

P.S. I dream of Thornleigh every night. I dream of driving through the gates, up the narrow winding path to our home. I can't forget her. Daphne, please resurrect her in one of your books. Perhaps through those pages she will live on.

Sealing the letter and burning it as instructed, I picked up the picture postcard of Thornleigh sitting on my desk. An intense longing for the old house caused an ache deep within my heart. What a shame she did not survive the fire.

Let her live on through pages.

Taking out a fresh sheet, I drew a sketch of Thornleigh and renamed her.

Manderley.